A Ghost
in the Music

A Ghost in the Music

by John Nichols

Holt, Rinehart and Winston   New York

Library of Congress Cataloging in Publication Data
Nichols, John Treadwell
A ghost in the music.
I. Title.
PZ4.N619Gh [PS3564.I274]   813'.5'4   79-657
ISBN 0-03-042576-X

FIRST EDITION

DESIGNER: *Joy Chu*
Printed in the United States of America
10 9 8 7 6 5 4 3 2 1

For Leo Garen

Corpulent Odysseus, good friend.

When last seen, he was slouched in a
smoking blue pickup filled with dry
piñon, rattling along an October
aspen-flanked dirt road one thousand
miles—and a million heartaches—beyond
the Hollywood pale.

L'chaim!

I'm sitting alone
By a pink telephone,
Waiting for someone to call;
But a ghost in the music
That's drifting like smoke
Doesn't know how to dial at all.

A Ghost in the Music

1 *"In a real dark night of the soul,"* once said F. Scott Fitzgerald, *"it is always three o'clock in the morning."*

That's when the phone rang, and I knew, even before fumbling for the receiver, that it would be him. Bart—otherwise known as my dad—Bart Darling. Sometime writer, theater and film director, actor, real-estate mogul, stunt man and poet, songwriter, perverse womanizer, masochist, health faddist, worrywart, child in a grown man's jeans—I always knew it was him when he called. At the hours he chose, the ring inevitably had an urgent, breathless quality to it, almost as if he were shouting into his mouthpiece long before I picked mine up. And often when I did press the apparatus to my ear, he was already in such high, loud gear that I could almost set down the instrument and listen to his actual voice traveling cross-country from wherever he happened to be situated.

"Pop—?"

"Marcel," he groaned—and he's the only person I've ever known who positively roars when he groans: "I'm in trouble!"

Talk about copilots—Bart's was Trouble. A high-risk player, he had spent his life teetering on the edge—of madness, bankruptcy, immense wealth, stardom. And even if he was not in desperate straits, he always claimed to be, for effect, because he hated boredom, because he wanted people to be excited by him, by his life: he needed everybody's attention. Personally, I often surmised that it was guilt which made him begin our phone calls with some declaration of disaster. A guilt traceable to me, to our relationship together. After all, I was Bart's illegitimate son who did not even use his father's last name, the only known offspring of his wench-drenched existence. And my guess is he usually felt he had to have a reason to call, justifying a simple need to chat by inventing one trauma or another, thus legitimately catching my attention; and, by depersonalizing his need, making it possible for him to reach toward me.

Over the years, I had gotten used to the histrionics. By now, I just accepted them as his way of saying hello. Always he was sick; an old girl friend had committed suicide; his prostate would be scraped on Monday. Such calamities I took with a grain of salt. And anyway, Bart exaggerated unmercifully. And he always survived. Including some tight squeezes that might have felled more ordinary men. I mean, over the years people had constantly told me that the way Bart lived, he should have been dead at thirty. But look at him—the rakehell! Fit as a fiddle and going hell-bent-for-leather at forty-seven, with a liquor bottle in one hand, and a gorgeous woman on his arm, howling like Hemingway, Ruark, Paul Bunyon themselves —never slowing down. Secretly, I knew Bart was a dozen times healthier than myself. I often had a vision of him sneaking wheat germ and honey early in the morning when nobody was looking. I knew for a fact that he jogged and swam, played tennis, and worked out in gyms whenever he could find them. And I occasionally suspicioned that all the liquor he downed was in actuality stage booze, water tinted with grape juice or food coloring.

I grumbled, "So you're in trouble, so what else is new?"

"No, this time I'm not fooling around, I ain't crying wolf; this is for real. Marcel, you gotta listen to me, my days may be numbered—"

Somehow, in our talks like this, I always felt like a grown-up confronting a not particularly ingenuous child. "Pop," I said, "do you know what time it is?"

"*Time*—?" He seemed amazed that that could even be a consideration. Didn't everyone else follow the same schedule as Bart Darling, i.e., no schedule at all? I could picture him dazedly glancing out the window, startled to discover stars, a full moon, and werewolves creeping. Or else, bewilderedly focusing on the room lights, he was flabbergasted to learn that a brightness he had mistaken for sunshine was actually General Electric induced.

"Geez," he said. "I didn't realize. I forgot. What time is it where you're at?"

Where I was at was New York City. Where he might be, I could only—with trepidation—guess. Was the sun still shining? His call originating from Rangoon? London? Azerbaijan?

I said, "Here it's three A.M. Where are you?"

"Me—? I dunno . . . oh, sure . . . in the living room." Again, I imagined him casting around, befuddled—surprised to find himself in an actual *place*. Confined by walls. Its temperature perhaps controlled by a thermostat. For when Bart got going, mainlining nervous energy and ideas and not a little sauce into the bargain, the actual world melted away, and he existed entirely inside his undisciplined noggin.

"Come on, Bart. I mean, what town are you in? What city, state, country? Are you calling from America, Xanadu, the moon—?"

"Very funny."

"Hey, I'm serious. Also, you just woke me out of a deep sleep. So I'd like to establish something concrete before this conversation is knee-deep in non sequiturs and malapropisms."

"That's my kid," he shot right back, petulant, feisty, also overjoyed to click into our teasing, argumentative gear. " 'Something concrete,' 'non sequiturs and malapropisms'— Christ Almighty! When are you gonna stop being a tight-assed, cynical, sardonic, New York City jew-bastard, nigger-loving, crypto-Commie neo-faggot intellectual bent on saving the world and, in the process, putting down your poor old daddy in snide and dastardly ways at every golden opportunity?"

I wasn't in the mood for it. Sometimes I really got off on our banter, and so did he. Yet often the raucous taunting hit me wrong, largely because it was just about the only way we communicated. And I resented that, for I had never really cracked through all the banter to find out what kind of person he was—"at heart," as they say.

"You're calling from the Coast?" I asked blearily. "Or Aspen? Or Palm Springs?" I was getting those vibes.

"I'm calling from Chamisaville. Where the hell else?"

"Oh. Well, at least that's established." Chamisaville being a gaudy little southern-Rockies town, half Chicano, half Anglo, a tenth Indian, inundated by four dozen art galleries and a half-hokey, half-for-real literary-artistic-resort tradition. In the shadow of beautiful mountains, enveloped by the clean alpine air at seven thousand feet, lay a hot spring and religious shrine renowned the world over. I had never been there. About eight years earlier Bart had worked on a picture in that area, and, enamoured of the mountains and the trout streams, he had purchased an eighteen-room adobe mansion and thirty acres of sagebrush land, adding them to his collection of nonhome domiciles. I say "nonhome" because Bart could never settle down for long in one place. He had a house in L.A., an apartment in New York, and shared an Aspen condominium with one of his best friends, drinking buddies, and co-pussy chasers, a quasi-successful screenwriter named Aldo Cunningham. Other than that he lived mostly on airplanes, trains, buses even, or in rented cars, and motels.

Above all else, I suppose, motels.

I was conceived in a motel.

This cataclysmic event occurred back in the summer of 1947, when Bart was an eighteen-year-old rising young theater genius, and my mom, Kitty Thompson, was the same age and hoping to become a creditable actress one day. Summer stock out in the Hamptons brought them together. According to Bart, who can't remember the name of the motel, a five-acre strawberry field lay right on the rear doorstep of their unimposing cabin. And after he'd come a few times, he swaggered out back, positioned himself in the exact center of that field (under a full moon), and emptied his bladder, feeling so "prime" he could have licked a dozen bears, with a couple of wolverines thrown in for good measure.

That's the way Bart talked, not me.

Then he claimed he picked a bushel (read *handful*) of fat juicy strawberries (those are Bart's adjectives again, not mine —Bart's talk was often *all* adjectives; he heaped them onto his speech the same way he splashed syrup on flapjacks or smothered his morning raisin bran under five teaspoons of brown sugar!), and he lugged those ripe berries inside to where Kitty was spread-eagled on a white sheet looking like something God had cooked up just for him. Hungrily, they demolished the fruit in commemoration of a lovely screw, passionately kissing each other with lips drenched in sweet red juice. Next, Bart smeared her beautiful white skin and lovely full breasts with leftover pulp, and they commenced humping again.

For years, Kitty offered no version of her own. God knows, she never loved Bart. They never even slept together again, for that matter. But something went wrong with one of his rubbers (as he tells it)—and there you have it. When I finally pinned Kitty down, recounting Bart's story of my less-than-immaculate conception, she laughed. "He didn't use any rubbers," she said. "That's not Bart's style. You just got to look out for yourself when people like him are around."

Kitty couldn't recall any strawberries, either. She remembered a dynamic and egotistical young man so eager to nail her that he stuttered making the proposition. But she was bewitched by his energy and went along with it. The affair occurred in one little drab motel room or another. Bart came fast, redressed quickly, and paced nervously around the room talking to her. He had a thousand plans, he loved Kitty, he wanted to marry her, but they couldn't get hitched because he was destined to be a great actor someday, or a novelist—

"Bullshit. It was a whole lot of bullshit," Kitty gently told me years later, with the sad look that invaded her eyes whenever Bart and the role he played in her destiny cropped up. "But he was very attractive, physically, and his vitality was so catching. Yet the man couldn't concentrate, you know? He was so eager to get on with it, that he couldn't truly focus on a damn thing, he was so impatient to have one experience over and the next one coming up."

Welcome to the world, little Marcel Thompson.

"Marcel," Bart pleaded (back in the present, again), "this time I think I've had it. I've hit bottom and there's no bounce. Lorraine walked out on me."

I would need not just to take off my shoes, not just an abacus, but a highly sophisticated calculator to tote up all the women who had walked out on my father. Beginning with my own mother (he had tried to "date" her again, she had refused), the various-sized female footsteps of countless thousands had created a trampled muddle in the dust aiming away from his life. True, he drew them like moths to a flame, as the saying goes. And they sure left with their wings burned, as the saying also goes. That inability to pay attention had plagued him all his life—whether to a book, a film, a stunt (inattention here had ruined his acting career), or a woman. Five times Bart had made it to an altar: no marriage lasted more than three years, I believe. He asked every woman to marry him, I don't know why—that was part of his style. Part of a need, too, that I suppose he recognized but never figured out how to fulfill. Guessing conservatively, I'd say he lost half the money he ever made ponying up in divorce settlements. Although given his sloppiness and prehistoric sense of responsibility, coupled with his devilish ability to make everything both emotional and financial *muddy,* it was just about impossible—following a decree—for those cheated and maltreated women to pin him down, actually extracting anywhere near what they and the law felt was their due.

Until quite recently, I really used to envy my old man all his wives, mistresses, casual affairs—all the women, girls, strumpets, broads who shared with him his "prodigious feats of sexual derring-do!" And oh he had introduced me to some lollapaloozas during the brief tête-à-têtes he and I shared over the years. I imagine you could multiply by ten the dozens of his exotic women I met growing up. Meaning, if nothing else, he sure got laid a lot. And with some preposterous beauties at that!

On reflection, maybe "beauties" is the wrong word. Pop liked flash, but he had zero interest in filigree, so far as I know. Make that pedigree. He liked his women funky, overtly sexy—God help them (in his book) if they did not possess big tits. He wanted male onlookers to drool. His voluptuous "poontang" originated from the pages of *Playboy;* and I have an impression that many of them were named Gloria or Lulu or Marilyn. Starlets, and bold stereotypes who teasingly reached for the Sybarite's balls in public. Often he leeringly whispered to me that this or that "cunt" was actually a high-priced hooker. Bart needed to look and feel macho, and whenever I was around, especially in my teenager days, he sure came on strong that way. And his women caused an ache in me I always resented, for I had none of Bart's flamboyant chutzpah with which to realize my lascivious dreams. For years I seriously fantasized about his air-brained femmes fatales. Even today, though I'm a mature twenty-nine and all grown up, as they say, with a divorce and two estranged kiddies of my own out there, maturing—as I did—without a daddy, I get occasional twinges over the blatant flesh he paraded before my yearning adolescent eyes.

"You called me up just to tell me Lorraine walked out on you?" I asked incredulously.

"We been together *for over two years!*" he hollered, mightily insulted by my contemptuous lack of tact. Bart was always offended to the core. The second he opened his eyes in the morning, he commenced suffering affronts. For starters, the sunlight was usually too bright—couldn't God have dimmed it slightly, knowing that last night's alcohol was still raising havoc in his fuddled brain?

"Don't you have *any* compassionate feelings?" he added.

I had to laugh. Him accusing *me* of insensitivity.

"It's not like Lorraine was just another ordinary bim," he

snarled haughtily. "I loved her deeply, I wanted to get married, I wanted to have children—"

I sputtered—but not too loudly. Though he was being his usual absurd and illogical self, I sensed a warning underneath it all. In fact, I had a presentiment that perhaps something was more out of whack than when he had called me on the tag end of a hundred similarly traumatic situations.

"Look, I'm sorry she left you, Pop. That's a real bummer. I never met her, but the letters you sent, the picture, she sounds like a very nice person . . ."

"When did I ever send you a letter?" Such curves were typical of Bart. Did I say lack of concentration? My old man was the most expert broken-field runner I've ever known. He could suddenly cut left when aiming right, veering off base at the drop of an innuendo; the man was as easy to deflect as a snowflake.

And he had me there. Almost. "You sent a letter last year," I protested. " With a picture of Lorraine in it." But that may have been the only letter I ever received from Bart. The telephone was his medium. He wrote so little that by now his written hand had become illegible. Occasionally, given that business matters often called for formal communication, he dictated to secretaries. But in his private life he never wrote things down. A habit I always took for one more proof of Bart's shallow nature. You see, I have a theory that at heart people too lazy to write, who always grab for a phone, really don't care.

"Well, I don't remember sending the letter," he said. Adding: "Yesterday I cracked up the Harley."

"You what?" Still groggy from being awakened, I had trouble making these transitions.

"I totaled the Harley. I hit a patch of sand, skidded off the road, knocked down a barbwire fence, and collided head on with a two-hundred-and-seventy-year-old cottonwood tree."

"Jesus, are you hurt?"

"Who the hell knows? I ache all over. Every time I eat a

bagel or knock down a slug of Black Jack, I start to vomit. When I try to fuck it feels like I got a slipped disc in my back."

"I thought you said Lorraine—"

"All right, already, so maybe that part's not completely true. But I really smashed up the Harley something awful. And I *do* feel like vomiting whenever I eat—"

"What did the doctor say?"

"Doctor, schmocter. What am I made out of, money?"

"You cracked up the Harley, and you didn't even see a doctor?" Was he lying, trying for the jugular of my sympathy, exaggerating hideously? Like: Had he *really* cracked up the motorcycle, for starters? Or, if he had, knowing Bart, perhaps that barbwire ripping, head-on collision with a cottonwood tree actually had been some ridiculous little brouhaha where he hit the front brake by mistake, dumped the cycle at two miles an hour, slightly twisted an ankle, and scratched the bike's ferring. Or, given that he really had clobbered himself and the Harley, his "no doctors" riff was apt to be all bluster. I could recall many a time that Bart had sneaked into the back door of a hospital or a doctor's office. But in public he was indestructible —even if he had his own steaming guts cupped in his enormous hands! Still, I'd always suspected that he played the quacks the same way he played his liquor and carousing roles: when backs were turned he was always sneaking carrot juice and soya bread, logging eight hours sleep, and sending half his gun molls and imitation Mae Wests out the rear window instead of screwing them, just to save up vitality for a public front that could make everybody believe he was thirty years old instead of heading for fifty.

Anything Bart fancied might be "good for his image" he magnified shamelessly. Anything that might be construed as bad for that same image, he underplayed dramatically. Talk about your con men and professional bullshit artists: my father had no conscience to speak of. Running it down even further, I might add that I always sensed Bart was ashamed of being such a flagrant hustler. I mean, no matter how jovial his mouth, raucous his voice, or flaming his cheeks, I always caught pain in my father's eyes. In the midst of the most bawdy hijinks or revelry, that timeworn cliché applied: he invariably looked alone.

I don't believe Bart ever meant to hurt anyone with his inconsiderate style. Being insensitive was instinctive, not deliberate, with him. The same goes for his impulsive, misshapen, totally undiscerning generosity. If he was flush, and if a benevolent gesture reinforced his image, Bart could part with his energy and his worldly goods like Christ giving away loaves and fishes. Naturally, his actions were the actions of a man who desperately wanted "to be loved" . . . or "not to be loved"— pick one. I myself used to trash Bart for his abject fear of the loving responsibility. But after my one marriage to just one woman for only six years, I had found myself leaning much more sympathetically toward my bitched old man.

As for the rest of his needs and desires: who can really tell? My guess is Bart never pulled rein on himself long enough to tote up a score, or figure out what all his cacophonous bluster was about—afraid it would add up to zero? Maybe. Or perhaps he just didn't want to bother. It could be he simply wanted to have fun. I've always been pretty scornful of people who want life to be a joyride. But that's what he was forever telling me, anyway: "Shit, Marcel, what is the point to any of this if it ain't *fun?*" Fun meant getting laid a lot, of course, and being rich and famous. My guess is it was also a bitter alloy of being at emotional, spiritual, and physical loose ends. For all of his forty-seven years, my father had been dissatisfied, horribly ill at ease with his haphazard, and all too often silly, progress through life. I could be wrong: maybe deep down where it counts he honestly didn't give a damn about the significance of things.

That was one of his pet phrases: The Significance of Things. A phrase inevitably uttered with a churlish sneer, as in: "Marcel, you'll spend so much time bending your brain double trying to comprehend, and then alter, The Significance of

Things, that your fucking pekker will shrivel up and drop off, your balls'll recede, and you'll become a soprano again!"

Needless to say, Bart didn't believe in God, or communism, or determinism, or any other ism.

"Except *j*ism!" he once hooted derisively, after I had tried to put a few Marxian talons into his tough, scruffy hide.

Call him eclectic; call him an enigma; call him a dazzling scoundrel. "Call him a son of a bitch," Kitty once said to me, laughing. " 'Cause that's what he is, pure and simple. An honest-to-god, dyed-in-the-wool, no-holds-barred son of a bitch."

From Chamisaville, his electronic voice sounded as cantankerous as ever: "I don't need doctors to tell me how I feel, Marcel. A couple of my own brain cells are still functioning . . ."

More in line with our accustomed ritual banter than to put him down, I said, "Wanna bet?"

His response was so typical that I felt tempted to speak his words right along with him. "My own kid," he moaned. "Kids got no respect for their parents nowadays. I feel rotten inside, you make a joke. Maybe I'm dying, but you got nothing better to do than cast aspersions. I'm so depressed I can't see straight, and you got to saddle up some kind of sardonic Lenny Bruce routine. Why do you fucking Reds love mockery? They got me on Thorazine, Benadryl, milk—you name it. And the movie's going haywire; I'm losing control of all the Hollywood idiots I'm supposed to be controlling."

"What movie? You're on location?"

"Of *course* I'm on location," he howled. "And I need to see you right away!"

I was still playing the game, because with him it had always been the game, so I said: "I'm momentarily tied up. I'm two thousand miles away in New York City, busy being a Socialist Ph.D. candidate."

"So stop saving the world for a minute, and save your old man. Don't forget, I saved your ass once or twice over the years—"

Fair enough. He had. His help had been mostly financial: bread for college, money for an abortion. And twice he had bailed me out of jail on movement busts. In fact, there were times in my life when he had heaped the dollars atop me like I was a Jacqueline Bouvier in some Onassian divorce settlement. Although I had always accepted the aid, I had generally resented the motive behind it, sensing that he was trying to buy my love, my loyalty, my *some*thing, because he didn't have the guts, or the goodness, to angle for my affection by baiting a hook with his own love. As I grew older and had my own emotional and loving fuck-ups handed to me on a silver platter more than once, I learned to forgive him for his crass materialism, becoming belatedly—in the process—much more grateful for those bucks he had delivered during my lean years.

He had also sent money to Kitty, albeit erratically, during my tykehood. She had accepted and resented his aid the same way I had later. She couldn't help feeling he was trying to buy his way out of a deeper responsibility for me. Yet Bart claims he made many heartfelt overtures to her from the day I was born. "I would of married her if she'd a had me!" he claimed. "Who wanted to marry an amoral, whore-mongering, egomaniac?" Kitty countered. Over the years, the cases each made against the other just tailed away into a mishmash of conflicting wounds, needs, and temper tantrums. Like I said, almost everything Bart touched turned into a bewildering muddle.

I said, "I can't save you or your movie, Dad. You know that. I never could. Don't be absurd. Believe me, it's not as if I didn't once have this fantasy . . ."

Which is true. In my younger days I often dreamt of catching Bart right at the dangerous peak of all his crazy stunts, plucking him safely out of thin air just before he crashed, or went out the second-story window, or hit those tree branches with his parachute only partially opened, thereby saving him from a broken arm or busted ribs, a concussion, or terrible burns.

He started singing in a buffoonish, drunken way (I'll bet

he even had his eyes closed and was gesticulating spastically): "If your *daddy* . . . seems like he's . . . about to *die* . . . You'll feel *better* . . . if you help him . . . or at least *try!*"

I could picture him doing his Johnny Ray imitation. For you could wager your last nickel he was writhing, even without an audience. I also remembered the first time I'd caught his Johnny Ray act, over twenty years ago, right after he had surrendered to the cops the time he kidnapped me when I was seven. Squad cars and floodlights surrounded the motel cabin in north Las Vegas where he had held me prisoner for five days; and the way he acted, I'm surprised they didn't riddle us with dumdum bullets. When we emerged, ostensibly to give up, Bart was waving a toy gun, threatening to kill all of them, and me, and then himself, in that order. But suddenly he realized that *they* weren't joking. Then he dropped his cap gun and kicked it away like a soccer ball, and pushed me ahead into the arms of the cops and Kitty. And with that, captured forever in my child's mind in the glare of their spotlights and the glitter of their shotguns and pistols, he gave a spastic jerk and went into his Johnny Ray imitation . . . and I'm telling you, we *all* just gaped, right through the first two verses of "Cry." Not until the second chorus did the police finally wake up, grab him, snap on the cuffs, and hustle him away.

Because after a fashion Bart was semifamous, my kidnapping, and his arrest, made the network-television news; we played on tubes from coast to coast. It would have been great publicity for his latest movie of that time, but for the fact that he could have gotten the chair for grabbing me and flying across God knows how many state lines during our colorful odyssey together. When she realized just how serious the charges were, Kitty almost shit a cupcake, did a one-eighty, and told the police the whole escapade had just been a family quarrel, a terrible misunderstanding. So they let him creep out the back door to his freedom again. And Bart never did get to give that dramatic speech about having but one life to give for his God and his country, a speech he had been planning to make from his courtroom box, or from the gallows, or from his place before the firing squad—the latter being a group he had planned to face, of course, without any namby-pamby kerchiefs binding his fierce, immortal eyes.

Kitty was so freaked by the whole adventure that her attitude about me and Bart changed somewhat. That is, she decided to grant him certain visiting privileges, hoping they might avert another kidnapping. Prior to the heist (or during my first seven years), Kitty had denied Bart the right to spend any time with me. Which hurt, because he had faithfully made annual pilgrimages to wherever we happened to be living at the time, begging for the privilege of tinkering around with me for a weekend or two, and possibly even transporting me out to his family's North Shore Long Island home, an edifice that happened to be the baronial mansion of one of our country's more ruthless robber barons.

As you can see, the plot thickens.

But, suffice it to say here that my mother, being the Communist she had developed into, had little sympathy for Bart's origins. And she sure as hell didn't want me corrupted by so much as one day in that opulent palace of iniquity. Kitty feared (pretty correctly, I might add) that my impressionable child's brain would be hopelessly contaminated (which it was—later on) by the magical grandeur of a fifteen-acre lawn, indoor tennis courts, and a luncheon table that seated sixty.

All those forbidden fruits became accessible to me after the kidnapping did away with the visiting ban. At last, upon occasion, I was allowed to spend a weekend or two at my father's boyhood castle. Fortunately, I proved equal to the task, rolling around as happy as a pig in shit in all that splendor during my childhood and teenage years despite Kitty's pinko brainwashing, and then turning full circle during my college movement days, reviling that in which I had previously reveled.

But these reflections were touched off by Bart's Johnny Ray imitation over the telephone.

"Pop, it's no use. In fact, it's hopeless. I can't leave New

York right now. And even if I could, what's the point? If I remember correctly, a couple of times in the past when I really thought you were in trouble and went rushing to your aid, I always wound up in a house full of weird creeps having one kind of outrageous party or another, and you hardly even talked to me, you were so preoccupied busting groupies or acting or trying to nail down business deals. And you weren't in trouble at all. You had just had a sentimental urge to exercise some obscure fatherly prerogative."

" 'Obscure fatherly prerogative'?"

"You know what I mean."

"But this time isn't like that," he protested. Actually, he had started to whine, even though all during my childhood he had repeatedly castigated me in my weaker moments by snarling "If there's one thing I hate in life, Marcel, it's a fucking *whiner!*"

And he added: "I'm trapped in an eighteen-room house surrounded by a bunch of manic morons who don't know the difference between a zoom lens and an optical printer! And every time I cough, I cough up *blood!* And I feel like an old man and I'm tired and I'm *scared!*" he babbled frantically. "And you're the only family I got that gives a hoot, believe it or not. Everybody else threw in the sponge long ago!"

He was laying it on a little thick, I thought. Still, he'd never admitted being scared before, and that gave me some cause for concern.

"You'll excuse me for being ever the Pollyanna, Pop, but you sound right full of piss and vinegar to me."

" 'Right full of piss and vinegar,' " he roared. "Who the hell do you think you are—Andy Devine? You listen to WJRZ one more week, they'll turn you into a 'Hee Haw!' hayseed. Ain't you got no fuckin' respect for *language?*"

That last comment was an old joke, and it always made both of us laugh, so we laughed—by rote—once more.

Then he said, "I'll send a money order for the plane fare tomorrow."

"*Don't!* I really can't come."

"The hell you can't. I'm sending the plane fare whether you spend it on plane fare or not. Go ahead, cash the damn thing, blow it on a broad and a bottle, see if I care. I never asked you for—what would you call it?—'Filial Gratitude'? I never even pretended that I *deserved* any. I never—"

"Pop, I'm gonna hang up, you're getting hysterical."

"—even asked you for a single God damn thing, as far as I can remember. Just maybe once every two or three years to be able to shake my own kid's hand, and catch up on old times, and maybe even receive a teeny-weeny crumb of respect and sympathy when I'm hurt, and when I'm down . . ."

I shouted, "*When are you ever gonna grow up?*"

That stopped him. The airwaves tingled.

Then his voice, very tiny and very far away, said, "Grow up?"

Incredulously.

And *he* hung up on *me*.

I lay there, slightly dazed, unable to recapture sleep, thinking about my crazy dad: Bart Darling.

I guess if I were to add up all the time we had actually spent together, it would only amount to several months. Even though I always saw him a few weekends every year after Kitty lifted the ban, there were some stretches, especially during more recent years, when we had barely communicated once or twice every twelve months by phone. And at the time of his call I hadn't actually seen Bart for over two years.

Still, the man and his style had had an enormous impact on my life. I tend to believe he would have made an enormous impression on me even without being my father. I mean, look how many people impress you even if you don't know them— famous men and women, of course: writers, film stars, heavyweight champions . . . And, in a perplexing way, Bart always seemed to me a little like Muhammad Ali or Charles Lindbergh. I say *perplexing* because Bart never even remotely became whole in a way that might have made him legitimately larger than life. He blew it all; his talent was horribly fractured; he never had two good days in a row. But he got under my skin almost as soon as we were allowed to spend time together, and forever after I had an awe of him: he was always more than just human.

And believe me, I'm no pushover. I've been to Hollywood. I've even been to some of those parties. I've met 'em all: Redford, Newman—pick a star. I drank champagne once with an actress who had the sixties by the balls in no uncertain big-box-office terms, and I wasn't very impressed.

But for a long time Bart had me really snowed. In my book, he cavorted around with the likes of Ernest Hemingway, Karl Marx, Che Guevara, Ali, Edith Piaf, Tina Modotti. It might be that he had me buffaloed by what he *almost* had, yet lacked, and could have learned to get, *if* . . . , but somehow tragically failed to learn. . . . It goes something like that in my head, and then I lose the drift.

The phone rang again.

I figured: Ignore it, he'll give up, he'll go get drunk, he'll have forgotten all about it come morning.

On the tenth ring I grabbed it, shouting, "Jesus Christ Almighty, man, what are you trying to do, *wake the dead?*"

The kind of voice that could have belonged only to a Coal Miner's Daughter or a Toddle House waitress in Savannah, said, "Marcel Thompson, is that *you?*"

I gulped. "Speaking. I'm sorry. But who's this?"

"Lorraine Waldrum."

I drew a blank.

"The Lorraine who just walked out on your rascal of a daddy."

"Oh . . . you." *Rascal of a daddy?*

I couldn't think what else to say, so she asked, "Are you all right? I'm sorry—I woke you up, didn't I? I forgot what time—"

"No, that's okay, really. I was just lying here, you know. I mean, barely five minutes ago my old man phoned."

"That's why I'm calling. About Bart."

"Oh. I see . . ."

"I'm not sure exactly where to begin . . ."

No doubt she was another of his cheap floozies: talk about sap and malarkey transmitted by wire! I didn't have to meet her to know what she looked like. Big tits, tiny waist, bouffant peroxide hairdo: another cock-teasing, uneducated, thirty-five-year-old teenybopper, with a perky little y'all voice, and an underlying cynicism making her weary beyond her years.

"Why don't you begin at the beginning," I said with a weary sigh.

"Just a minute—" Her voice changed remarkably, instantly hard and no-nonsense: authoritative. "What do you mean by the tone of what you just said?"

I sat up, opened my eyes a little wider, shook my head once to clear the cobwebs, and blurted, "Nothing at all—I didn't mean anything."

"I don't know you," she snapped, "I only know Bart, and I've lived with him over two years now, and I know some things about him, and maybe that also means I know some things about you; that's debatable, of course. Still, I've often observed that assholeism tends to run in families. So don't you start getting snide and cavalier with me, sugar, because I can hold my own with the heavyweights, I'm warning you."

I said, "Please . . . it's three-thirty in the morning. If you don't mind, I'm pretty groggy."

"I'll get straight to the gist of it, then. I love your father, but he's so full of shit the cowbirds peck at him from sunup to sunset, and that's why I finally left him for good, two days ago. If you know Bart, you'll know that what he did next was a big old theatrical play for my sympathy, your sympathy, and everybody else's sympathy, but I got a hunch it backfired on him. He drove that humongous Harley of his off the road, through a barbwire fence, and smack-dab into a cottonwood tree, and he was still out cold when the ambulance picked him up twenty minutes later. It wasn't 'til eighteen hours later he finally came around—I guess that'd be this morning. He didn't break any bones, but the doctors at the Our Lady of the Sorrows Hospital, they claim he probably for sure has a concussion, and they'd like to do a bunch of tests to see what happened to such internal organs as his kidneys. Soon as he woke up, though, Bart threw a shit-fit and stomped out of the hospital. He went straight to the film location without even stopping by the mansion to shave. I went over to the Big House to try and coax him into going back, but talking to that rockhead is like trying to handle chopsticks with a boxing glove. He called me a whore and threw an Andy Warhol at me, so I told him to fuck off and go die with the chickens, see if I gave a good God damn. And that's my story about your old man. And the only reason I'm calling you is he blabs about you a lot, and maybe you could make him see those doctors and quit being so dad-gummed puerile and theatrical, and take care of himself a little, because maybe this time he's gone and done some real damage. The man is *not* immortal, as well you may realize."

"That's it?"

"That's all she wrote."

"I didn't think it was that serious. Bart always cries wolf."

"That's Bart." And suddenly her voice changed again, becoming gentle. "He's a lost soul for sure, but Jesus . . . sometimes he comes so *close.*"

I think that was the first time I ever heard anyone besides myself, and especially a woman, speak of Bart in tones almost approaching reverence . . . and love.

I said, "Well . . . what do you think I ought to do?"

"That's your problem. I just thought it was important for you to know. And to also understand that I'm not returning to that two-fisted, double-dealing, son of a bitch, no matter how bad he tears himself asunder trying to make me come home wagging my little old tail behind me."

"Then maybe I should come out . . ." Suddenly, in my head, a thousand things commenced boiling. Excitement over seeing Bart—there was always that, almost an illicit excitement, like visiting a whorehouse (which is part of what he was often running whenever and wherever I happened to cross his path on his turf)—and the logistical problems of leaving New York for a while, getting someone to pick up mail, feed the cat, take care of my tutoring chores for a week. I'd have to call Nancy, letting her know I wouldn't pick up the kids and take them to Washington Square this Saturday (guilt! guilt! guilt!), and ... and so on and so forth. Airline reservations, plane tickets, all the garbage that is second-nature stuff for everybody in America except me.

"If you decide to come, Marcel, maybe we'll meet, have a drink together, who knows?"

Click.

I said "Okay," and then hung up too.

And looked at my watch: it was four o'clock in the morning. So I congratulated myself, for I had made it through *l'heure Fitzgerald* yet once again.

2 Funny, how nonindispensable we usually turn out to be. I had children to father each weekend, NYU students to tutor, a university assistantship, a Ph.D. thesis in the works, and a cat to feed . . . and yet none of that stood in my way. A week ago I had felt so intricately mired to the destiny of everyone and everything within my orbit, that it had seemed I might never escape the fourteen-square-block area in which I ran my patterns. Now, when I actually confronted my obligations in each situation, it turned out that the biggest obstacle to boarding a plane headed west was finding a taker for Jules—the cat. But once a friend agreed to feed him for a week and keep her window closed so he couldn't hit the fire escapes, I was home free.

I felt slightly dismayed that it had all transpired so easily. How come, at my age, and considering my expertise, experience, and personality, I wasn't needed more?

In the East Side Terminal, still on Manhattan, the jitters began. They worsened on the ride out to the airport. By the time I was buckled into a seat and staring at the No Smoking sign I wanted to leap off the airplane, grab a cab, race home, retrieve my cat, and never again venture so far afield.

Too late, though. Settling back my head, I gritted my teeth, inhaled, and held it—and then we were airborne. I hate airplanes. I hate anything over which I have no control. At least in a car I would have a last-second chance to swerve, or duck, or swan-dive into the back seat: I was, in part, responsible for my own safety. But in an airplane—? I hated flying for the same reasons I was afraid of hallucinogenic drugs and had somehow developed a mind-set making it impossible for me ever to become truly drunk. I'm *terrified* of losing control.

We swooped up safely to an altitude of thirty thousand feet, where I opened my eyes, venturing a nervous glance earthward. All America—patchwork fields, rivers, and pretty—lay below. And I experienced a sudden ecstasy, feeling safe for the moment and glad I had dared to make this effort.

Cruising along with semi-impunity, then, zipping across America in just a few hours to rendezvous with my crippled father, I remembered other transcontinental jaunts that had taken days. Back when I was almost twelve, Bart had chauffered me cross-country for the inauguration of President Kennedy. Kitty and I were California-ing it in a tight little bungalow for a year while she worked on her Master's at Berkeley. The way I recall it, Bart simply showed up one day (wearing threads resembling a three-piece white Pierre Cardin suit) seated behind the wheel of an enormous burgundy-colored automobile sporting white leather seats, mahogany dashboard paneling, and a TV sunk into the back of the front seat, and told Kitty: "Let him come. It'll be good for his education." If Kitty had known that a woman who would ride along with us was waiting at an Oakland bar, she never would have delivered me to his careless tutelage. But he guaranteed the trip across America would be magical for me, would only take a few days, and that ten minutes after the inauguration I'd be on an airplane winging home in time for the next school day. So she let him whisk me away in his flashy "niggermobile," as he called it. Already, though I had barely logged over a decade on the planet, I attacked him broadside for that type of racist remark. Bart retorted loudly, "That ain't racist, Marcel, that's just *cultural,* for cripes sake!" Then he laughed, saying, "Hell, boy, don't you know? Some of my best friends are white folks!"

That trip occurred a few years before the stunt accident. Bart was at the height of his high rolling, making good money in Hollywood acting, producing, directing—you name it. The girl waiting for us at the Alibi Inn was a big sensual chatterbox, Kyrah Pattachinsky. I don't recall if she was in films, or in chorus lines, or just another pretty babe to be seen on the arm of whoever happened to be in the shekels down Los Angeles way. But she laughed a lot, and after a while I got to thinking of her as a small-time nightclub torch singer, because she had a pretty sexy voice: we sang songs together halfway across America. She and Bart shared a fairly good rapport, as any fool kid my age could see. They squeezed and jostled and poked and prodded each other a lot, told dirty jokes, squealed with laughter, and, in general, friendlied up a storm. As for myself, I spent the first five hundred miles camped on the rear seat, gooning at the boob tube, utterly flattened by the idea of Imogene Coca and Ernie Kovacs and Jack Paar and Lucille Ball in the back seat of a lush rocket whooshing me at eighty miles an hour across the continent. Fact is, too, I was starved for television: that's one cultural accouterment Kitty never allowed into our humble digs—not until after I had split, and suddenly she found herself so lonely at nights that by the time I returned for my first visit from college she already had a little black-and-white job on a roller tray at the foot of her bed.

Hitting Reno, Nevada, with Bart and Kyrah Pattachinsky was like inspecting oil wells with John D. Rockefeller or shooting straight pool with Willie Mosconi. Reno, Times Square, Miami Beach—the Big Time—Bart's kind of action. Where it was flashy and phony and open twenty-four hours a day, and reeked of sin and funky people, chorines and murderers and money (and if you were hungry you could always get a Wimpy's hot dog or a MacDougal Street sausage or a South Philly cheese-steak): Bart had always been attracted to that kind of scene. Preposterous false fronts, overblown egos, carnival banter, miniskirts, slickly nyloned female legs, and big boobs: oh, how he loved the noise, the barkers, and the gun thugs patrolling all that glitter!

Bart gave me Coney Island on July Fourth, dozens of Rangers hockey games, Blaze Starr and Candy Barr, and two championship fights! He actually drove me up to Lewiston, Maine, to see Muhammad Ali deck Sonny Liston in the first round of their second fight. He also made sure that we hit

Yankee Stadium in the summer of 1960 to see Roger Maris hit a home run on his way toward the Babe's record. Another event my father insisted I relish with him was that 1963 World Series when the Dodgers blew the Yankees out in four straight: Bart even made sure that I got to shake the hand of Sandy Koufax, Number One on my list of boyhood idols. We attended Giants football games, back when they were a team to be reckoned with. And Bart hustled me, underage, into many a murky jazz joint—the Five Spot, Slugs, the Vanguard, the Page Three— in order that I might hear such monoliths as Stan Getz, Memphis Slim, Thelonious Monk, and Charlie Parker, without a working knowledge of whom he did not believe I could survive.

Other immortals I have known, thanks to my impulsive father, include Lenny Bruce, Janis Joplin, Tiny Tim. I mean, in person, Out There— "The real thing!" Bart always howled. "Nothing else compares to the real thing!" Make that the Real Thing. And oh how he loved slipping the maître d' a fat and crinkly double sawbuck just to make sure we had ringside seats—Nothing But the Best.

"If you ain't gonna go first class," he liked to counsel, "why the hell go at all?"

Understand, this peculiarly analphabetic manner of speech came from a man who had been born with a silver shovel in his mouth, and who had once had three years toward a high-and-mighty Bachelor's degree in English literature from none other than Harvard, if you please!

And he had grown up dining with vice-presidents and secretaries of state, and playing croquet of a summer Sunday on a fifteen-acre front lawn!

Meanwhile, back at the oasis—

"The Arabs were smoking their camels and eating their dates."

That was one of the first dirty jokes I ever learned; naturally, Bart told it to me.

Another one of his favorites, which became one of my

favorites, too, when I was a kid, was the translation of the Lucky Strike LS/MFT slogan: "Loose Sweaters Mean Floppy Tits."

I mention this lowbrow semimoronic trivia only because I have a memory of myself and Bart and Kyrah Pattachinsky— me in the back seat of that burgundy-colored yacht watching some fabulous giveaway quiz show on TV—floating into the neon rigamarole of Reno giggling our heads off over a spate of inane jokes in the mode of those two IQ busters above. And I, for one, had never had so much fun in my life.

Also, I had never been so free. Kitty kept a pretty tight rein, and one thing she sure as hell would not sanction was the sort of free-for-all capitalism Reno offered. Already she had instilled in me a fledgling consciousness of money, capital, and the nature of class society and class struggle. And, although essentially a gentle woman, Kitty was very firm in her convictions: we lived our lives according to frugal Marxist principles. I respected her immensely, and meant—sincerely—to follow her example when I grew up.

Meaning I was just about as repressed as any other little puritan my age would have been, so I gobbled up whole hog Reno's cheap glamour, glittering facades, fancy ladies, gambling dens, and frontier follies!

Probably we weren't in town but a few hours. Yet it made the powerful kind of impression on me that the sight of American soldiers with fixed bayonets knocking down my wife and child on the steps of the Pentagon would make only a short seven years later. I don't mean the terror part, I mean *in the guts.* Bart fetched me a bunch of silver dollars, and when nobody was looking, I clunked them all into a slot machine. I gooned at Wild West peep shows in Harrah's Club—the death of Jesse James, the shooting of Wild Bill Hickok!—and watched Bart and Kyrah play blackjack and shoot craps. Cowboys cluttered the town, and I gawked openly, for I'd never seen a cowboy before. By the time we left, I half expected a gigantic mushroom cloud from some down-range testing to unfurl against the purple desert horizon as "Eastward-Ho!" we headed toward the crowning of Camelot.

I figure it was in western Kansas that one of my early Great Voyeuristic Adventures vis-à-vis Bart took place. Happening to look up from the TV set for a moment during an ad, I discovered that Kyrah had disappeared. Then I noticed Bart was hunching his shoulders peculiarly, and tipping his head back weirdly. When I leaned to my right, I could see that his eyes were half closed. Strangely dazed, he grimaced and muttered jerky little things I couldn't quite decipher. Not only that, but *we were barreling down the fucking left-hand side of the road straight toward the big red bulldog-led cab of an enormous Mack truck!*

Talk about your Too Paralyzed to Speak syndrome! Only at the very last moment did Bart open one glazed eye and deftly swerve onto our side of the macadam, allowing the semi to shudder by with a tooth-rattling *whoosh!* I've never been able to forget.

Unfazed, Bart continued hunching and grimacing. Lips pursed, he nodded his head, then shook it, let out a soft whistle, and muttered "Attaboy, girl—!"

I leaned forward, parking my nose delicately on the rear edge of the front seat. Rolling one eyeball discreetly forward, I peered over the ledge . . . down to where Kyrah Pattachinsky's starlet curls were bobbing in his lap.

The most incredible thing to me then was that he had her almost naked. Her sweater was accordianed up under her armpits so he could fondle her breasts. And her skirt was wrunkled around her waist so that when he tired of her tits he could reach down her back to her butt and hook one finger, the middle finger—he always called it his "social finger" (Bart *was* obscene!)—up her anus. A moment of erotic fury ensued, him with that one claw in her tugging so hard he lifted her ass off the seat, bending her spine back toward her head, his teeth gritted fiercely, and when he came the car wobbled all over the highway at ninety miles an hour, at which point I thought for sure we were goners.

Bart sagged, Kyrah did too, and I eased back carefully, my heart pounding—fibrillating, no less! I spent hours, it seems, blinking my eyes, trying to make sense of the meaningless scrabble on the tube.

Too soon for comfort, Bart said, "How's it going back there, slugger?"

"It's going just fine, sir."

"Whatcha watchin'?"

And the thing I couldn't believe, is, his voice sounded normal. As if nothing more exciting than five-o'clock tea and cinnamon toast had just happened.

I said, "Watching? Sir?"

"Yeah, what program you got going back there?"

I stared hard at the TV. A bunch of people populated the screen, moving around, talking; they had familiar faces, familiar voices, and the familiar canned laughter sounded with moronic regularity. But damned if I could make any sense out of it all!

"I don't know, sir. It's just a program."

"Well, why the hell don't you turn the idiotic thing off and take a glaum out *there!*" he bellowed good-naturedly. "That's America out there, kid! Land of the free, purple mountain majesty, I pledge allegiance to the flag of the United States of *America!*"

Kyrah's head popped up; she and Bart burst into "The Star-Spangled Banner." By the time they were halfway through it I had recovered enough to join in. After that, Bart taught me his version of "America":

> *My father was a spy,*
> *Caught by the FBI,*
> *His name was Joe.*
> *He was on a mountaintop,*

When shot down by a cop,
They le-eft hi-im there to rot—
God bless my ass!

Then I fell asleep, and when I awoke, Miss Kyrah Pattachinsky had vanished—poof!

Bart had dropped her off in Kansas City so that she could
catch a plane home to Los Angeles.

And you may be wondering at this point: Whatever
became of Kennedy's inaugural?

Well, we arrived in Washington fairly pooped, and with
bad sore throats stemming partly from two days spent singing
every rock 'n' roll song ever recorded between 1954 and 1958.
Bart and I shared that talent: I guess I had gotten mine by
osmosis from him. Have I mentioned that he was a good singer
and musician, who, in 1956, formed a group called the Glitter-
bugs that cut a rock record, "Blinded by Love," which actually
basked for six weeks on the charts, in the sunshine of the Top
Fifty? The rest of our sore throats had come from halting the
car every four hours to do roadside exercises in minus-twenty-
degree cold. My dad, the health freak, insisted on this kind of
regimen, whether we caught our deaths of pneumonia or not.

So we arrived in Washington one day before the inauguration, and holed up in a Georgetown mansion I think Bart said
belonged to a Mafia personality, or to a politician temporarily
detained at Leavenworth. The place was empty, but its refrigerator harbored a "bodacious cornucopia of rare goodies" (quoth
B. Darling), including a dozen bottles of champagne on the
bottom shelf. My enormous room had beautiful mansard windows from which I could stare down at the Potomac. A marvelous sunken tub was the bathroom's main attraction.

Overwhelmed by the luxury, I spent most of my short
sojourn there stuffing my face, watching television, and taking
baths.

In fact, I watched the inauguration on television. Having
gone out the night before, Bart rolled in at 4:00 A.M. drunk as

a skunk with a typically statuesque lady named Charley (from Charlotte) Grapp on his arm—later I learned from Bart that she was "a big-time ecdysiast." Their debauching eventually woke me, and naturally I pattered on my innocent little feet downstairs for another mind-blowing glimpse at yet one more orgy. When I reached my station at the butler's window of the pantry, I could see immediately that the two lunatics in the kitchen were engaged in some no-nonsense High Old Times, to say the least. Seated on a low chopping-block table located about mid-kitchen, Bart had his head tilted back and a tin funnel in his mouth: she was dancing Salome-like around him, splashing champagne into the funnel. My idiotic pop sputtered, joked, gurgled, and giggled: booze spattered every which way. By the time I arrived, both of them were drenched and so raving happy they seemed like madhouse goofballs to me. Between dishing up Bart's champagne slugs, Charley staggered all over the place like a delirious heavyweight out on his feet. She slammed into cabinets, swept pots and pans off a counter, and body-blocked the refrigerator so hard its door swung open. All the time she incoherently whooped and hollered so mirthfully tears flowed from her heavily mascaraed eyes, raining along with the champagne upon her temptingly soaked bosom. Pretty soon Bart spit out the funnel and chanted: "Take it off, take it off, take it alllllllll off!" Then he cupped his hands at his mouth and began playing a stripper's tune, making the sound of a sly and slurry coronet. And in the crackpot jargon of my irrepressible old man, "She sure knew how to pop them patooties!" About halfway through her act, Charley unzipped Bart's fly and, again in the argot of my frenetic daddy, "Out jumped the Big Fella!" All during the strip Charley continued losing her balance, colliding heavily against things. But in between these clumsy sorties, she shed her sopping vestments with such tantalizing gusto, I almost passed out. As soon as she had twirled her panties twice around an index finger and sailed them off to the top of the fridge, Bart heaved up, going for her like Fred Biletnikoff lunging for an end-zone pigskin. She was a big woman, but Bart manhandled her like I imagine a lion might manhandle a rabbit. In no seconds flat he had her spread-eagled over the chopping block, directly facing me, and was batting at her from behind . . . and with that I ran for the hills.

I just barely made it back upstairs!

Next morning Charley was as chipper as a pink canary in Honolulu after a hurricane (thanks, and a tip of the hat once more to Mr. Bart Darling of Hollywood, New York, and Chamisaville), when she tripped into the den where I was glued to the box watching the inaugural parade, waiting for the presidency to change hands. Looking good in a man's blue terry-cloth bathrobe and male slippers, she had not even bothered to wash her face after the night before, though her mouth was freshly decorated with aluminum-pink frosting. Nonchalantly she flipped a cigarette between her lush lips, lit it, and plopped onto the couch beside me, saying "How they hangin', slugger?" We proceeded to watch the show together, during a saturnalia of eating: Cokes, baloney-and-cheese sandwiches, grapes, ice cream with powdered Nestlé on top. Although I was properly awed by the lady's dimensions, false eyelashes, and glossy lipstick that glistened like nitroglycerine, not to mention by my vivid recollection of the night before, I also liked her a lot. A friendly sort with a Kewpie-doll voice, she laughed overtly and often, and seemed really to enjoy life, her role in it, the whole shebang. Every time they zoomed to a close-up of Kennedy, she three-sixtied her eyeballs, giving a funny gutteral sigh while exclaiming: "Oh boy, would I ever like to slip one of my grubby little paws into *that* joker's skibbies!"

Later on that afternoon, when Bart surfaced, they hustled me off to the airport. On the way, we stopped at the house of somebody Bart knew who had an official program, and he gave that to me, making me promise never to tell Kitty I hadn't actually seen the event in person.

(Since then, I have lied so often about having actually attended the opening moment of Camelot that I can almost feel exactly how cold and windy and bright it was, and how Kennedy and Jackie and the kids looked, and what color Robert Frost's liver spots were—stuff like that. In fact, it takes a super-human effort to remember that I was not actually a grandstand spectator; I saw it all on television, wolfing down a thousand monosodium-glutamated junk foods I was never allowed at home, seated beside a comical stripteaser who kept joking about the new president's genitals!)

Then Bart put me on a plane, and that was the first time ever I flew across the United States all by myself.

Which brings us back to the present, in an airplane again, crossing America once more, this time ostensibly to "save" my floundering father.

Maybe to salvage whatever was left of him is a better way of putting it.

For Bart had changed some during the intervening years since he piloted me across the continent in that throbbing flamboyant car; and he had skidded a ways down the proverbial hill. Yet before filling in the more recent background, perhaps I should dwell briefly on the man's origins, where he came from and why, and what happened to make him what he became—insofar as I know, that is, or have been able to educatedly guess. Though, of course, much—let's say most—of my knowledge about Bart originates from the horse's mouth itself, and Bart never could tell a tale without embellishing it to the hilt, or just outright unconscionably lying his ass off. Hence, I wouldn't bet a plug nickel on how much of what I know is stretched fact or true fiction, because for most of his lifetime Bart was hilariously, single-mindedly, often tragically engrossed in creating himself as a legend. Being mythical, larger than life, wholly *original* was something he wanted much more than to be rich (he was born *that* way!), or to be famous in his field, or to be respected. "Respect," he once told me, "is for dead generals. What do I care for the respect of a society made up of puny, psychotic, scared-shitless, money-grubbing little worms?"

Of course, such an attitude might be one he adopted long before I got to know him, when he may have realized that, for one reason or another, he possessed neither the talent nor the temperament to amount to more—in his chosen trade and assorted avocations—than one more (albeit splendiferous) phony hill of beans.

He—better yet, "It"—began with Herbert Marovich Darling, H. M. Darling, according to the Seymour Melmans, Charles Beards, and Matthew Josephsons of our crippled, and crippling, empire. Among other things, the man was a banker in cahoots with J. P. Morgan, H. P. Davison—that crowd. He also coined the infamous paraphrase: "I never met a sucker I didn't like." The Darling estate bordered (still borders, for that matter) the Davison estate, Peacock Point, near Locust Valley on the Island's North Shore, about an hour east of New York City. Bart grew up in a mansion that had fifty-six servants during the peak years; his bedroom windows faced out on a spacious lawn, majestic walnut trees, and, fifteen yards beyond a seawall, Long Island Sound. His youth was a Gatsbyan dream —too bad he hated it so! He was kicked out of a Connecticut prep school—Choate—and attended various private institutions overseas, notably in Switzerland. At one time in his life he could defend himself in four foreign languages: French, German, Italian, Spanish. Just about anything he wanted he could get, simply by pressing a bedside button (connected to maids; to the kitchen; to the stables; to the garage, where a fleet of black station wagons and limousines were at his disposal; to his father) or just by asking for it. Tall, handsome, athletically inclined—of course he played football at Harvard and was a member of Hasty Pudding. Bart hobnobbed all his youth with the sons and daughters of Roosevelts, Lindberghs, Coolidges, and Morgans. When he reached twenty-one he inherited a trust fund worth a million or more.

Bart responded to his good fortune by abusing it flagrantly from an early age on. Restless, headstrong, almost obscenely energetic, he thought the Darling estate—Dolphin Bays—was boring. His elders—nevermind that they were undersecretaries of the navy, presidential advisors, hot-shot Republicans, and

African big-game hunters—he viewed as stuffed shirts, pompous asses, predatory idiots. He was always in trouble, always running away, always disappearing. By the time he reached eighteen his face was scarred from automobile accidents. In fact, from fourteen on he drank like a fish, and by his early twenties he had totaled no less than seven automobiles and gotten three debutantes pregnant out of (way out of!) wedlock. Against the family's wishes, he raced stock cars and motorcycles. He even earned a pilot's license, then lost it for being drunk in an airplane that crashed on a North Shore golf course only moments after perilously buzzing a high-school football game, causing panic among spectators and players alike. The woman with Bart in that airplane happened to be the wife of a well-known, highly respected Glen Cove magistrate.

Although captain-elect of the Harvard football team, Bart never returned to college for his senior year. Due back at the university early for fall practice, instead, after giving the finger to Dolphin Bays, he hit the road with a theater troupe, wound up in Provincetown, directed some plays, acted in others, and worked up a nightclub routine in which he sang, danced, cracked dirty jokes à la Lenny Bruce and Redd Foxx, and did a comical *Hamlet* spoof. Soon he landed in New York City. By then I was already around, having been conceived the previous summer. Learning of my existence, Bart asked Kitty to marry him. She pointed at his bride of exactly three months, one Thelma Gascoyne, an alcoholic actress (in the Bankhead mold) twice his age, whose greatest claim to fame seems to have been a short-lived affair with Eugene O'Neill. Immediately, Bart divorced her, and begged again for Kitty's hand. When she rejected him, he had a nervous breakdown and spent four months in the Bowery tottering at death's door before his own father—an austere puritan who often rode the morning subway from Penn Station to Wall Street—spotted his own boy slumped among day-old newspapers in the corner of one car of the Seventh Avenue Express, and dragged him home, nursing Bart back to health.

Soon as he could, Bart gave Dolphin Bays the backside of his heels again, and tried to join the Communist party, not because he knew (or cared) a whit about communism, but because he thought his membership might soften Kitty toward him. And anyway, he never missed an opportunity to thumb his nose at his family. "The Commies *needed* this boy," he once told me. "They needed every recruit they could get, because the rest of this rabid country was girding its self-righteous blood-thirsty loins for McCarthyism and the Cold War."

The Communists, however, wouldn't touch him with a twelve-foot pole.

So he became semifamous, instead, as a director of off-broadway productions, and as a first-rate, yet highly tempera-mental actor, singer, dancer. His poetry came out in little magazines; he also had a go at painting. And at writing: first plays, then screenplays, then for television. Bart never really hit the big time because he rushed everything. He couldn't stand to polish. Halfway through one idea, he'd veer off to tackle another. He could nurture nothing, he had no patience with revisions. Bart knew how to work like a dog on somebody else's finished material, but he could not sit still for his own. Too, the man was so involved in creating himself as a legend that little time remained to become a wholly serious creative person. You might say that he had a terrible fear of becoming the least bit ordinary. Naturally, he continued to drink prodigiously, and became entangled in outlandish fornications. "He was known for being quite a stud," Kitty said, "but not for being a lover." Also, Bart hated anything organized, despised all institutions, and threw his money away, ashamed of it, apparently, trying to make his fortune dwindle faster than it could earn interest for him, and never entirely successful at that. He continued to have numerous accidents—in automobiles, on motorcycles, or just sauntering down the sidewalk dead drunk. He blew some important gigs by fighting with the big-shot theater, art, and literary people involved, often burning bridges even before he had half finished constructing them. Bart cultivated an extravagant disrespect for anything establishment. He had a terrible chip on his shoulder; nobody knew quite why. And although the general consensus was that he possessed extraordinary talents, everyone also agreed he was self-destructively sabotaging those skills, exhausting his reserves, demolishing his own gifts (and most of the projects he brought to half flower) in much the way early southern planters had used up cotton land then abandoned it and moved on—Bart was constantly forsaking things, projects, people, and Moving On.

Somehow, the movies got made. Guessing conservatively, I'd say in the fifties and early sixties Bart starred in at least a dozen B pictures, most in the swashbuckling Errol Flynn tradition. As a matter of principle he would not work in "serious" films. This prejudice had to do with some of his blacklisted friends, the hypocrisy of intellectuals, his belief that almost all "serious art" was just clever veneer disguising empty self-indulgence, anyway. "So why not do the vapid shit up front?" he liked to say.

In his cinema outings, Bart always insisted on performing his own stunts, a stubbornness that never sat well on a man so accident-prone. Yet it is why—after wiping out in a simple motorboat stunt during a moronic movie about daredevil hydroplane racers—Bart later could still get work, and mighty lucrative work it often turned out to be, on many late-sixties and seventies pictures, where fantastic violence was big box office. Fearless stunt men—a few, anyway, and including Bart —were able to become stars in their own right; several—Bart again among them—even turned up on TV occasionally, doing Johnny Carson or commercials. And Bart had gigs in such fat grossers as *Earthquake, The Towering Inferno,* and *The Poseidon Adventure.*

As I mentioned, for my first seven years Kitty wouldn't let Bart see me, give me a present, or even pat my fuzzy little head. She wanted no such undisciplined, self-destructive madcap in her careful life, which was proceeding in an altogether different direction from his. Though she stayed in theater for many years, taking small roles, working backstage, Kitty finally left it altogether to practice her beliefs in the sweatshops of Lower Manhattan, Brooklyn, and New Jersey, where she felt the roots of her communism would best be nurtured.

Bart couldn't stand not getting what he wanted, especially if the object of his craving was a woman. Therefore, two or three times annually he showed up wherever Kitty and I were living, dressed to the nines, blasted out of his gourd, toting roses, and inevitably spouting Dylan Thomas, begging her to marry him, shack up with him, or at least pardon him. She never tumbled to Bart, though she did finally allow him some visiting rights. Providing he took good care of me, stayed off the sauce, refused to lavish me with presents, and was a good example for me by his own exemplary behavior. "You better tell her I'm a paragon of virtue," he always threatened just before sending me home, "or else next time our paths cross, buster, I'll knock your pimple-strewn little block off."

If recollection serves, nearly every time Bart was about to get hitched, or had just divorced another beauty, he appeared at our house crying in his beer. Down on his knees (literally!), he would beg Kitty to save him from his next disastrous marriage by becoming his bride before he could execute another futile plunge. Or, having blurted out all the gruesome details of yet another savaged romance, he would sob that she, and only she, could save him.

My mother shook her head, sobered Bart up, gave him a couch for the night, and then quietly indoctrinated him with Marxist theory, which he could only take in small doses before dashing—howling!—out the door.

Bart had telephoned her sometimes, late at night, threatening to bump himself off if she would not allow him to become the legitimate father of their own son.

Once, he had even fired a gun near the telephone, let the instrument clatter to the floor, and left it lying there. "Ten minutes later," Bart said, "the goddam East Los Angeles Rescue Squad appeared at my doorway: Kitty had dialed them!"

She never recounted that story. Kitty abhorred gossip in any way, shape, or form. She just told me that she hoped I understood the sorrow and loneliness gripping Bart, and how important it therefore was for him to know that I loved him. No matter what, I should always try to deal with him compassionately.

Suddenly, high in the air, a most startling thing occurred! Seventeen years after Bart had asked me (somewhere in Kansas? in Missouri?) what program I was watching in the back seat of that burgundy chariot whizzing us toward the Kennedy inaugural, I remembered (for the *first* time!) that it had been a "Honeymooners" rerun, featuring Jackie Gleason, Art Carney, Audrey Meadows, and company.

The realization caught me so by surprise, that immediately —breathlessly!—I asked the stewardess for a drink and downed the liquor in two gulps.

Then I ventured a glance earthward: could that have been Kansas way down there? When the plane inclined slightly leftward, my heart sank; I leaned way to the right, trying to correct our tilt. And, as my skin grew clammy from the usual cold sweat, I swore that if we alighted safely, I would take a bus back to New York and never leave the ground again!

Naturally, Bart loved airplanes. In fact, he once bragged: "I wouldn't mind dying in an airplane. What a gas to be cruising along way up high at eight hundred miles an hour and run smack-dab into some kind of invisible brick wall—*blam!!!!* Etherized twenty thousand leagues above the world!"

Because such thoughts made me sick to my stomach, I quickly switched channels and, paddling somewhat frantically through the debilitating ooze of my plane-tormented imagination, I struggled back to Lorraine Waldrum, wondering about her again for a little while, speculating on the kind of guts it took to cohabit, however fleetingly, with my old man. Was Bart somebody special despite his hang-ups, outrageous behavior, and complete lack of loyalty? And fun to be with on occasion? And—this may sound off the wall, given his sexual proclivities and multitudinous conquests, but—was he a good lover?

Taking everything about that manic ruffian into consideration—was it worth it?

A sudden fatigue knocked me out. Falling asleep, I had a dream. My father and I stood on the edge of a wide field bordered by a white fence over which rose vines tangled, Kentucky style; in the distance stretched a rich vein of trees. Overhead, the sky was Magritte blue, occasionally stroked by an innocent filament of cloud. In the field, large shiny horses—mahogany colored, palomino, jet black—galloped around silently: I doubt their hooves actually touched the ground. They were beautiful and young; their muscles glittered. Bart had a high-powered rifle, and every now and then he would raise the gun and fire, and a horse would topple to earth with brutal clumsiness, kicking up a cloud of dust when it crash-landed, dead as a doornail. Soon, only three horses remained. At that point, Bart offered me the weapon: "Here, have a shot. It's fun." I shook my head no . . . *even though I desperately wanted to kill one of those horses.* But I couldn't let him understand this; it terrified me to think he might find out. Bart seemed not to notice, however. He shrugged, said "Suit yourself," and casually planted another high-powered-rifle bullet in the brain of a galloping mare.

I awoke just as our wheels struck the runway.

3 I sat there with my eyes closed, deflating, letting the fear drain, trying for a final calm moment before Bart and his frenetic entourage hit me like a ton of bricks. Drinking, carousing, moviemaking, endless rap sessions, sleepless nights—I cringed. I didn't want to meet his hysterical Hollywood gang. I blanched, contemplating the upcoming heartaches, arguments, and Lorraine Waldrum follies: all the usual Bart Darling catastrophies and bizarre adventures. So I enjoyed my lone stab at peace while passengers lurched and bumped, pushing for the exits. In fact, so great was my relief at being safely earthbound again, I actually fell asleep. A stewardess nudged my shoulder, saying "Sir—?" Groggily, I opened one eye.

"We've landed. It's time to get off now."

"So soon?" I'm constantly surprised by my wit in situations that really aren't funny at all. "Do I have to?"

She chilled me with a vapid Muzak smile, and drifted away. I roused myself, said a fond farewell to the deserted and deceptively tranquil fuselage, then sauntered out of my flying tomb into a red-carpeted tunnel that led to the terminal building.

Bart's ambush caught me by surprise. Somehow, in this type of situation, I never saw him until it was too late. He had a knack for attacking from my blind side, enveloping me in his lethal bear hugs before I could raise an arm for protection or knee him in the groin to discourage his jovial greetings. Bart was one of those sadists whose handshake popped knuckles and dislocated elbows. In fact, during the course of a normal conversation he constantly gripped my biceps or shoulders and slapped or thudded his ham hand against my thighs. Walking along, his arm was always around my shoulders. He punctuated his speech with sharp index-finger jabs to the solar plexus. Often I staggered clear of our conversations black-and-blue all over! Many's the time I've wondered how he avoided mangling women while screwing them. Because he was a regular Lennie from *Of Mice and Men,* Bart was. Wherever, whenever, however, the man inevitably left a trail of wounded creatures in his wake!

Purely and simply, "If it don't crack ribs, it ain't a heartfelt hug!" is the way Bart looked at it.

About two steps into the main waiting room, therefore, he had me in his anaconda squeeze before I knew what had hit me. My shoulders seemed to collapse inward until they Siamesed at a point one inch below my Adam's apple; my spine threatened to snap, leaving me paralyzed for life! And although I'm no jockey-sized person, my feet were swept off the ground as he employed one of his gimmicks for establishing Instant Rapport, i.e., his foul mouth:

"You old son of a cum-sucking bitch, Marcel! Damned if you don't look just about as good as pussy in a peignoir! How're the old nuts, kid, full of dynamite? Shit on an everlovin' stick, boy!"

Setting me down, he grabbed my cheeks between the thumb and forefinger of each hand, and nailed me with a big slobbering European-style kiss on the mouth—*Mmwaaanch!*

I gurgled, "Bart . . . Jesus . . . *please!*" And coughed, embarrassed, and wondering how many ribs had punctured my lungs.

Then, just as I realized that another person—a diminutive female—was playing this scene, Bart announced, "Kid, I want you to meet Lorraine."

A little honky-tonk hillbilly about as substantial as a piece of dandelion-seed fluff settled into my arms. She kissed the tip of my nose, a look of real teasing merriment in her eyes. "Welcome to the monkey house, Marcel."

I said, "I thought you guys—"

Lorraine dropped back beside my father. "We did. But you know how these things are . . ."

Though I would have placed Lorraine in her mid- to late-twenties—there was a lot of experience evident in her eyes—she looked younger. Dressed in a baggy gray sweater, tight jeans, and white sneakers, she resembled a half-starved waiflet fresh from the Appalachian coalfields. Plenty of mascara defined her small green eyes, but that was about it, cosmetically, on her face. Her cheeks, her forehead had scattered pockmarks, not from acne as a kid, but rather from some man-made disaster, I guessed, such as shattering windshield glass. She had a slightly turned-up nose and thin lips permanently caught in a sly and sardonic smile. As for the style of her dusty brown hair —picture a field-mouse nest at harvest time, short tufts of grass and cotton kicked apart by a sickle bar or a tractor wheel. A hundred comparisons leaped to mind: she was a ragamuffin pixie, a refugee from *The Little Rascals.* Or a poor man's Jeanne Moreau, as I remembered her from the opening scenes of *Jules and Jim.* I don't know what made her so instantly attractive—certainly not her body. Five feet tall and no more than ninety pounds, she had a positively concave chest and no hips: I believe "scrawny as a jaybird" is the metaphor that applies. But she sure had *it,* whatever *it* was. Because all I had to do was see that insouciant gum-chewing redneck imp standing there beside my old man, nestled under his enormous arm like a wild bird under the wing of its mama, to fall head over heels in love!

As for my father, the Human Hurricane, he was more or less his usual outrageously domineering self. Still, something was different; I noticed that right away. I couldn't tell exactly how Bart had changed, but he appeared vaguely transformed. Of course, with him, nobody could accurately ascertain what kind of shape—both physically and mentally—he was in. The hydroplane stunt that had gone awry, hurtling him aflame into the drink, had partially melted his features into such a set of permanent pain it was impossible to assess his real emotions or reactions to more recent physical traumas.

He had once been a remarkably handsome man. Even Kitty had admitted that: "He could've given Clark Gable a complex, Marcel." And the thing is, he was still very good-looking in a powerful, not quite grotesque, way. Fine surgeons and expert grafting had healed his face: all the old robust contours survived. Bart had a massive head, a square jaw, thick lips, and a pained, wonderfully savage smile. Once-bushy eyebrows were scraggly now, laced with scar tissue. Piercing, and always slightly startled-looking, his small blue-gray eyes flanked a large, hawk beak. Though never warm, his eyes usually appeared intensely interested. And then came the skin across his cheeks, forehead, and gathering jowls. That shiny skin glistened like Christmas; it seemed fragile and effeminate, belying his rugged features. I sensed I could dramatically wound him simply by touching his transparent and delicate face. Bart resembled a big, and yet curiously diaphanous, wild man.

His muscles bulged under a snappy, short-sleeved custom-fit shirt buttoned just once, at about the navel (leaving exposed most of his hairy, tanned chest). His pants were expensive, cream-colored, and slightly flared. He wore no socks and had the rotten taste to flaunt a pair of white-suede loafers. On one wrist—a slim digital watch. On one beefy finger—a chunky diamond-studded ring. A tiny gold band sparkled in his left ear: a gift, he insisted, from Marilyn Monroe. Long bushy hair that had grayed considerably since last we'd met almost covered his big ears.

I said, "Three nights ago I get a phone call, it's the end of the world. Lorraine has taken a powder. Pop has cracked up his motorcycle and is on death's door. Everybody's hit bottom and there's no bounce."

"Things change." Bart threw an arm around my shoulders, and, with a jerk like a train starting, he headed us off toward the baggage area. "The only sure thing in life, kid, is that there's no such thing as a sure thing in life."

"You got me out here on a ruse! You're a liar, you're a cheater! You're healthier than fucking Adelle Davis!"

"But I really split," Lorraine said as we careened along a corridor toward the baggage room. "I can't help it if I haven't completely cut the cord. I only came down for the ride . . ." She cracked her gum so loudly I jumped, thinking it was a gunshot.

"They always return," Bart said. "They can never keep away for long. Once they've been diddled by a god, mere mortals can never satisfy."

" 'By a god!' " Lorraine groaned. "Listen to the human ego rant and rave. By a crippled gorilla is more like it!"

"Wait a sec! Ho! Whoa!" Bart squeezed us both tightly against him with his massive arms. "I got a son here thinks the world of me. So can the obscene crap, Lorraine. Marcel looks up to his father, he admires me; don't say anything to burst his bubble. You want to trash me, go be an iconoclast on your own time."

"Listen to the big words. Your father knows a million big words, Marcel. He's a walking dictionary. When Einstein died they transplanted his brain into the head of Bart Darling."

"You better believe it." Bart puffed out his chest. "All my life I've been destiny's intellectual darling—!"

And yet, something was wrong with Bart: his walk teetered, it harbored a dozen tiny hitches that betrayed his natural rhythm. A barely perceptible hesitation, an awkwardness had been appended to his motion. If nothing else, Bart had always traveled (at least physically) with almost sublime coordination across the surface of this pitfall-strewn earth. But now he seemed a trifle off-balance, unsure of his body, as if his audio radar were out of whack, or his depth perception had been sabotaged by astigmatisms.

I guessed his recent motorcycle accident was to blame, even though he showed no visible wounds, other than a slight bruise along one cheekbone. Yet on Bart's face you could never tell, because the scar tissue fluctuated through all gradations of color, depending on the weather, or the surroundings, or his mood.

At the baggage console, when I reached for my suitcase, Bart knocked my arm away, continuing in his hyperbravado role:

"No two-bit East Coast ashen-faced shrimp should be forced to lug his own bag, not when a man-mountain like me is around."

"Life isn't tough enough," Lorraine said, cracking her gum, it seemed at least once between every word. "He wants to aggravate his hernia, now. Or maybe put a wrenched shoulder on top of his concussion and punctured lung and God knows what else from the motorcycle accident."

"It's a suitcase, not a shipment of lead ingots," Bart retorted. "If you don't carry things in life, you lose all your muscle tone, you get flabby, your timing collapses, you blow the stunts. It's dangerous not to stay in shape."

"But I suppose it isn't dangerous to play with rattlesnakes every day—huh? That keeps your muscles toned?" And to me. "The only muscle tone Mr. Man-Mountain here has lost is the muscle tone between his ears, if you ask me."

"Rattlesnakes? What's this about rattlesnakes?" I asked.

"The fucking Big House was full of them," Lorraine complained as we headed across the main lobby. "There were cages all over the living room. There was a goddam aquarium full of rattlesnakes on the kitchen table! Why the hell do you think I split?"

"They're for the picture," Bart groaned. "I got to have those rattlesnakes for the picture!"

"So he has to start a rattlesnake zoo? Jesus! I wake up in the middle of the night, they're all buzzing! I try to pour milk on my Cheerios, it's like burglar alarms going off in New York City."

"What do you need rattlesnakes for in a movie?" I asked bewilderedly.

Bart opened his mouth, but Lorraine said, "Let me explain. There's this guy—see? He's the hero. He's a dope pusher. And he offs people with rattlesnakes whenever they get in his way."

"Sounds like another Bart Darling special."

With his free hand, my father cuffed me so hard in the back of my head I nearly fell over frontward. I said, *"Hey!"*

Bart said, "Don't give me one of your lectures on art, schmuck. I don't want to hear it. The artists in this country all got their noses crammed up each other's bungholes. I don't want any part of it; I don't need it."

Lorraine said, "That's another thing. At heart you're just an arrogant prick."

They meant to be funny, they were kidding; but underneath they weren't that funny, or just kidding. A real bitterness, routinely camouflaged, underlay the repartee.

"Arrogant prick—?" Bart discarded the suitcase and grabbed her. That is, he snagged an arm as she bolted, jerked her back, and in one second flat had raised her up over his head, hoisting her the way male cheerleaders heave up their female counterparts at college football games. Naturally, just about everyone in the main concourse stopped and stared at them.

Very calmly, Lorraine said, "Let me down, Bart, you big lummox, or you'll be sorry."

Beaming, Charles Atlas addressed me: "The thing I never understood about the laws of nature, Marcel, is how come a guttersnipe as tiny as a mosquito will take on something as large and as powerful as a horse or a human being."

"You'll be asleep, sugar, and I'll drive a carving knife down through your heart," Lorraine said, surprisingly together, I thought, for somebody in her position.

Bart began walking across the lobby toward a garish indoor fountain.

Lorraine said, "Don't you dare!"

My father continued heading for the water. Beside him, I begged, "Hey, Pop, come on—cool it, man, everybody's looking."

"Let 'em look. Find a hat. Pass it around. Charge admission."

"You're crazy. You're crazier than ever. You've flipped. You're nuts."

Lorraine said, "If you don't put me down, Bart, I'll scream."

"Go ahead and scream," he said placidly as we reached the fountain.

"Pop, look over there, see those two cops? They're giving us a very evil eye. If you throw her into the fountain we'll get arrested, and believe me, I didn't come out here for that. So just set her down like a rational gorilla, would you please?"

Lorraine screamed: "Help! Murder! Police!"

The two cops launched themselves briskly in our direction.

Bart said, "Shut up, goddam you!"

I retreated from them. Oh, to be back in the airplane, afraid only for my life! Bart was still holding Lorraine over his head as the two cops, both youngsters barely over twenty, arrived. One of them said, "Mister, what are you *doing?*"

Setting Lorraine on the floor, Bart dusted off his hands. "What do you mean 'What am I doing?' I ain't doing squat. I was just carrying my wife a little ways, that's all. She had polio when she was a kid, and don't walk so good. Why? There's a law around here a guy can't carry his wife if she had polio when she was a kid?"

"There's laws against being a public nuisance," the other cop said. "There's laws against disturbing the peace," his partner added.

"You should arrest my wife here, then. She's the one who hollered, not me. I was just carrying her around, that's all. Honest, I didn't make any noise."

"We'd appreciate it if you all would leave quietly," the first cop said tensely. "Then there won't be any trouble at all. Nobody wants trouble."

"Nobody *ever* wants trouble," Bart said, taking Lorraine's hand. "But it's always those people who say they don't want any trouble who cause all the trouble."

"Now hold on a sec, mister—"

"He's sorry," I blurted. "I just got in from the East . . . it's very emotional . . ."

But Bart was plowing right along, oblivious to the danger, and I could see that neither officer relished a tussle: they let him go. Snagging my suitcase, I followed them outside, where Bart immediately gave a porter ten dollars to go fetch the car, an ostentatious play I found in poor taste.

"The man could use a sawbuck," Bart said, countering my protest. "In this country you think it's easy being a nigger?"

"*Hey!*" I shouted, falling right into his trap.

"Hanging around you it isn't easy to be anything." Lorraine tried to be stern and angry, but her eyes glittered playfully.

Bart said, "If I could ever invent a way of getting women to shut up I'd be a millionaire overnight."

Lorraine explained to me: "He spends three hours a day, including on weekends, studying how to be a racist *and* a male chauvinist pig."

"I believe you."

"Don't believe anything she ever tells you, Marcel. Every time this little girl opens her mouth, a bald-faced lie jumps out. If she was a wooden puppet her nose would be ten feet long."

"Ay, look who's talking!"

Bewilderedly, I asked, "Are you guys always like this?"

"Like this?" Bart pondered a beat. "I dunno. *Just* like this?"

"Actually, sometimes it's different," Lorraine said. "Sometimes, for example, I hit him." And, without warning, swinging with all her might, she slugged Bart in his enormous belly. But he saw it coming, and had the split-second foresight to flex. Her hand bounced off harmlessly.

"Ouch!" Immediately, she added, "Dammit, Bart, if you've messed up my picking fingers I'll murder you."

"You and who's army—?"

And I turned out to have been wrong about his vehicle: I had guessed Cadillac, but this week's wheels was a beige diesel Mercedes splattered with mud and so dented it seemed to have been pummeled by a baseball bat.

"Pop, do you still drive like you always drive?"

Placing his enormous hand, fingers splayed, against his chest, Bart opened his eyes innocently wide and dropped his jaw in astonishment. "Me? Like I always drive? What kind of a question is that, Marcel?"

"You know what I mean. Like an insane person."

"Who—*Bart?*" Lorraine cackled sarcastically. "Not him. He's the prince of the cautious drivers. Milk and honey on the highway. Mr. Velvet."

"Wait a minute. Hey. Lay off it, you two. Why all the maligning? I'm almost fifty and I never had a fatal accident!"

I said, "If you don't mind, I'd just as soon drive."

"Oh no you don't!" Bart leaped behind the wheel. "I can pilot this thing as well as anybody."

"Pilot?" Lorraine winked at me. "Get the reference? Pilot? Y'unnerstand? *'Pilot'*—?"

Approximately as queasy as when I'd entered the airplane, I opened a rear door, but Lorraine grabbed my arm. "Hold it, Marcel, I'll sit in back. You take the death seat."

"I don't want the death seat. I really don't."

"Take it anyway," she ordered, slipping by me into the Mercedes. Before I could further protest, Bart reached across the front seat and yanked me into his car. On the way in, my head clobbered the door frame with a loud clang! Literally, I saw stars. I also hollered *"Shit!"*

Bart said, "Oh wow, I'm sorry. I didn't mean—"

I flared. "You *never* mean it! You just grab things and

yank them too hard, or back up into them because you forgot to check the rear-view mirror, or trample them because your head was turned gooning at a good-looking 'broad'! But you never *mean* to do it, it's always an accident! One hundred fucking accidents a week! Your wake is strewn with bodies because you never think—!" I must have been exhausted to blow up that quickly.

Twisted in his seat, feigning abject puzzlement, Bart addressed Lorraine: "What'd I *do?*" he griped. "What makes me such a master criminal?"

"You did what you always do, sugar." And, abruptly, I heard a note of fatigue in her voice. "You blew it."

Bart said, "Hey, Marcel, I'm sorry. I'm just excited . . ."

Naturally, I relented immediately: I was ashamed. "It's okay, man. The problem is I had a long trip, you know? I'm feeling kind of tender, that's all. I'm sorry . . . I shouldn't . . . it's very hot . . ."

"Well, let's hit the road, then!" He popped the clutch, and we took off. As he turned, accelerating and spinning the wheel, the centrifugal force slammed both Lorraine and me up against the passenger-side doors. "Hi Ho Silver! *Away!*"

"Slow down!"

"I know how to drive this car."

"But it's the other people who will cause an accident," I whimpered weakly.

"Let them look out for themselves!"

Lorraine tapped my shoulder. "Ease back and enjoy it, pal. Nobody's ever going to teach this old dog new tricks. Didn't he explain to you he was trying to commit suicide?"

Bart's head snapped around. "Cut that suicide shit, Lorraine. It isn't funny."

"No," she said icily, "you're right. It isn't funny."

"Well, let's drop the subject, then. Do you *have* to crack that gum?"

"Do you *have* to drive eighty miles an hour?"

I fumbled in the space between the seat cushion and the

door, but came up empty. I asked, "Where's the seat belt, at least?"

"I took it out," Bart said.

"How come?"

"It got in the way."

"Well, do you have a parachute or anything I could put on?"

"Very funny."

I begged, "*Please* slow down."

He braked so hard I nearly lurched into the windshield. And, with an almost nasty gleam in his eyes, Bart guided us along at a dangerously slow speed, about fifteen miles an hour.

Lorraine said, "Marcel, I want to introduce you to your father, Henny Youngman. Or is it Rodney Dangerfield? Mr. Comedian. Joe Funny."

I said, "I'm not talking anymore. The hell with it. If we all get killed it serves everybody right."

"What we all need is a beer." Bart swerved into the dusty lot of a roadside tavern. "I'll get a six-pack."

I cried out, "No!" but he was gone already, galloping into the bar.

"What's the matter with a six-pack?" Lorraine wanted to know.

"Other than careless speeding, the only thing that makes me deathly nervous in a moving vehicle is messing around with liquor in it."

"Bart can drive this car blindfolded with a beer in one hand, his arm around a lady, and his knees steering."

"That's comforting."

"You need to learn how to relax, Marcel. Take these things in stride."

"But he breaks things," I complained. "He's stupid. He's had a dozen accidents."

I suppose she felt that she had to defend him a little. "Well, yes, I guess he's crazy. But the man is incredibly alive, Marcel. Wait'll you see how he's running this film circus. He's like a madcap general. He can juggle fifteen problems at a time and manipulate people all over the block. He makes it work, God knows how . . .”

Bart already had two beers open before he reached the car. Pausing by his door, he guzzled from one can, downing it without a pause. Flushed, he crushed the aluminum can in his mighty fist, tossed it over his shoulder, and mounted the driver's seat with all the gusto of a movie cowboy leaping off a barn roof onto his rearing stallion.

I couldn't keep my fat mouth shut. “Hey, you can't litter like that.” I popped out, and self-righteously circled the growling Mercedes. Bart beeped, making me jump as I bent over to retrieve the can. When I settled back in, Bart addressed Lorraine. “Sweetheart,” he said. “I'd like you to meet Benny the Boy Scout.”

“Well what's the point, Pop? Why go out of your way to litter?”

“I'll tell you why.” Bart laid down twenty yards of scratch on our return to the racing oval. “There's many poor folks in this hard old world whose only method of scoring an honest buck is to canvass our highways and byways collecting aluminum beer cans. Which, by the way, earn something like seventy-five cents a pound. And if it weren't for generous litterbugs like me, those impoverished malfortunates would starve to death.”

“Oi vey! I don't believe it.”

“Come on, ease up, enjoy the scenery!” Bart snapped on the stereo tape deck, I suppose to drown me out: the Eagles, *Hotel California.*

The trip north—conforming to the script of almost any voyage with my father—was an outrageous adventure. Bart proceeded in fits and jerks, his mind totally preoccupied with relevant or irrelevant chatter, the landscape, the stereo. Always avidly gesticulating, his hands rarely touched the wheel. He kept swiveling his head in every direction except the one in which we were aiming; at least a dozen times I slammed my braking foot against the floor, or grabbed for the wheel, or uttered a cry. Bart invariably recovered in time, guffawing: "Hey, take it easy, Marcel, *relax.* I know how to drive this Nazi pussymobile. Jeepers, man, I'm a *pro!*"

I asked, "Then how come Lorraine is lying down in the back seat?"

"Because she's tired."

"Because she's scared shitless," Lorraine contradicted. "I swear, if we get home alive, I'll never ride with you again."

Bart threw up his hands and wobbled all over the road. "The younger generation," he wailed, "ain't got no respect for their elders!"

Every ten minutes he swerved onto the loose gravel of a highway turnout in order to read historical markers. Most of them concerned a local pueblo, a famous church established by the early Spaniards, or other pertinent lore involving Coronado, Juan de Oñate, or Kit Carson. An amateur student of the area's bloody past, Bart maintained a nonstop patter, prolific with facts, on the picturesque life along the northern Rio Grande from the early 1500s to the present. My father's style bore little resemblance to the musty putterings of a collegiate history professor, however. A typical paragraph chock-full of racy information worked its way out of Bart's mouth in obscene bursts that soon had me giggling despite my discomfort over his nonchalant mannerisms behind the wheel of our speeding deathtrap.

"Dear old Kit Carson," Bart mused salaciously. "He came into this area toting a sixteen-inch hard-on with a bayonet strapped to the end of it, and poked it into every redskin that so much as eyeballed him funny. After he killed all the Pueblo people he could find, they sent him over to Navajo land where the motherfucker laid down a blanket of honky murder and pillage across the Canyon de Chelly. Anybody who survived that wound up down south in Fort Sumner, New Mexico, picking corn kernels out of their own shit to survive. That son of a bitch sure had a knack for genocide. Shoot, they all did. When Coronado's expedition tied into the Pueblos, it was like running a rotary lawn mower over field mice. Then the church goose-stepped in and nailed every surviving heathen it could locate to a bloody cross . . . Whoops, hey! We almost missed the highlight of our journey!"

The Mercedes fishtailed, skidding sideways as Bart braked, hanging a ninety-degree right turn onto a dirt road heralded by a sign reading: PRAIRIE-DOG VILLAGE—ONE MILE. We barreled over the rutted road at fifty miles an hour, enveloped in a violent dust ball. We all jounced horrendously, banging our heads against the ceiling. Fighting the wheel, gunning us up to sixty, Bart shouted "Whoopee!" like some kind of devil-may-care rodeo rider.

"Pop, you're gonna wreck this car!"

"So what else is new?"

"Well, it's conspicuous consumption, that's what it is!"

Addressing Lorraine, Bart shouted, "Lorraine, I want you to meet Mr. Thorstein Veblen here!"

She rolled her eyes, giving him the finger. And he laughed; oh, how he laughed. I had forgotten how my father could laugh. I suppose I never met anybody who reveled so much in his own childish shenanigans. His laughter cavorted forth in rollicking yellow bursts; it tumbled around inside the car like daffodils in a washing machine. "The thing about Bart," Kitty once told me, "is that no matter how much you may dislike the man, it's hard to condemn him for his style. Unlike most of the rest of the world, usually he's actually having real, honest-to-goodness fun."

Again, we skidded—the usual one-eighty-degree (stomach-sickening, automobile-tilting) slidearound—to a stop in the middle of nowhere. When the dust cleared, it became obvious that we were indeed parked in a scruffy prairie-dog village of twenty-five or thirty mounds. Bart killed the motor, popped open three beers, and handed one to Lorraine, another to me, which—this time around—I accepted. I was parched: my tongue had almost started swelling. Fear performs miracles in my mouth.

Bart tied into his beer like a he-man doing a television ad for Gusto as Lorraine said, "Well, here we are."

I said, "Where are we? And why are we where we are?" Bart belched. "You'll see."

Lorraine said, "He's a mighty white hunter. He's gonna shoot himself a prairie dog. It makes him feel more macho. Like: His gun is a penis. And all those harmless little critters out there are cunts, broads, chicks, tomatoes, and bimbos."

His grin a cross between Kirk Douglas and Liberace, Bart polished off his beer, chucked the can out the window, and leaned across me, opening the glove compartment.

"Pop, I really wish you wouldn't throw those beer cans out the window. At least not while I'm in the car."

His hand emerged from the glove compartment clutching an enormous, long-barreled, .357 Magnum pistol.

I groaned, "Oh shit, you're kidding."

"He thinks he's Clint Eastwood, Marcel. The gun is merely a logical extension of the man's alter ego."

"Bart, seriously, you're not going to start actually shooting prairie dogs?"

He extended his arm lackadaisically out the driver's-side window, aimed at a prairie dog, and fired.

I shouted, *"Jesus Christ!"* at the same instant he exclaimed, "Dammit, I missed!" With a chirp and a flick of its tail, every varmint out there dove into its burrow and disappeared.

I cried, *"Pop, what's the matter with you? This is a fucking state park!"*

"Hey, lower your voice, Marcel, would you? We're all together here. You don't have to shout."

"Yeah," Lorraine gruffly mimicked Bart's voice. "No need to shout, folks. This here journey is a cool, calm, collected, and laid-back operation."

Without hesitation, Bart pointed the gun at her. Lorraine leaned forward, taking the barrel tip into her kiss-shaped lips.

I squeaked, "Don't do that ... *please.* "

Lorraine's eyes locked onto Bart's. They held it that way

for an astonishing, sexy, and frightening moment. Bart's smile half died into a bemused and quizzical grin; his face was crimson and damp, his eyes appeared beautiful and worried, filled also with a startled, aching look that seemed like love. Lorraine's green hillbilly eyes sparkled with a lot of things: defiance, love, taunting despair, suspicion—I don't know how to describe it. Braggadocio was in there; likewise a confident challenge. To love her and love her straight, maybe . . . or else. But I can't really explain it; it took me by surprise: her toughness and wisdom. I suppose she had the most attractive, character-riddled eyes of any woman I ever met. I saw a film once on coal miners and their women, a documentary entitled *Harlan County, U.S.A.* Lorraine had eyes like some of the wonderful, courageous women in that film.

She made a kissing motion and drew back her head. The gun snout glistened.

"It's hot, Bart. It damn near scalded my lips. I can taste gunpowder."

My father winced as if in pain, abruptly dropped his eyes, and faced forward. With the gun settled casually in his lap, he explained matter-of-factly to me:

"See, here's the rub, kid. Everybody in this state hates prairie dogs, because prairie dogs are the number-one nuisance to just about every agricultural or cattle operation we got going here—them and coyotes. And the residents of this state have spent a billion dollars and a couple hundred years trying to eradicate those furry little sons of bitches so that some day something besides sand and mesquite will grow around here. So when the state takes my tax dollars to make a little shithouse park for the protection of these useless critters, that gets my dander—as a law-abiding God-fearing, constitution-revering citizen—*up.*"

Lorraine said, "They also carry plague. There's one . . ."

"Where—?"

"Over there." She pointed.

Bart fired. And missed again.

I said, "You don't even take time to aim."

"It's harder to hit 'em if you aim. Too self-conscious. You just have to make like you're pointing your finger." He crumpled another beer can and gave it the old heave-ho. I started to protest: "I really wish—"

Bart suddenly kicked open his door and jumped out. And not only did he collect Lorraine's can and his own, but then he began to wander about picking up everybody else's tin and aluminum refuse. I groaned, "Oh no . . ."

"Isn't he clever?" Lorraine spoke loud enough for Bart to hear. "Hasn't he got just about the most huggable, lovable sense of humor this side of Bob Hope and Archie Bunker? Isn't he just about *the* most original and exciting human being you ever set your teeth into?"

Bart swerved over to the car, dumping two dozen beer cans, a bunch of bean-dip and custard tins, and several cellophane potato- and taco-chip wrappers through my window. I brushed all the crap onto the floor, grumbling, "Whenever you're through mocking me, Pop, I'm tired, I'd like to get home . . ."

"But this is a state park. And I always like to leave this kind of place neater than I found it, so that other folks can enjoy it, too. If we all do our bit, we can make America a cleaner and healthier land to live in."

Lorraine giggled and in a friendly manner tousled my hair. "Grin and bear it," she said good-naturedly. "I gotta admit he's a regular asshole, but he sure has a fine personality. And," she whispered conspiratorially into my ear, "he also happens to be a terrific dancer."

"I don't know whether to laugh or cry," I said ruefully.

"For two and a half years, sugar, I have done a lion's share of both."

Bart returned, and had us going sixty, it seemed, even before his left foot had entered the car. He and Lorraine started singing crazy songs together, tunes with titles like: "I Was A-Lookin' Back to See If You Was A-Lookin' Back to See If

I Was A-Lookin' Back to See If You Was A-Lookin' Back at Me." Also: "Does Your Chewing Gum Lose Its Flavor on the Bedpost Overnight?" And once more with feeling: "Your Tears Are the Rain That Makes Love Grow." They hooted and hollered, cornballing it up royally. Yet they also sang together in a hoarse country harmony—mocking the genre while also taking it seriously—that literally gave me goose bumps, it sounded so good.

A powerful tension existed between them, I could tell. Yet rarely had I seen my father able to enjoy himself with another woman the way he could literally gambol with Lorraine. It was as if she lacked all the attributes he'd always demanded of his women, especially all those lush physical requirements; and what remained, in Lorraine, was this strange, real, live, *human being*—which might have been an original experience for Bart.

With no warning (as usual), my dad sailed off the road again, wobbling at fifty miles an hour down another potholed dirt track, plunging us into a beautiful little valley of damp alfalfa fields, apple and peach orchards, and picturesque adobe houses.

"Hey, slow down!" I yelped, the needle certainly stuck in a groove on my record. "You'll kill us!"

"If I slow down, Marcel, I won't ever get where I'm going."

"Well, where is that gonna be at this breakneck speed?"

"Dunno," he laughed, sparkling for a second like newborn ecstasy. "But I feel good enough to lay golden eggs!"

"Suppose when we get there," Lorraine said, "there is no there there?"

"Thanks, Gertie . . ."

We nose-dived to a spectacularly brazen halt in front of a small adobe chapel surrounded on three sides by apple trees heavily laden with ripening fruit. Bart popped open his door, crowing, "Everybody out. We are now going to view a native structure of some cultural importance!" Jacking open the rear door, he bowed low, ushering Lorraine to the ground with a royal flourish of his arm. She curtsied and did a clever two-step, a sort of cocky riff with old-fashioned tap-dance overtones, and then sashayed into the chapel.

Self-consciously, I reconnoitered the landscape for Local People. I wanted to tuck myself up into a turtle shell, becoming invisible. I couldn't stand feeling like such a gross interloper. Talk about Ugly Americans personified! I had truly forgotten just how obnoxious Bart could be on someone else's turf. Whether it was conscious egotism or not, he was an arrogant chauvinist who appropriated everyone else's territory as his own.

He bounded into the pretty little church, goosing Lorraine on his way past her. She squealed and swatted at him, but missed. Bart strutted right up an aisle flanked by simple wooden benches to the altar. Me, I halted two feet inside the doorway, assuming all the hypocritical reverence I could muster. God forbid that I would offend anybody who might turn up!

My father actually grabbed the enormous, blood-spat-tered, thorn-bedecked santo of Christ dominating the altar and held it out for Lorraine's inspection. With one of her bitten fingernails, she traced a bloody trickle down a leg as Bart pontificated loudly:

"Believe it or not, this statue was carved by a little old sheepherder named Domingo Luna in 1702. It's one of the oldest and most cherished bultos around these here parts. And it must be worth a stinking fortune in gold!"

I whimpered, "For Pete's sake, Pop, please put it down."

"When we get married," Bart blathered on his way out, "I think this here's the place to do the nuptials, qué no, Lorraine? Afterwards, we could all take off our clothes and cavort in the orchard . . ."

Lorraine came up behind him, tucking her skinny arms around his waist, squeezing him tightly as she peeked around one arm, humorously eyeing him as she said, "That'll be the day."

He made a playful face, then shouted, "Hey! Hold on a sec!"

Diving into the Mercedes, Bart emerged with a Bolex 8mm camera, and aimed it at us, focusing. I squinted and made a self-conscious face. Lorraine threw her arms around me, placed her cheek against mine, and grimaced at the camera. Then she hooked an index finger in one corner of my mouth and tugged it out so that I'd look more grotesque. With her other hand, she shot Bart the finger.

"What does that pass for," he asked, "originality? Your IQ? Your number of legitimate parents? Do something creative. Go ahead. Walk over there, both of you, pick an apple, be interesting."

Lorraine moved to do his bidding. Foolishly, I protested: "Bart, this isn't our orchard, this isn't our property, these aren't our apples. What if—"

"G'wan, g'wan," he interrupted, waving his hand impatiently. "Jesus, are you ever uptight. For somebody who doesn't believe in the myth of private property, or surplus value, or planned obsolescence, or maximum feasible profits, you sure seem to have an unholy reverence for private ownership of the means of production."

"That's not the point, and you know it."

"Go pick a fucking apple!"

I hurried over to the tree under which Lorraine was standing, dappled in sunlight, looking for all the world like a Victorian sprite from the brush of a modern-day Howard Pyle. She held out a cherry-red apple, offering it to me as if it were her love, or a hundred beautiful days in a row, or a valuable talisman. Her expression was bemused, sad, translucent. A mysterious puff of scented air—sagebrush, ripe apples, mesa dust—rippled her fuzzy hair. She flicked a mosquito off her nose. Her tough, vulnerable radiance clubbed me behind the knees, and I almost sank into the rich grass.

Lifting the apple from her hand, I gestured with it at Bart, saying, "There, are you satisfied?"

My father laid the camera on the Mercedes's hood. "I'm gonna get *me* an apple," he said defiantly, charging toward us.

One apple wasn't enough, though, not for Bart. Inside five seconds he had Lorraine holding up the front of her baggy sweater, forming a cloth bowl into which he dumped glistening fruit as fast as his fumbling fingers could pluck it.

I retreated, still casting about for Enraged Locals. I hissed, "Hey Pop, cool it. This really isn't our orchard. Those apples don't belong to us. You can't simply walk onto somebody's land . . ."

My voice trailed off hopelessly. Slumped into the car, I hunched down as far as possible, placed a hand over my face, and squirmed.

Oh how I squirmed.

Looking up once, though—they were taking such a long time!—I caught them kissing, Bart's right hand behind her head, his left hand up under the sweater that she held tightly with one hand: it bulged with apples.

I honked the horn!

"Hold your water!" Then Bart had another bright idea. "Hey, kid, grab the camera, take my picture!" And as I got out to do his bidding he picked three more apples and began to juggle them; I focused on him, and pulled the trigger.

Twice Bart circled Lorraine, clowning with the fruits. Then he fired them into the sky, snatched her up in his arms, and ran toward the Mercedes while Lorraine frantically clutched the apples to her chest. Despite her efforts, a few squirted out as they approached, bouncing around Bart's enormous boat feet as he galloped toward me, and I continued taking their picture.

They had almost reached the car, when something awful happened. I have seen documentary films of big-game hunts where fleeing animals have been filmed in slow motion at the moment they were hit by high-powered rifle bullets. Everything sagged, muscles instantly lost their shape, rippling with a hel-ter-skelter powerless rhythm as the moose, deer, or antelope collapsed. The same thing happened to Bart; I witnessed it through the camera's reflex lens. His mouth shaped a startled O as he crumpled, dumping Lorraine out of his arms in a cascade of apples. "Hey—!" she cried, crash-landing awk-wardly as Bart hit his knees, breaking his forward fall with both hands. And then, summoning a superhuman effort, he threw himself up on one knee, and, his face horribly contorted, thrust upward like a diver pushing off the bottom of a swimming pool, lunging aloft toward air. His features contorted in a silent shriek, Bart regained both feet. He gasped, a wounded whoosh of air from deep down in his lungs where it had been trapped. And on the heels of that he exclaimed, not without wonder: "Holy mackerel!"

Lorraine said, "Bart are you all right?"

"Shit yes, I'm all right!" Though obviously hurt, he con-jured a disarming smile. His beefy hand landed in her hair, tousling it bewilderedly. "Sure, I'm fine. Christ! I just hit a pothole or something. Lost my balance."

But tears had formed in his eyes.

Lorraine suddenly hollered: "God damn you, Bart Dar-ling! You're the stupidest human being I ever knew! I hate your chickenshit, pigheaded, childish guts! I hope to hell you *do* kill yourself! *You* don't give a good God damn, so why should *I* give a shit? Or anybody else for that matter? Go ahead, pick me up again, run me up to the road, why don't you? Go ahead, drink another beer—why not? Let's stop at the next liquor store and buy a bottle of bourbon; how would that be—pretty good?"

Bart fluttered one hand hopelessly at her, urging her to shut up. "Hush," he croaked. "Don't say those things. Come on, Lorraine, don't be mean . . ."

"Let's all get drunk and drive that fucking Mercedes at a hundred miles an hour up the gorge road!" Lorraine wailed, tears splashing out of her eyes now. "Why don't we do that,

Bart? Isn't that what you want? Why wait until Saturday when you parachute into the fucking gorge? Why not let me save you all this trouble, I'll take that pistol and put a bullet in your idiot, retarded brain!"

Bart groaned, "Hush up, Lorraine." Then, leaning over, he cuffed her face almost gently. "Don't talk like that . . ."

She jumped up, actually spit (real spit!) at him, and stomped away.

"Don't go!" I called

"Let her be," he said. "Leave her alone. You can't do anything. Let's go, let's get out of here."

"But . . ."

"She'll hitch home, she's done it before. Come on. Get in the car."

"But . . ."

"No 'but's,' Marcel. Christ on a crutch. For once just leave it *be*."

"I don't understand . . ."

"Ignorance," he said, starting the Mercedes and peeling away from the chapel, "is bliss."

We nearly sideswiped Lorraine on our way out. But neither she nor Bart seemed to notice.

I said, "You're both crazy."

In his most bored, most ugly voice, my father said, "No shit, Dick Tracy."

We traveled north, humping it. I became terrified again. Because with just one hand flopped laxly over the wheel, my lead-footed father was propelling us at sixty-five along a narrow, dangerously winding road bordered by cliffs on one side and by sheer drops of as much as four hundred feet on the other side. Straight down we would have toppled, into turbulent white water pounding between enormous boulders! Bart paid little or no attention to the road. Pissed off, fuming, all his attention was turned inward. The stereo blasted out one acid-rock group or another. Convinced I might crack, if not from the reckless speeding, then from the racket, I turned down the radio's volume. But he twisted it loud again, warning me, "Don't touch this, Marcel; keep your hands *off* it!" And so for twenty miles, heart in my throat waiting to die, I offered no further protest. For whatever reasons, he had lured me out here to kill me, and nothing I could do or say would stop him now. Whereupon all at once I became incredibly calm. As if, now that death was a certainty, I had nothing, really, to worry about.

I had started to sense a rhythm to his speeding madness, when he slammed on the brakes, almost skidding into the useless tin guardrail of a narrow pullout two hundred feet above eternity.

"It would be a pity," he said calmly, "to pass up this beautiful stretch of water without catching a trout or two for supper."

"You're not going fishing!"

"Who says?" Already, he had the trunk open and was piecing together a spinning outfit.

I said, "Can't we simply go home? I mean, I just flew across the country in an airplane sweating from terror every inch of the way, and I haven't stopped sweating yet. And I'd just as soon—you know—go straight home, shower, change clothes, relax—"

He smiled. For some reason I thought of Dylan Thomas, his ingenuous profligate's features, his innocent, hurt, world-weary, sensitive eyes.

Patiently, as if addressing a dim-witted three-year-old, Bart said, "Listen, Marcel. I got no idea how long I'm gonna live, or what's going to happen to me just around the next bend. We might collide with a semi, and I'll be paralyzed for the rest of my life, never able to lift a rod again, or experience the beautiful thrill of hoisting a big mean brown or a lovely rainbow out of these gorgeous waters. Now, there are businessmen and sportsmen all over this country who spend billions of dollars every year simply trying to reach a river like this, full of fighting fish, and on such a day as we happen to have going for us right

63

now. And I believe it would be a crime not to take a few minutes from our busy everyday lives in an attempt to experience the kind of thrill that some people never have the luck to know, not in their entire lifetimes."

I said, "I'm worried about Lorraine. Let's go back . . ."

"Lorraine, believe it or not, is a bigger girl than you are a boy, Marcel. She can take care of herself."

Reluctantly, I mumbled, "How long are you going to be down there?"

"Not long. Maybe ten minutes."

"You'll never catch a trout in ten minutes."

Bart winked. And as he circled the car again, he said, "Son, if you don't wet the fly, you sure as hell won't catch a fish. Now, why don't you traipse on down here with me . . . and bring the gun."

"The gun?"

"If you want the rod, I'll use the gun. Maybe a ten-pound lunker will rise to the surface after a frog swimming from one side of the river to the other."

"I'll come. But damned if I'll bring the gun."

I trailed him over a rockslide to the river's edge and sat on a boulder while he cast a black-and-white Dardevle lure, probing among opposite shore rocks for a brown or a rainbow. Bart fished as he lived, though, unable to cast more than twice from any single location. Hence, he traveled up the riverbank at a rapid pace. I let him go, glad to be away from the car and free of my tempestuous father for a moment. Although sunshine still glinted off half the river, the high gorge walls made afternoon shadows elongate rapidly. A chubby gray dipper bird skimmed by; I inhaled deeply, letting out air very slowly.

Startled, my eyes focused on Bart. Back already, grinning like a demented jackal, he had an eighteen-inch trout dangling from his index finger.

"I don't believe it!"

Tickled pink by his luck, Bart crowed, "Stick with me, kid, and I'll teach you how to believe in miracles."

"It's a plant! You had a paid peon hiding in the bushes with that fish!"

Bart said, "Every time I head for the capital, or return from somewhere, I toss a lure or a fly into this stretch, because it looks so good it seems you can't possibly miss. But this is the first time in six years I ever caught anything!"

Blamming his chest with his free hand, he hollered "Eeyow!" Picture it, yet: that enormous goon in a custom shirt, snazzy slacks, and white-suede loafers, with the scar tissue on his troubled radiant face shining as if some brazen Tinker Bell had shot it full of pixie dust!

Kneeling, using a silver initialed pocketknife, he slit open the trout's belly. Making another incision under the jaw, he fastened onto the cutaway tongue with his thumb and first two fingers, ripping down hard, severing the pectoral fins and releasing all internal organs from the body cavity. Tossing away the guts, he doused the trout in river water, thumbed out the back kidney line, said, "Let's go," and scrambled swiftly up the rocks. I stumbled after him, carrying the rod he had forgotten.

Lorraine was sitting in the back seat of the Mercedes. Bart said, "Hello." I said, "Hi." She said, "Howdy." And we pushed on without another word.

Cresting the gorge ten minutes later, Bart made a pit stop at yet another rest area. "Feast your souls, kiddies!" He killed the Mercedes's engine. The motor crickled, cooling, as we confronted the panorama. Mesa land, unbroken sagebrush as placid as a becalmed ocean, stretched away on every side, looking pearly and cool in the waning sunlight. Distant western mountains rose from the earth with a soft, undulating motion. Nearer to us, though still west of the highway, ran the Rio Grande Gorge, a dark jagged crack in the plain. Directly in front of us, thirty miles distant, loomed the Midnight Mountains, their highest peaks six thousand feet above the valley floor. At their base, we could make out tiny dwellings and trees of the irrigated land comprising Chamisaville and its satellite villages. Beyond, we could see clearly up along the mountain chain for at least a hundred miles. And on our right, close by, ran the southern Midnight Mountains, heading down past the gorge. Sunshine illuminated some ridgelines; isolated rain clouds misted along other slopes. The western horizon was growing golden, as clear as honey, but up north more scattered rain was falling. It seemed so wide, so total, so all-inclusive—a natural Cinerama: peaceful, majestic, passionate, calm.

Bart stepped out with the Bolex. Starting in the east, he swung slowly and carefully west about one-eighty degrees, filming the scene. "I always stop here," he told me when I joined him. "And I always shoot a few feet of film, same way every time. Someday I'll put all these short takes together in a film—it might be an hour long, possibly even longer. And what a magnificent film, too! This panorama never twice admits to the same mood."

Leaving the camera on the front hood, he wandered away from the car, crossing the gravel to where sagebrush began. And, oblivious to passing cars, Bart took a leak. Having followed him, I summoned the guts to do likewise, because I was tired of trashing every last one of his obnoxious actions.

I asked, "What was she talking about, back there?—Lorraine, I mean. When she mentioned parachuting into the gorge."

"Oh, it's just a little gag we have scheduled for Saturday," he said nonchalantly.

"Why do you have to parachute into the gorge?"

"It's in the script," he replied, flicking urine droplets off the tip of his penis.

"It sounds dangerous. At least Lorraine really thinks so."

"Lorraine don't know watermelons from acorns when it comes to the danger factor in stunts."

"You're forty-six, forty-seven years old, Pop. You're no spring chicken."

He grinned strangely, a child's caught-in-the-cookie-jar affectation, and wouldn't face me: he trained his gaze on the mountains. His voice, when he spoke, sounded absentminded, almost woozy.

"I'm not afraid. There isn't anything about it gives me even two seconds of concern."

"But why do you have to parachute off a frigging bridge into the Rio Grande Gorge?"

"See, what happens," he explained patiently, "is this character, his name is Tony Phelps, and he's a pusher, all right. But he's, like, this sort of Robin Hood of the dealers—know what I mean? He makes a lot of money bringing stuff into the country, but he uses that money for some very benevolent purposes. I mean, he's a semiattractive, anti-hero who's tried it in straight society, but straight society never gave him a break. He grew up in the ghetto, was unjustly jailed on a one-to-life in California—like George Jackson. Had the shit beat out of him in the pen, finally escaped, and turned to crime: it was the only way to survive, given his record. Anyway, he brings some bush up from Mexico and lands at this tank-town airport, the Chamisaville airport. Goes into town for one of those obligatory nights, you know: booze, a nightclub, a sexy broad—a hooker. Then he heads back out to the airport the next afternoon. But meantime somebody squealed and there's a stakeout on his plane. They drained the gas tank, there's a half dozen cops running across the tarmac to nail him. But in this shoot-out, he escapes from the plane. Fortunately, he's got a little auxiliary chute on his back, and is toting a suitcase loaded to the gills with a hundred Gs. He makes it to a car, commandeers the vehicle, and careens out of there in a hail of hot lead, onto the highway leading to the gorge bridge . . . which only happens to be five miles west of the airport. I mean in real life. So anyway, just as he hits the span, the pursuing pigs shoot out his tires. He skids all over the place, does a roll, maybe, and comes out of the car okay, still lugging the suitcase. Then he realizes he's still wearing the chute, and jumps over the railing—just like that. Yanks the cord, and he's home free.

There isn't access to the gorge for ten miles on either side, and it's close to nightfall anyway. His plan is to follow the river, going into the water whenever there's a posse near, and by dawn he's thirty miles away from where he floated into the gorge."

"It sounds like a really morally uplifting picture."

"It's what the traffic will bear."

"What do you mean?"

"It's what people will pay to produce because it's what people will pay to see. You know: Clint Eastwood, Burt Reynolds, that kind of garbage. I'm gonna make a million dollars . . ."

But there was sadness in his voice, the melancholy of a man who perhaps once believed he had the potential to be a giant. Instead, he had spent most of his life cavorting among dwarfs. For Bart there had never been a true outlet. I was embarrassed for him, and I suppose he knew it. Because he said:

"Aw hell, you're right, I guess." He grinned again, almost shyly, and looked so strange. That painful, vulnerable scarred face of his, and all the curly gray hair, made him resemble a middle-aged little boy, like Norman Mailer, or—again—Dylan Thomas.

"It's a living," he said. "And it's being in action. As long as you're in action . . ."

But his voice trailed off.

I had a vision of my father as some kind of beautiful animal —a bear, say, or a rare silver arctic fox—in the zoo, trapped in an alien environment, all its beauty and energy useless, on display and nothing else, unable to merge or consummate with an environment equal to its own capacity for being larger than life.

About ten miles away a tiny plane flew toward the Chamisaville airport. Whenever it tilted slightly, sun reflected sharply off it, causing a gemlike glitter. We both tracked it for a moment before Bart spoke:

"When I was a kid, it just about killed me that I couldn't

fly. I used to stand out there on our enormous front lawn for hours trying to will myself aloft, into the air, just six inches off the ground, *anything* to be airborne. Impossible to believe that I couldn't make a run, and take a little hop, and start soaring. I had dreams all the time of flying, of drifting around the estate, over the lawns and cars and gardens, over the swimming pool and the tennis courts, over the beach, and over Long Island Sound . . . until I disappeared out there, lost among the gulls. I would wake up from those dreams with an incredibly intense, almost erotic feeling . . . from having been able to fly. It drove me crazy that I couldn't fly—when I was five, seven, even ten years old. It seemed horribly unfair. It was one of the most disappointing things I ever had to deal with, that. I still sometimes wake up in the morning with a terrible nostalgic ache in me about it. I can't get over being disappointed, feeling that it's unfair. Isn't that strange? I mean, I'm a grown human being . . ."

He faced the car where Lorraine smoked a cigarette, her lackadaisical attention held by the far landscape.

I asked: "What about you and Lorraine?"

"Who knows? I love her. I gotta figure out a way to make her stay."

"I think if you quit trying to kill yourself it might help."

"You don't understand," he protested. "I'm gonna live to be a hundred."

"You say."

"She's pregnant. She says if I keep stunting she'll get an abortion. We had a big fight about that—it's one of the reasons she split. I don't like the idea of an abortion. Believe it or not, I need that child. She says she doesn't want it to grow up without a father. But I try to tell her . . ."

He lapsed. I prompted: "You try to tell her what?"

"I try to tell her she's full of shit."

Then he addressed me earnestly.

"What nobody understands, Marcel, is that I'm indestructible. Feel this muscle, would you?" He made a fist, bulged his bicep. "I'm so fucking powerful . . ."

"And—?"

"And I don't know how to convince her it'd be worthwhile. I'm so old, she's so young. I mean, look at us . . . wow! What do we have in common? But something there really works. I don't understand it. Even three years ago I wouldn't have looked at a little twat like her. What has she got that I ever craved? Sometimes I don't even believe it myself—I'm in love with this half-pint scarecrow who doesn't even have *tits.*"

He chuckled, bent over, selected a slim weed, peeled it, and stuck it between his teeth.

"But I really love her, kid. Don't ask why. I don't even want to screw around with the broads anymore—I'm serious. I mean, something happens when you get older. You get lonely from being alone. I don't want to be alone anymore. I want to live with her. I want her to have that kid. I want to be the father for somebody like I never had a chance to be a father with you. I want . . . I'm so hungry. You understand—hungry? I got an appetite, suddenly in my life, for being *ordinary.* I don't even know where it came from . . ."

He faltered. Over there, Lorraine snapped her cigarette out the window.

"How can I tame her?" Bart asked petulantly. "You know what she said the other day when she told me we weren't gonna be married? You know how she put it to me?"

"No."

"She said, 'I'm sorry, Bart, but I never wanted to sign on as a pallbearer at your funeral.' She said that."

"I don't blame her."

"Up yours. Let's go." He strode angrily back to the car, and I had to hustle, catching up.

Impishly, Lorraine said, "Well, did you solve it?"

"Solve what?"

"The riddle of the universe."

"You better believe we did." Bart gunned the engine prior to shifting into first.

"Oh—so what's the answer?" she asked.

As he popped the clutch, Bart quoted from a Tom T. Hall song: "Faster horses, younger women, older whiskey, and more money!"

4 Lorraine had moved out of the Big House into a seedy, overcrowded little trailer court a half mile north of town. Despite Bart's insistence that she have dinner with us, she wanted to be dropped off there.

"I need to practice, you guys. In three hours I gotta make like Loretta Lynn at the La Tortuga. I better calm down beforehand and find the right mood."

"The temperamental artist," Bart scoffed. "Three hours of zen and yoga to prepare for songs like 'I Can Still Hear the Music from the Restroom.'"

But he drove her there and pulled off the highway, parking outside the ornate green archway gate to the cheesy Sundance Trailer Court. Lorraine lived about eight heaps down the narrow lot—in a vomit-pink-and-silver job, Number 12. Her car, a 1965 Chrysler convertible that looked as if a firebomb had gutted it, was parked outside.

The court itself was shabby and depressing. A few scrawny Chinese elms provided meager shade; ratty dogs and half-naked kids played desultory games in the dust. I had an overwhelming impression of TV aerials, diaper-loaded clotheslines, and rattletrap cars, half of them without tires, up on blocks. Nearly inert adults had been discarded everywhere: fat slobs, women in curlers, undershirted men—all drinking beer. The icing was flies and garbage. We had arrived at the banal, grubby end of a sadly deteriorated daytime-television world.

"I still don't see why you can't at least chow down with us," Bart said. A hint of panic half transformed his eyes. If he let her go now, would he ever see her again? "I mean, hey, don't forget, it's Marcel's first banquet . . ."

"Don't 'hey' me, sugar. Marcel will survive without my august presence," she quipped, giving me an efficient good-bye peck on my left cheek. Seconds later, leaning through the open driver's-side window, she tapped her tongue lightly against his lips.

"Well," Bart said uncertainly, "we'll catch your act later on."

"You do that." Mockingly, she flounced her skinny butt at us as she took exaggerated sexy strides, heading for her new home.

Bart beeped the horn and she stopped. He yelled, "If you ain't got it, don't flaunt it!"

Lorraine whirled and stooped, snatching up a small stone; she flung it at the Mercedes. The pebble actually bounced against our windshield.

Bart cried, "Watch it!"

And Lorraine pulled a silly, wonderful stunt. With the cigarette dangling from her lips, she did a funny modern dancing riff, a quick combination of tap, soft-shoe, and vampy blues, just a dozen moves or so, executed perfectly, with sexy precision and syncopated slurs in all the right places. She included a cute and sensual bump-and-grind flourish that was powerfully nostalgic and alluring. And ended it in a boop-boop-be-doop jerk of her hips and shoulders that seemed pirated from Marilyn Monroe's act in *Some Like It Hot.*

Then, launching a finger at us, she sashayed arrogantly offstage toward her derelict digs.

"You break my heart!" Bart laughed.

"Suffer, sucker!" she called gaily, trailing smoke, refusing to look back. "I'm a real killer! I pour water on drowning men!"

We watched her kick a dented fender on her convertible, scoop up a scruffy yellow tomcat that had been sunning itself on her rickety plywood stoop, and march through her unlocked door into the dismal trailer.

Bart released a deep sigh. I said, "She sure is a pistol."

"You can say that again."

"She sure is a pistol."

He made a sound, half grunt, half bellow, and attacked me, tackling me the way he had when I was a kid, hitting me with great exaggerated motions, his blows so soft I barely felt them. Enveloping me with his enormous bearlike body, he cursed and threatened a dire massacre. "I'll tear you limb from limb, you schmuck. I'll disembowel you on the spot." It was play-wrestling, play-acting—he had always done that. How well I remembered his throwing me all over rooms or lawns without ever once causing any damage other than the stomachaches I got from the giggles when he tickled too hard. I had loved that gentle mayhem, when I landed in a hundred rag-doll positions as harmlessly and softly as if I'd been a pillow. The worst wounds I ever sustained were occasional abrasions on my cheek from the rough stubble of his chin . . . when he attacked me long ago, trapping me in slow-motion, infinitely compassionate explosions of love.

Now, of course, he couldn't throw me about much. Especially within the confines of our car. He merely shouted, gurgled, and flung a half dozen sham punches, then rocked away, saying, "Don't fuck with me, Marcel, or I'll rip your arms out of their sockets; I'll squash your head!"

He breathed heavily from the brief exertion; his face had become alarmingly red. I said, "Pop, you're crazy. You really are. You know that, don't you?"

"Crazy?" He started the car and made a dangerous U-turn on the crowded highway, heading for home. "Crazy, he calls me. My own son . . ."

His motorcycle, what remained of it, was enough to give anyone the willies.

I whistled softly as we walked away from the Mercedes parked in back of the Big House. "I don't understand how you came out of it alive, Pop."

"I don't either." We circled the wreck and, using the major back door of his eighteen-room adobe palace, entered a large kitchen full of remarkably gaudy and outwardly original human beings engrossed in various stages of eating and drinking their suppers around a large aluminum-topped table.

"All *riiight!*" somebody said. "The prodigal returns!"

"Hey everybody!" Bart announced, flinging an arm around me. "This is my kid! His name is Marcel! Be nice to him; he's a very sensitive human being!"

A general "Greetings!" commotion ensued as maybe fifteen or twenty outlandish-looking people welcomed me into the fold. Several long-haired men wore headbands, dirty jeans, and leather shirts. Others, outfitted in cowboy hats and turquoise jewelry, appeared clean, phony, Hollywood Western. Most of the women seemed young, pretty, and buxom, their bodies provocatively decorated by a white cotton peasant blouse, a squash-blossom necklace, a shiny purple velveteen vest. One bizarre sexy girl, who came across hard and 1950ish, had on a bright tight jersey, a short skirt, and sheer stockings. The scent of marijuana was so strong it almost fogged the air.

Very quickly, Bart introduced me to a dozen characters. "Randy, this is my kid. Randy's one of our special-effects maniacs. John, meet Marcel . . . assistant director. Marcel, Kathy . . . she's a hair stylist. And this is Deborah . . . she plays a prostitute. Over there, the one with the beautiful tuchus, that's Allison. She wears glasses because she's a bookkeeper, believe it or not." A Larry, a Devon, and a Michelle followed; they nodded, saying "Put 'er there . . . good to see you, man . . ." in friendly, noncommittal ways. Bart kept slapping and touching everybody, shaking hands, patting shoulders, giving out squeezes. Gently, he cuffed a cheek, or gave a swift sexy kiss to a woman. He poked a dozen guts, moving through them— his crew, his professional family for the time being—like an agile quarterback in a football backfield during the execution of an intricate play. Effortlessly, he led me through that crowd of film technicians and hangers-on and gophers into the daylight of a baronial dining area occupied by some more Beautiful People, among them a dark-skinned lady, a blue-jean-jacketed Ivy League type who resembled an urbanized lumberjack, and two very New Yorkerish men in custom-made suits and hundred-dollar maricón boots.

"Mel . . . Charley . . . Bubba . . . Veronica . . ." A cameraman, an assistant editor, a script advisor, a makeup person. They were drinking beer from goblets; two of the men smoked cigars. Veronica had a short joint in a roach clip poised at her delicate fingertips. Lazily, she joked, "Bart, I didn't know you were old enough to have a grown son." Diamonds would have melted in her mouth!

Half the dining room was usurped by a fat, plaster-of-Paris woman bathing in an old-fashioned eagle-claw bathtub full of polyurethane water on which a rubber duck floated. Though in the style of George Segal, I doubt the piece had been done by him. A bunch of paintings, prints, and photographs by well-known artists, among them Andy Warhol, Jasper Johns, Alice Neel, and Helen Frankenthaler, decorated the room in a baroque, haphazard manner. Helter-skelter, Bart had accumulated art all his life; many people hanging on his walls here (and in New York and L. A.) he counted as personal friends.

As we marched through a large room occupied by a jumble of electronic amplifiers and other assorted equipment at one end, and by a lumpy secondhand couch and an old Baldwin grand piano at the other end, I said, "Don't any of these people have last names?"

"What for?" he asked blithely, charging up rickety, uncarpeted stairs ahead of me, still carrying my suitcase. "You seen one, you seen 'em all."

"Yeah. But people feel unfinished to me if I don't know their last names."

"They go through my life so fast I barely have time to learn their *first* names!"

On the second floor, corridors aimed off in three directions. A hairy little man wearing one-way sunglasses, madras Bermuda shorts, and tennis shoes, backed out of a door, still addressing an occupant inside the room. "I know she can't add two and two," he said sarcastically, "but who's asking her to be a mathematician?"

As we passed him, he adjusted his shades. Bart said, "Jerry." And Jerry did a half-pointing little chop with his index finger, greeting my father with one word: "Later."

I asked, "Who's that?"

"Jerry."

"Jerry *who?* Jerry *what? Jesus,* Pop!"

"Jerry Fazzina. Jerry my director. That's who. He's a cokehead married to that gorgeous girl who didn't know I was old enough to have a grown son. She's not old enough to have a grown husband. They've been on the outs for two years; they only communicate by writing notes. He's screwing my lawyer's secretary, Shannon Markson; she's doing a number with Bubba Wilson, one of the cigar smokers down there. Maybe you heard of Bubba. In his real life he's a painter from Topanga Canyon. One day somebody told Bubba he could shove a paintbrush up his ass and do better. So he stuck a brush in his anus and invented rectal realism. He's got a brother named Frank, also on the picture, who invented the cardiac bass. He's a singer, a guitar player, you know. To save money on a bassist once, he hooked a mike to his chest, amplified his heartbeat, and played to that rhythm. If he wants a faster beat, he jumps up and down to make the old ticker pump more rapidly. That was his equipment you maybe noticed in the music room. The lady sitting on the bed in the room we just passed, that's Lily Enright, his— Jerry's—Rolfer. We got three Rolfers on this film, two psychic healers, and a bearded guru in a pear tree, who also doubles as a sound-sync technician. Running a fucking movie these days is like trying to pilot Noah's ark. I gotta import a ton of peanuts every day to feed the animals!"

A battle-scarred calico cat snoozed on a sagging double bed in my room. Other furniture included a dusky mahogany bureau and a full-length mirror on the closet door. The walls were bare except for one small Cézanne print of Collioure

Harbor. My eastern windows gave onto a magnificent view. Beyond an area where the Mercedes, several pickups, two jeeps, and a half dozen other assorted vehicles were parked, stretched miles of untouched mesa leading up to rambling Midnight Mountain foothills. A half mile away, at the end of a row of cottonwoods bordering an irrigation ditch, stood a small, windowless religious edifice with weeds sprouting from the dirt roof, a Penitente morada. To the left, close by the house, a large corral housed sleek Arabian horses munching on bright-green flakes of dry alfalfa.

In a yellow room across the hall, the window looked down on a grassy courtyard where a man in a black European bikini and Acapulco sunglasses was playing Ping-Pong with a very tall teenage girl wearing gold hoop earrings, a silk blouse under a leather vest, and a nondescript ankle-length skirt—no shoes. Beyond them, a medium-sized swimming pool held no water. It had gone to ruin; frizzy grass clumps surged from cracks in the tile floor and walls. A tiny apricot-colored toy poodle raced around the bottom of the pool, unable to get out, barking its head off.

I asked, "Who are those people?"

"That's Julian—he's a driver. If anybody wants to go anywhere, he drives them there. He's Brazilian, he can't speak a word of English. So if you want to go someplace, you got to learn Portuguese. He also takes film to the bus every evening, and brings back the developed rushes. There's about a three-day delay getting the shit back from L.A. The girl's name is Kitty Spencer, she does macramé and holographs. She also knows French, which Julian speaks a little of. So essentially she's an interpreter."

"Hired especially to accompany Julian?"

"Actually, she's Julian's girl friend. To get a driver who can't speak English, I had to put his girl friend on the payroll."

"What about the dog?"

"That's Lily Enright's mutt."

"What is it doing down there?"

"I dunno. I guess she left him there this morning. That pool is a good dog pen." Bart shouted down to the Ping-Pong players: "Hey Kitty, see if the mongrel has water, would you? And if his food dish is empty, go find a package of baloney or something in the kitchen, okay? C'mon, Marcel, I'll give you the rest of the tour."

His own quarters, at the end of that hall, were as large as the downstairs dining room. A battery of French doors opened onto a wooden balcony, enclosed by an ornate carved balustrade, on which sat a small upright piano. The room itself was a mess. Manuscript pages, books and magazines, a portable typewriter, and rumpled satin sheets were reflected in a ceiling mirror over his mighty waterbed. Somebody had lipsticked an enormous, absurd smiley on the mirror. Lithographs, paintings, snapshots, posters, silly trinkets, deer and jaguar heads, and a large stuffed lake trout chaotically plastered the walls. In one corner, a gilded birdcage on a white pedestal held two delicate Japanese finches. Ashtrays heaped with cigarette butts, half-empty drink glasses, and more magazines cluttered the top of an enormous color console television. Clothes lay in violent piles around the floor; scattered among them were dozens of hardcover and paperback books. He had a large desk, a stereo, and another cassette recorder on top of the stereo. The room also contained several filing cabinets, and an 8mm movie projector aimed at a sheet tacked against one wall, under which lay a Martin guitar. Beautiful Navajo rugs were barely visible beneath the garbage blanketing his floor.

I said, "What if it rains on that piano?"

On his way to a small refrigerator camouflaged by copies of *The New Yorker* and a two-week-old *New York Sunday Times,* Bart replied glibly, "Nine out of ten times the thing gets wet."

From the minifridge he selected a Coors, offering it to me —I shook my head. Punching open the top, he took a hefty swig. I asked, "Who's the cartoonist on the ceiling mirror?"

"That's Lorraine, bless her sardonic little heart." He

belched. "It's been up there for over two years. She drew it the first night we shacked up together here. She claimed this bed and that mirror were the most ridiculous sexual accouterments she'd ever seen. Most nights we slept in that room you've got. She hates waterbeds, mirrors, and big rooms. And big houses. Says it feels like her body is echoing all the time."

I said, "I think I like Lorraine a lot."

"You would. She's your type."

"What do you mean?"

"Well, appearances notwithstanding, she believes in all the old ethical verities. You know, like true love, faithfulness, commitment, sex because you love each other, not just because you're into balling . . . crap in that vein."

"There's something wrong in that?"

"Well . . . it makes her hard to handle sometimes. As you may have noticed."

Downstairs again, he showed me the library, a square, windowless space with unpainted, rough-cut lumber, floor-to-ceiling bookcases against every wall. A half dozen Salvation Army easy chairs were arranged with no particular rhyme or reason; fluorescent ceiling bulbs made the atmosphere aluminum white. A shirtless, bald, and fierce-looking little man sat cross-legged in one chair, reading a book called *How to Win Through Intimidation.* "That's Cass Attaturk," Bart informed me on our way out. "He used to ride with the Hell's Angels. He's our Special Advisor on Drugs and Collisions."

"You're kidding!"

"Honest injun, sweetheart." He gave the three-fingered Boy Scout sign. "I think his subtitle is Violence-Authenticity Expert."

Two 35mm Moviolas were quartered in another room, surrounded by several tables and much cutting and editing equipment. Shelves were stocked with dozens of film cans: discarded pieces of celluloid littered the floor. A flustered-looking man and a woman with an enormous Afro prowled about, muttering under their breaths while puttering with strips of film the way I picture semihysterical stockbrokers often fidget with their Bache quotation tapes.

Bart announced, "Millie . . . Brad, this is Marcel, my kid. Millie's an actress who gets murdered by Doberman pinschers. Brad is the chief editor responsible for cutting all this glop into some kind of semi-intelligible moron food."

Brad grumbled, "I wish I was back in L.A. Trying to put something together in a jury-rigged pit like this is like trying to fuck the hypotenuse of an isosceles triangle."

I said, "What?"

"Don't mind Brad." Bart gave his editor a spontaneous bear hug that made Brad's eyes bulge. "He talks like a Polish washerwoman."

"I don't want to do the Doberman scene on Tuesday," Millie said. "My boyfriend, Craig, he's flying in that day. I don't want to do that scene in front of him."

Bart embraced her. "Baby, is it on the schedule for Tuesday?"

"Screw the schedule. I don't want him to see me like that."

"Tell him to come a day later."

"He can't."

"Why?"

"Because that's when he got booked on the peanut flight."

Bart said, "What's the dollar difference between the peanut flight and a first-class ticket?"

"I don't know. I bet a hundred dollars."

My father said, "I'll give you a hundred bucks out of the general fund. Call Craig to come a day later. And do me a favor—go to Doris or Allison in bookkeeping tomorrow morning and tell them I said to release the bread. When you get a chance, too, you might have Chuck or Teddy take you around the Dobermans. Chuck says they're trained not to maul or bite, but it would help if they got used to you a little beforehand anyway."

Brad said, "That's no sweat. Eddie called me earlier today. He says Bert Margolis can have two more five-seven blond

Afro'd girls here in ten hours if the Doberman shot goes haywire."

"What does he mean by *that?*" Millie shrieked.

"It's his sense of humor," Bart explained. "Pay no attention. Where were you brought up, Brad, in a sewer?"

Brad squinched his eyes, hunched his shoulders, and jiggled a bit, wheezing, which, I take it, for him, passed for laughter.

"Another thing," Millie said. "No bare nipples."

Bart sighed. "What do you mean, no bare nipples?"

"I'm not exposing my nipples when those dogs slobber all over me. I don't have to do that. It's not dignified."

"Aw hey, Millie," Bart said warily. "It's in your contract, you know that. What the hell do you think the public is paying to see, your face?"

"I could care less about the public. What about my family? What about my boyfriend? What about my *kid,* if we ever have one?"

Bart was all patience. "Look, do me a favor, let's not discuss it now. Go talk to Eddie. He's got all the contracts."

"Eddie's a son of a bitch."

"I know, I know. That's what he gets paid for. He also knows everybody's rights. Everybody signed a contract. Everybody read the script and knew beforehand, right? Eddie explained it to you, about the nipples. He explained it to your agent. He explained it to your boyfriend. If you signed to do the movie, you signed to expose those pretty tits."

She snapped, "A plague on you, Bart!" And stalked out in a huff.

Brad said, "How can I work in this nuthouse? Where's my privacy? Not only do you expect me to start cutting this clunker before shooting is finished, but every five minutes some two-bit actress staggers in here and starts pawing all over my film, trying to ascertain if there's more of her tits than the contract called for, or if Mel tried to sneak in a beaver shot. I'm an artist. I've read Hegel and Kant."

Throwing up his hands, he winked at me, hunched over and wheezed for a beat, then wandered unperturbedly out.

Bart drained the beer he had commenced upstairs, opened a cupboard housing another midget refrigerator, and selected a new Coors.

I said, "Did you know there's a Chicano boycott against Coors?"

He answered, "*Et tu, Brute?* You got a contract forbidding me from drinking the kind of beer I like to drink?" In almost the same breath, snapping on the Moviola and gazing critically at the tiny screen projecting a stretch of film, he said:

"Here's a scene we shot on Monday. It's not bad. Rick Bates, the actor there, he plays the Robin Hood pusher. The woman he's punching around is Marcia Gadbois. Casting found her in some topless joint on The Strip—she's not a half-bad actress, but that's not why she's in the picture, as you can see."

It was a brutal scene. They were in a motel room, arguing, the actress dressed only in her bra and panties. Bart had the sound off. The woman took a poke at Rick Bates, and he slapped her a half dozen times. She fell against a night stand, opened a drawer, and pulled out a small pistol. He grabbed a bottle off the dresser, and broke it over her head: glass shattered, blood blossomed across Marcia's face as she collapsed backward onto the unmade bed. The camera held on her for a beat, then she opened her eyes, shrugged, and, as she asked a question that must have been something like "Did I do okay?" she tucked one breast back into the bra.

I said, "Jesus, doesn't that hurt?"

"Hardly. It's a breakaway bottle. Hurts about as bad as a snowball."

"It *looks* horrible."

"It's supposed to look horrible."

I said, "What do people get out of all this sadomasochistic bullshit?"

"Aw hell, Marcel; it's entertainment. They gobble it up.

Nobody takes it seriously. Everybody knows it's just the movies."

"I really don't understand, though, why you risk your life in this kind of jerk-off exercise."

"Well . . ." He pondered that for a moment. "One of the charms of crap is it has no pretentions. Crap is crap. Phony from the word go. Everything is up front."

"Still, to risk your life doing it?"

He nodded. And for a second lost the grip on his manic energy; he seemed almost pale and fatigued. "I guess," he said slowly, letting the words out as if he wished they could be more profound: "I guess the reason I do it is it's fun. I don't try to justify it or anything. It's merely fun."

"But if you die one of these days doing a stunt in a vehicle like this, won't that be sort of like dying in a bad joke?"

"Dying, period, is a bad joke. It doesn't matter how or where. Why surround it with a whole shitload of irrelevant blather? As a matter of fact, why even bring it up? What is this, the morbidity sweepstakes? *Jeez!* Between you and Lorraine . . . C'mon, let's get out of here!"

We had barely entered the courtyard when Bart blanched and faltered. All color drained from his face. He gasped and seemed about to faint. The Ping-Pong game was still going full tilt: the ball clicked loudly against the table. From a dozen open windows a dissonant music issued into the grassy patio area: somebody plinking the piano, a Willie Nelson song from the *Red Headed Stranger* album, and Linda Ronstadt. Flute notes carried to us from farther away. Many people were conversing faintly. And a male peacock, tail feathers raised and spread, turned the corner and halted, eyeing us.

I touched his arm. "Pop, are you all right?"

He burped. And color—almost bright red as broadcasted through his delicate, transparent scar tissue—flooded his features. Making a half-hearted gesture at the house, the peacock, and the surrounding grounds, he said: "This sure would be a piss-poor excuse for a last stand, though, wouldn't it?"

"Sit down for a second. Why don't you quit drinking that beer?"

"Marcel, if I could I would but I can't so I won't. Sorry."

"All it takes is a little willpower."

"Willpower!" he snorted derisively. "Where were *you* brought up in, Communist China?" And he whapped the back of my head, though not hard. Another silly, affectionate gesture, albeit of annoyance, and awkward as all his physical gestures toward me were. Because he didn't really know me very well; we didn't know each other.

I said, "What's with the peacock?"

"Ain't my peacock." Bart swayed as if dizzy or drunk. "It showed up one day behind the wheel of a chartreuse Carmen Ghia. It feeds on chameleons we have flown in special from Costa Rica every Saturday."

Making a pistol of one hand, Bart pointed it at the posturing bird, and said, "Bang. C'mon. Let's go hunt up some grub. I'm so hungry I could eat a tank."

The sole survivor from that kitchen-supper crowd was a woman named Kathy. She sat at the aluminum table smoking a cigarette, sipping on a glass of red wine in a crystal glass, and reading a Tin Tin comic book. Looking up as we entered, she half smiled, said "Hi," and returned to her story, paying us no further attention. Her beauty, up close, floored me. Wheat-colored hair framed a broad Slavic face with misty green eyes, round cheeks, and voluptuous apricot lips. She looked very sexy in a mischievous, lazy way. I struggled hard not to pay attention to her while we rustled up some food.

Clicking on a portable TV beside the stove, Bart tuned into the evening news. He was demolishing a can of beer every two minutes, it seemed. We located warm chicken legs, some posole, and salad, and heated up Safeway tortillas. As usual, Bart wolfed down his meal, gobbling phenomenal quantities so fast I thought he'd choke on every bite. The man annihilated his dinner and crumpled beer cans seconds after opening them, set-shooting the remains across his kitchen into a garbage can.

People kept arriving and departing. First a man named Monte Gershwin informed us, "We got three dummies and the chutes all rigged up, Bart. Bill says maybe sometime late morning, while we're setting up the auto stunt at the bridge, we might drop at least one off, if that's cool with you."

"Will somebody be down there to pick them up?"

"Oh sure. Cliff's flying up from the capital with a helicopter first thing in the morning; he'll have it out there by then."

"Did you clear it with the town council, the county commissioners, and the state cops?"

"Randy and John got it all taken care of."

"What about the car?"

"Randy and Gil are all finished with the interior reinforcement, seat belts—you can check it over whenever."

"You tell them to make sure there's less than a half gallon of gas in that vehicle," Bart growled.

"Don't worry."

"I'll check it out early in the morning. Did they get the kind of tires I want?"

"Does a bear shit in the woods?"

"Are they shaved?"

"You bet."

Allison the bookkeeper popped in. She said, "Veronica wants a thousand dollars advance."

"Tell her to pray for it—Jesus Christ! I'm running a business here, not a charity. What does everybody think . . . ?"

Eddie Cobalt, Bart's lawyer, a short, muscular, and inordinately handsome man who could have doubled for Raf Vallone, paused briefly on his way through the kitchen to inform Bart, "Anybody tell you they got Gadbois down at the hospital? Snakebite on her thigh."

"*Snakebite?*" my father roared. "How in the name of—?"

"Chuck says she was at the animal ranch, doing a number with Teddy, and he started playing with one of the snakes. He feels terrible. Cheerio . . ." And he split.

Bart raged, "Idiots!" Then he screamed: "*Shannon!*" A

moment later his lawyer's secretary, a mousy-looking little woman appeared. "Hey, find out what's happening with Marcia at the hospital, would you? And see if you can catch up with Eddie and have him get in touch with me about our responsibilities in this thing, huh? I forgot to ask and he didn't have the generosity to offer. And if Teddy's at the hospital, tell him I want to see him right away. If I'm not here I'll be at the La Tortuga listening to Lorraine. And I want to see him *tonight,* before I retire. And do me one other favor, Shannon: tell him to keep his fucking snakes in their fucking cages. And ask him why didn't he milk the goddam things? He's supposed to milk them twice a day!"

"Roger . . ."

"I don't believe it," Bart groaned. "The pathetic Humane Society won't let you pull out their fangs anymore. And then you get a friggin' bevelhead for an animal keeper, and a two-bit actress who gets off humping among the serpents . . . The world is full of nincompoops!"

It went like that for another ten minutes or so, until, shortly after John Holbein, the assistant director, had checked in looking for Vaseline because Lily Enright had dropped a cigarette on Jerry Fazzina's buttocks while Rolfing him, Bart cried, "Let's get out of here while the getting's good; Lorraine should be starting any time now."

"Pop, I'm tired, I don't want to go to a bar, I'm sorry."

He said, "Marcel, when are you ever gonna learn to let it all hang out? You're too timid, boy! You'll wake up at sixty-five and realize that the Parade made a left turn down the block twenty-five years ago, and it ain't *ever* going to pass your reviewing stand."

Kathy looked up from her comic book. "The trouble with you, Bart, is you don't understand that everybody else in the world is just a regular little old human being."

He went "Uffh!"—kicked back his head, grabbed my arm, and literally yanked me out the door.

On the way to the Mercedes, he said, "You oughtta try

some of that on for size, if the mood hits. She likes you, I can tell. Could you feel it? Generally, she's butch. Her and what's-her-name, Veronica, they had a thing going until Jerry latched on to Veronica, and I suppose they still got it going anyway. But she's bisexual, sometimes. I knew a guy in L.A. named Jo Jo Handelman who blew his brains out over her last year. She's so soft and quiet, but she's got power—you know what I mean? It'd be like fucking a slow-motion avalanche."

Completely thrown, I cried, "What the hell are you talking about?"

"Kathy. The girl in there during our supper."

"Bart . . ."

"I'll tell her you're interested." He squealed backward then jammed the stick into first and nearly sideswiped a pickup on the way out. How it had gotten there I don't know, but yet one more beer can occupied his fist.

"Pop . . . please . . ."

"If it weren't for Lorraine," he said. And, for no reason at all, he beeped his horn at the darkness. His face—the set of his features—was caught between intense pain and real ecstasy. "If it weren't for Lorraine!" he repeated, his laughter sounding almost like a sob. *"If it weren't for Lorraine!"* he bellowed.

"Don't you ever stop shouting?"

"Why should I?" he laughed happily, and I realized his motor was really humming. He was soaring, in fact. I wondered if he had just popped a pill or tooted something. He seemed so impossibly high, vigorous, vital. After such a long day, with all the drinking and the emotional Sturm und Drang, how could the manic pace currently riding his charged-up bones be anything other than artificially induced?

I said, "At least turn down the tape deck."

"You're old before your time, Marcel. You're a little old stoop-shouldered gray-haired fuddy-duddy!"

With the hair on the back of my neck standing up from the fright instilled by a quarter-mile ride with my hyper dad, I tumbled free of the Mercedes and staggered dutifully after Bart into the La Tortuga. There I sank gratefully into a Naugahyde couch, ordered a double shot of bourbon, and withdrew, watching the show. It was a crowded bar, very smoky, very noisy, very dark. Irritating electronic *boings!* from TV-tennis games sounded between acid-rock and cool-country jukebox selections. We had only been there a few minutes when Lorraine elbowed through the crowd. She plunked herself onto Bart's lap. Kissing his lips, she peered briefly into his eyes with a deadly earnestness. Then she kissed her fingertip, and, reaching across the table, touched the fingertip to my nose. "How was dinner, you guys? Marcel, you look awful. Bart, you look drunk."

I said, "Dinner was very quiet, very relaxed. We watched TV, held court for a dozen lawyers, actresses, prop men, bookkeepers, and animal keepers, and dealt with a rattlesnake bite and a mad Rolfer who attacks people with lit cigarettes."

Lorraine tossed her head. "Yeah, but I mean, did anything out of the ordinary happen?"

With the queerest strained look on his face, Bart muttered, "You ain't killing that kid."

"Says who?" Angrily, she got up, unplugged the jukebox and the TV tennis, arranged herself on a spotlighted stool in one corner, checked the tuning on her acoustic guitar, twirled several buttons on the amplifier system into which her double mikes were jacked, and started singing "Bridge Over Troubled Water." After the first verse, I understood that she had a real voice, a truly exceptional way of singing: Lorraine was a pro. In fact, her husky and provocative voice and delivery style were so good I really did a double take. I actually sat up and listened, and almost immediately resented the noisy bar crowd, which couldn't have cared less. But Lorraine simply let her eyes glaze, fixing her gaze on a spot in the smoke above the patrons' heads, and sang the song with a remote and perfect feeling, as if she were on stage at Carnegie Hall or the Grand Ole Opry.

I let out a long slow breath. "Wow, she's really good."

Glumly, down off his high as fast as he'd ascended it, Bart said, "You noticed?"

The phone rang at the bar; a barmaid called over the crowd for my father. He ambled over there, talked for a minute, and returned gnashing his teeth. "Kitty Spencer," he said miserably. "She's got popcorn for brains."

Because I was tired of his movie entourage scene, I didn't even launch a half-hearted query about the latest outrage.

He offered an answer anyway: "That fucking poodle in the swimming pool. It's barking its head off, so some idiot on the second floor leans out the window and takes a shot at the swimming pool with a twenty-two. Kitty wants to know if I think she should fetch the dog out of the pool and lock it up in the pantry!"

Lily Enright and Cass Attaturk spotted us and headed our way. Lily was in her mid-forties, and peered sardonically at the world through thick-rimmed glasses. She wore an almost matronly summer suit, and resembled a hard-driving, hard-talking, very hip career yentah. She had a perpetual cigarette between her fingertips. Cass wore rose-colored sunglasses, love beads, a sheepskin vest with no shirt underneath, tight powder-blue flare-cuffed pants, and Wellington boots.

Lily said, "I hear old what's-her-face got bit on the whosit by one of those whatchamacallits."

Bart rolled his eyes. "What's the word from the hospital?"

Cass said, "Onomatopoeia."

Bart screwed up his features: *"Huh?"*

Cass grinned and stared coldly: "That's the 'word.'" Pointing his finger at Bart, he mouthed a silent *Pop!*

To Lily, Bart said, "Who hired this clown?"

Lily shrugged, made a he's-a-crazy-ding-dong motion with a finger at her temple, and tugged on Cass's vest: "Come on, sweetie, let's go sit over at that table."

After the Simon and Garfunkel number (à la Wanda Jackson), Lorraine sang "Help Me Make It Through the Night,"

"Queen of the Silver Dollar," and "Behind Closed Doors," never once smiling, and with no in-between patter. Nobody paused to extend her the courtesy of listening. A woman named Betty Malenkov stopped by the table for a second to talk with Bart about tomorrow's eating arrangements: she had some problems locating organic bran, yogurt, and tofu for the half dozen vegetarians working on the picture. Before she had finished, Bubba Wilson showed up, full of breathless news: cops had descended on the Big House. Neighbors had summoned them in response to the gunshot fired at the barking dog in the swimming pool.

Bart said, "Where's Eddie? He's supposed to take care of this bullshit."

"Nobody knows. He went out, remember? Shannon said he found some local nooky. She said she hopes he chokes on it."

"Well, do me a favor, Bubba. Try and find Connie, and if they arrest anybody have her withdraw a few hundred bills from the safe and go down to the fucking jailhouse and bail them out, would you?"

Lorraine finished up her first set; she flopped into a chair across from me at our table. "Jesus, I'm bushed already. Order me a brandy Alexander, would you please, Bart?" And she asked me: "Well, how did you like it?"

I told her she was wonderful. "But why in God's name are you singing in a place like this?"

She shrugged. "It's what the traffic will bear."

Bart said, "Next set, why don't you shut up this crowd of ingrates. Do 'Amazing Grace.' A cappella."

"I'm too tired . . ." Lighting a cigarette, she inhaled deeply. And then, her eyes on him, narrowed suspiciously with concern, she exhaled slowly.

"What are you doing," she asked Bart, "drinking yourself into a stupor?"

"I'm unwinding. I had a long day." I noticed that his eyes were bloodshot now. His whole body had slumped, his torso seemed contorted, all out of shape, feeble, and aged.

Lorraine said, "What you're supposed to do, love, is go home, tuck yourself into bed, and go to sleep."

Forlornly, he said, "How can I without you?"

"I'm not spending another night in that madhouse."

"I'll come to your trailer."

"No you won't."

"Why?" he pleaded pathetically. "What have I done to deserve . . ."

Leaning over, Lorraine took his hand in her calloused fingers and rubbed his flesh while she spoke. "Sweet Bart, gentle idiot, stupid little boy, I just can't take it anymore, I really can't. Two years ago it excited me, your rampant energy. Now it scares me because I love you. At first, I really wanted to go along for the ride. But now I realize I'm too young, I don't want to go down with your ship."

"You don't understand . . ." he whimpered.

"I don't have to understand. I just know that when I'm with you I love you so much I want to run away. I don't want to be within a thousand miles of you when it happens."

"Nothing's going to happen."

"Comets burn out," Lorraine said.

" 'Comets' . . . 'comets'? What do you mean, 'comets'? What is this shit? *True Romance* magazine? *Redbook? Jack & Jill?*"

Cooly, to me, Lorraine said, "Why don't you take him home?"

"How?"

"Pick up his hand, lead him out the door, and drive him home."

"What about you?"

"Tonight I really want to sleep alone. I'm tired. You wouldn't believe how tired."

So it happened that I drove a Mercedes for the first time ever. Like a wounded man, on the edge of total exhaustion,

Bart slumped in the seat beside me, his head dropped back, eyes closed, mouth eerily open. Like an enormous, rough pietà. Twice, on the way home, I said, "Hey, Pop, are you okay?"

The first time he roused himself a little, grunting, "Me? Yeah, sure, shit . . . child's play."

The second time I had to prod him again, "*Pop—?*" before he responded. "Huh? What?"

"Are you okay?"

"Happy as a clam," he whispered. As if all the neck tendons had been severed, his head lolled uselessly against the headrest.

Pulling in at the end of a line of vehicles parked outside the kitchen door, I killed the engine. "Bart, we're home."

He opened his eyes, staring at the ceiling, but said nothing, didn't stir.

I asked, "Are you gonna be sick? You look awful . . ."

"Home," he said slowly. "Be it ever so humble . . ." And after that: "You know something?" he said, still without moving or taking his eyes from the ceiling.

"No, what?"

"I am a Remarkable Human Being."

"Pop, if I don't crawl between some sheets in the next two minutes, I think I'll die."

"So go. Nobody's stopping you."

"What about you?"

"I think I'll sit here like this for a while. Feels comfortable. Soak up a few nocturnal bennies."

"Are you all right? You really look weird."

"Course I'm all right. I didn't get to where I am today by being fainthearted."

"Can you move?"

"Course I can move. What do you mean, 'move'?"

"Well, your body looks frozen. You look paralyzed. In the past three minutes you haven't even blinked."

"Watch closely," he said, teasing me. "To prove to you I'm okay, I'm gonna blink my right eye—you watching?"

"Bart, do you have to?"

"I said, 'Are you watching?' "

"Yeah, I'm watching."

"The right eye, now, you watching *closely?*" He blinked it. "There. Are you satisfied?"

"It's chilly out here. I wish you'd go inside and hit the hay."

"Leave me be, Marcel. I feel great. I feel lazier than I've felt in ten years. I feel positively drunk with erotic calmness. I'm getting a hard-on. I think if I just sit still long enough, tonight's the night I'll learn how to float."

"You're crazy."

"Look who's talking."

"I'll see you, then."

Bart whispered, "Hey—!"

"What?"

"She's really something, isn't she?"

"Lorraine?"

"Yes ..."

He smiled, his eyes kept staring at the roof of the car, and he didn't move one iota.

"She's great, Pop. Good night." As I started to walk away, he either said, "Take care," or "Take care of her"—I couldn't distinguish which. I was so weary I barely had the strength to lift the latch of the kitchen door. Passing through the dining room, I lost my balance and nearly fell into the bathtub with the plaster-of-Paris woman and the plastic duck.

Yet I had advanced beyond fatigue and couldn't sleep. My ankles, kneecaps, and thighs ached, my head throbbed, my eyes stung. I trembled from what felt like coffee nerves; I was thoroughly strung out. So I lay there unhappily, listening to drowsy night sounds. A television movie played somewhere; a woman laughed. I smelled marijuana: smoke fumes from the drug were a persistent mist seeping throughout the Big House.

The longer I awaited sleep, the more I became aware of my own heart beating irregularly, pumping blood erratically through my veins and arteries. On several occasions I caught myself with clenched fists, or with my teeth clamped together so tightly that my jaw hurt. When lying prone became painful, I sat up, straining unnaturally to decipher the night stirrings around me. So much rustling, muffled movement, faint voices and music; radios, TVs. Horses puttered contentedly in their corral near my open window.

Eventually sounds drifted, died away, settled into silence. Then I heard my father downstairs, plinking out a tune on the music-room Baldwin, a lonely melody, repetitive and bluesy. The music touched me, hitting chords that could have produced tears. I pictured him down there, all alone at last, experimenting in the cool summer gloom, able for a moment to tinker with something simple and easy: he had it all to himself. I felt powerfully drawn toward Bart, and experienced a nostalgic ache. For what we might have shared together, over the years, if we'd been able to spend time together. And simply for the concept of Father, which I'd never known. The *Saturday Evening Post,* Norman Rockwell concept, I suppose, of the smiling pop with a baseball glove or a fishing pole—who knows? Perhaps the ache was just for Bart, aside from his relation to me. For if he had been closer to me he never would have been that kind of old man, of course. So the ache was dissociated from all that. Call it a simple compassion for that awkward, self-destructive person downstairs ... and the tough little singer who, by threatening to take a powder, was trying to force him to save his own life.

Slipping on jeans and a sweater, I joined Bart. No lights burned. My father was silhouetted against the bay window beyond his piano. In the darkened dining room a man and a woman sat at the table smoking pot, conversing in low voices. Choosing a chair near Bart, I said nothing. He sang a verse of his song:

I can still feel the mood
Of you wandering through
Those cool empty rooms of my heart.
There's a ghost in the music
That's drifting like smoke
Through an echo of times that still hurt.

"That's a lovely song."

"You think so?"

"Yes I do. Really."

"Naw. It's sentimental crap." He chuckled.

"It's lovely sentimental crap."

"What happened to you," he asked haltingly, "you got brainwashed by Walt Disney? Rod McKuen? Kahlil Gibran?"

"Come on, Pop."

After pondering for a moment, he decided what the hell. "I wrote it for Lorraine last year. It ain't half bad when she does it."

"Are you writing many songs?"

"Here and there. You know. When the muse ambles close enough that I can grab her and rape her."

I asked, "What happens after this movie? What will you do?"

He fiddled with three notes. "Oh, little bit of this, little bit of that: I'll keep my hand in."

"Another movie? More stunt work? Writing? Real estate?"

Bart laughed softly: "A.) All of the above. B.) None of the above. C.) Some of the above."

"Please. It always seems like I never have any idea of what you're doing."

"Oh, let's see . . ." Scratching his head, he turned his back on me, facing out the window. "We oughtta have this thing wrapped and halfway cut by the end of September. In October I spend two weeks in Costa Rica, I think it is, gaffing sharks for a picture Mac Ivory's coproducing—remember him? You met him once at the Brentwood house. That night what's-her-name —Jayne Mansfield—fell accidentally on purpose into the swimming pool. Then I'll be back in L.A. for a while, riding herd on Brad and taking care of a billion and one little details. Middle of November I fly to Spain to help Jerry blow up a train for a picture he's doing over there. I'm also supposed to dive fifty or sixty feet off an exploding replica of an offshore oil rig. If I survive?—well, who knows? Naturally, I'm hoping Lorraine will be tagging around with me all this time . . ."

He jostled a smoke loose from a pack on the piano and lit it. He worked on the weed for a while, without speaking, occasionally fingering a sweet little blues riff on the piano, and I didn't interrupt his mood by speaking. Finally, he quit tinkering, took a last inhale from his cigarette, and held the smoke for a long time, thinking, his head cocked in a peculiarly evocative way, remembering.

When he spoke, strands and curlicues of white fluff fluttered out between his lips. He had so much smoke, down there deep in his lungs, that for almost the first minute of his story the words were accompanied by those spurts of smoky filaments from that single heavy drag.

"The first summer Lorraine and me hooked up," Bart said quietly, "I kind of took a vacation from the Los Angeles scene. Bought a big old white Cadillac convertible with a hundred thousand miles on it, and I reckon we put another hundred thousand on it before the fling petered out. I was her manager, you know, even though I didn't know shit from brass enchiladas about booking the redneck honky-tonks she wanted to play. I always had a pocketful of dimes, though, and a million schemes."

He cocked his head. "You listening to me?"

"Of course I am."

"Well . . . Lord. That sure was a primitive summer." He shook loose a fresh cigarette and lit it by scratching a sulfur match on his thumbnail. "We lived in that car, slept in it, hanky-panked in it, ate in it. And hit every county, parish, you name it in Texas, Louisiana, Arkansas, Mississippi, and part of Oklahoma. It was crazy and wonderful. She played in some bars so funky they weren't much more than outhouses with neon moons in the doorway. It was a whole other America, down there. People actually ate grits and hush puppies and chicken-fried steaks. I saw *cotton* fields. We survived mostly on peanut butter, white sandwich bread, Hostess Twinkies, watered bourbon, and fish fries. Lorraine taught me everything I know about bass casting: she was brought up pulling small-mouths out of Ozark cow ponds. We even ate rattlesnake a couple of times; I killed 'em, she cooked 'em. God, we had some laughs. We had some high old times. We decided her name ought to be Lorraine Luray, the Arkansas Nightingale, so I painted that in gold script on both doors, along with a fancy, jewel-studded guitar and some musical notes."

He spit some tobacco flakes off his tongue, and played a short run, jazzy and slow, moving up the keyboard with tenths.

"I picked up the crabs somewhere and I remember being drunk and having giggle fits together in the back seat of that monster Cadillac parked at night beside some old flatland reservoir with Lorraine bent all over me making like Doctor Kildare, wielding a flashlight, some rubbing alcohol, and tweezers, claiming she was an African big-game hunter."

Bart rocked dreamily, flicking ashes on the floor.

"Shit, I never felt so young or so innocent before. Our time was gentle and funny, and I suppose a little pathetic, too. We boozed from sunup to sunup and made love just about all the time. We would pull off the road in the middle of the day, or in the middle of the night. Or else we'd look up a motel in one little tank town or another and rent it for twenty minutes, take a shower, and hit the road again. I pissed blood half that summer, and I was always sucking on copper pennies soaked in vinegar—Lorraine's remedy—or on dry aspirin . . . for toothaches. For some reason, we had decided never to see a doctor. We drove with the roof down in rainstorms, and skinny-dipped in a million little creeks and rivers. And while she sang, I usually lolled around among the customers getting drunk on the house and digging the scene. Such a lack of responsibility! Oooo, that was sweet."

Bart laughed—openly, honestly, downright *merrily.*

"I remember one day we stole a bushel of peanuts from off the porch of a country store. But they were green, and we didn't know how long they should be roasted, and threw them all away. Then I developed coughing spasms and began spitting blood into handkerchiefs, and it got bad. So finally she took me to the hospital in Dallas, and I was there almost three weeks, recovering. That was the end of the fling. But what a wonderful, irresponsible summer. We loved each other like a couple of babies. And you know something? I didn't ever want to return to the real world again."

Dropping his cigarette, he crushed it beneath his foot—his bare foot, I noticed: he'd removed his shoes somewhere between the Mercedes and the piano.

Bart mused: "Sometimes I'm lying in bed and I remember driving along the Texas highway at night with Lorraine beside me stroking her guitar and warbling a few bars of this or that song, both of us staring at the deserted road up ahead . . ."

Shifting, he shook loose yet another cigarette.

"Or she'd be cuddled beside me, sound asleep. And I'd be listening to country-and-western music on Bill Mack's Open-Road show out of WBAP in Fort Worth-Dallas. Once, even though the gas gauge read empty, I wouldn't turn off for a refill —you know why? Because I didn't want to disturb the mood. I just kept going, and I think I believed that even after the tank was empty the car would keep humming along that starlit highway on nothing but the *momentum* of that peaceful idyllic mood. But finally the inevitable happened: it ran out of gas. So I steered carefully onto the shoulder and waited, without moving, because I didn't want to awaken Lorraine. My need—and oh it was a powerful need—was to sustain that mood, you know? Because for one of the rare times in my life I was so overcome by feelings of love for another human being that I wanted to prolong it until the next century, or die right then and there so I could feel that way forever. I know it sounds corny as hell, but that was a damn near religious experience.

Rising smoke caressed his cheeks, ambled through his hair, and rose upward.

"I sat there with my arm around her, absolutely immobile, until she woke up around dawn."

Bart coughed and made a touching, apologetic motion with his hand.

"Well, lessee," he rasped, his voice sounding peculiarly squeezed. "I'm also working on a TV script with a guy named Joe Sinclair for 'Starsky and Hutch.' On spec, maybe it'll go, maybe it won't. Other than that I'm gonna spend four days around Thanksgiving playing golf in Acapulco with Phil Wyandanch and Mort Cheesman—remember him? I think you met Mort once in New York. When we went to the World's Fair. He lost a leg in Spain in 1938. Now he's a member of the John Birch Society. He plays a good game of golf, though, for a one-legged Fascist."

Bart swiveled and thoughtfully rattled off an arpeggio.

"What else? Sometime around Christmas I guess I'll be a pallbearer at Mort's funeral: Acapulco should be his last curtain call. His body is riddled with enough big C to deck an entire metropolis. Polyps on his pancreas; six weeks ago they cut off his balls. Can you imagine that? Somebody cutting off your balls . . ."

He let smoke out of his lungs with an almost delicious slow-motion control, savoring the taste as if it were his last heavenly breath on the face of this earth. Then he went slack; I waited. The woman in the dining room raised her voice slightly: "The trouble with him is he wouldn't know how to pull a laugh out of a chocolate mousse if one bit him in the ass." The calico cat that had requisitioned my bed earlier hopped onto the piano, and settled about two feet in front of Bart, primly licking her chest and shoulder fur.

Demoralized, my father said, "Actually, sometimes I don't feel much like doing anything these days."

He puttered over the piano keys, the muting pedal depressed. Then, presenting his back again, he faced his courtyard where the Ping-Pong table gleamed brightly in calm moonlight.

"To tell you the truth, Marcel, most of the time I really don't know what in hell is going on around here. All these movie people—where do they come from, what do they want from me, what good are they? Personalities seem to materialize out of some bizarre ether and then hang around for a while until they disappear and someone else takes over. I know their names and their jobs; I know what I'm supposed to tell them to do. Every now and then I even recognize a face: so-and-so the actor—years ago we did off-broadway together; such-and-such, my lawyer—five years ago we gambled on some crazy futures; Joe Blow from San Diego, a sound technician—we used to visit the Baja together, big-game fishing; Ursula Nitwit, the infamous fashion-model-turned-sex-starlet who once gave me a sloppy blowjob in a changing room at Bonwit Teller. I dunno, I really don't know. Sometimes I get really low, I feel frozen inside, I'm scared, I seem to be losing the thread. That's how come it hurt so bad when Lorraine—"

Making a hopeless gesture, he played several sentimental Sunday-morning-hangover-blues ripples along the keys.

"I want that kid, Marcel. I want something *real* ..."

Softly, he sang another verse of the song he'd written for her:

> *I'll never regret*
> *The love that we shared,*
> *Or the way that you held me in bed;*
> *But a ghost in the music*
> *That's drifting like smoke*
> *Tempers new temptations with dread.*

I said, "It's obvious she loves you—"

"Hey," he said abstractly. "Wasn't that some trout we caught this afternoon? Did you ever see such a beautiful fish in your life?"

"What happened to it? I thought we were going to eat it for supper."

"Oh shit. I forgot," he drawled without emotion, his fingers absentmindedly picking up a Gershwin melody. "I reckon it's still in the trunk of the car."

"Let's go stash it in the refrigerator."

"Naw, it's too late now. Not fresh anymore." But then he reconsidered. "Actually, we better fetch the goddam trout before it begins to rot in earnest." And he lurched up again, lumbering through his house and out the kitchen door, with me right behind him.

Silvered by the cool moonlight, Bart held the fish up almost reverently; we both admired it.

"All my life," he intoned regretfully, "I've enjoyed killing things. But I never have cared much for eating them—especially the fish. Ain't that curious? I mean, I wonder why I can never throw them back in the water? Sometimes I've actually bashed them silly and then tossed them away into the bushes—beautiful trout like this, even lunkers that were bigger. All my life I envied those purists who could haul a big trout to shore, take out the fly, and release the fish. But somehow I never really feel I've caught one unless I kill it."

A Siamese cat materialized, its white fur glowing phosphorescently; it rubbed up against Bart's leg. Leaning over, he dangled the fish to it. Excitedly, the cat sniffed around the stiff rainbow, then bit it, tugging hard, and Bart let go. Backing up, the Siamese dragged that large trout past the twisted Harley Hog to the corral and in among the Arabian horses. Safely protected by lunar-cast equine shadows, it began to devour the gift. At ease in the white moonlight, the horses seemed not to notice the intruder. As it worked on the meal, the cat shone eerily, as if its fur were charged with poignant electricity.

Bart said, "Heaven only knows, Mr. Allison."

"Why did you say that?"

"I don't know. It just happened."

He was almost out on his feet. His face, captured in a near stupor, gleamed dully. God he looked old. Like a sixty-year-old man, or even older. I shivered.

Bart whispered, "You gotta help me win her back." Essaying a step toward the house, he almost stumbled, but caught himself. "I want that woman. I need her. I want our child. I want to *rest* . . ."

"You're exhausted, you have to go to bed."

"I hate going to bed. I can't sleep. The only way I can sleep is with pills, and I hate pills. And sometimes even they don't work. And *then* what am I supposed to do?"

I followed him through his mansion and up the stairs.

"And anyway, I'm not tired enough yet," he said. "I need to be really tuckered before I can sleep."

I stopped at my door. Bart continued along the hallway into his brightly lit room. I kept an eye on him a while longer. He snapped on the television, only raised a test pattern, but left it flickering. He almost pitched over while opening the mini-fridge and fumbled for yet another beer. And sat down at his balcony piano, where, with one finger, he moronically plunked out notes with no pattern, no melody. Occasionally, the pauses between notes lasted almost a minute. I quit spying and went to bed again, this time so drowsy that I knew I would be asleep in seconds. But I couldn't quite go under. After hearing a single note I failed to slide all the way into oblivion, because I was awaiting the next sound. For five minutes I had one ear half-cocked, fighting sleep . . . and always another note came, and then a long silence. I awaited those notes the way I had awaited his rare letters and occasional phone calls when I was a child.

For those communications, I suppose, were among the most important events of my childhood, however infrequently they occurred.

I hovered on the edge for a long time, anticipating those forlorn musical cries for help issuing from my father's insomnia.

5 I had a dream about Bart.
He was on that big Harley of his, floating down a deserted country road at night, illuminated by brilliant silvery starlight. It was springtime. I couldn't hear the noise of his motorcycle. His frantic curly white hair exploded like sunshine off his head. His little gold earring glittered. And he was laughing. He had the face of a clown who had walked into an airplane propeller: his little blue eyes clung to the bridge of his catastrophe of a nose like scared blueberries. But he was laughing; he looked so exhilarated. His giant frame was clothed in an iridescent cowboy shirt—unbuttoned down almost to the waist—that sparkled as if a rainbow were being repeatedly exploded within the fabric. The sleeves were cut off at the shoulders, exposing mammoth biceps and forearm muscles. A snakeskin belt that boasted an enormous silver buckle inlaid with colorful cheap stones kept up his faded Levi's. Knee-high purple-and-white elaborately carved and stitched mule-ear cowboy boots sheathed his size thirteen feet. In the orchards, on either side of the road, trees had recently exploded into white and pink bouquets that looked like rare popcorn creations.

In fact, as the motorcycle careened at sixty miles an hour along the solid white center line, it suddenly entered a swirl of petals caught in the wind, a thick blossom whirlpool that entirely covered, and more or less obliterated, the road. Bart stood up, joyfully bellowed "Sheeee-it!" and took his hands off the steering handles to try and catch some of the incredible floral snow. Just as he did so, the road made a seventy-five-degree curve leftward. Catapulting out of his ecstasy covered with apple-blossom polka dots, my father registered the turn, but refused to believe what he saw. Then, muttering "Aw, for cris-sakes," he dropped back onto the big foam-rubber seat, and, at the last moment before leaving the road, he really gunned the gas, leaned a little forward like a man on a jumping horse, jerked up the front wheel to miss a rotten log by inches, rode the rear-wheel jolt, and for another split second, going up, Bart strained as if he actually thought he could zoom over the low pines and become a bird or a plane and sail away to safety somewhere.

It was horrible. I screamed as the bike bounced end over end down a steep slope, Bart somehow entangled in its mecha-nism. The bike crash-landed with a great spray of water in the center of a small, shallow pond. Things hissed, steam rose, one wheel protruded. Bart kicked out a leg, a hand, his face emerged; sputtering, he fell back underwater. Then he disentan-gled himself from the crumpled bike and stood knee-deep in the muddy water. Swaying, he banged his tilted head to get the liquid out of his ears. He looked befuddled and dazed. The wind gave a last little whip and disappeared into the darkness. The air changed, growing sharper, real cold. A last few apple blos-soms fell from the night, landing on the water, spreading faint silvery circles. Then, what had been in the air all that spring evening, real snow, began to fall. First a few flakes, indistin-guishable from the apple blossoms, except they melted when they touched the water. And for a minute, awed by the delicate and incongruous weather, my father made no move. The snow-fall thickened and became regular, floating down languorously through the crisp sweet-scented air . . .

I woke up scared and with an ache in my heart. Bart had been captured in such a poetic and vulnerable moment. I lay quiet for a while, in the sunny morning stillness, wanting to reach back into the dream and pluck my father from it, into safety. I had never in my lifetime thought of him as fragile. He had always been so rambunctious, fierce, macho. Yet I awoke from that dream feeling as if my father's buoyancy were sus-tained in this life by a substance as fragile as the dust upon a butterfly's wing; he was a human being held to this world by a bond as delicate as the silken thread of a tiny floating spider.

With that, I experienced a sharp flashback to one of those startlingly vivid days of a more romantic yesteryear. With a clarity that stunned me briefly, taking me as much by surprise as had the revelation that it was "The Honeymooners" I had been watching while Bart and Kyrah Pattachinsky engaged in overt sexual shenanigans on the way to Kennedy's inaugural, I recalled my kidnapping at age seven. In particular, I remembered the five days we had spent together in that north Las Vegas motel cabin.

I could picture him again, feel him again, and hear him again so clearly that goose bumps prickled along my ribs and my neck hair seemed charged electrically. A gigantic, gruff, weeping, boistrous, stuttering man paced the little room with the curtains drawn, haphazardly trying to make a case for himself to my blithering seven-year-old sensibility. Profusely, he declaimed his fatherhood, insisting he was ". . . a good guy. I would never hurt you, Marcel," he pleaded pathetically. "Look at me, what do I look like, some kind of monster? Honest injun, kid, I'm just a regular human being. How come your ma doesn't understand that?" Every time he reached into his pocket, or his suitcase, or ran out to the car, he produced another little bribe: a Duncan yo-yo, a baseball cap, a water pistol. One afternoon we had a marathon water-gun fight in those cramped and shuttered quarters. It was the kind of battle a child wishes would never end. We skidded and slipped on the drenched floor, and wound up entirely naked, blasting each other while hiding under beds or squatting behind the open doors of closets. "See?" he hollered gleefully, crouched fetallike on all fours, guarding the back of his head with clasped hands as I pumped water at him: "I'm just a regular person, I'm a good guy, I'm your fucking *daddy!*"

We sneaked out for meals, patronizing a greasy spoon down the block until the fuzz located our whereabouts and closed in. I had never dined in a café or restaurant before;

buttons almost popped off my shirt in celebration of my grown-upness. Bart ordered me cheeseburgers, milkshakes, and ice-cream sundaes—*for breakfast!* I gawked at that enormous and ridiculously flamboyant human being who claimed paternal distinctions. It was like going from no father at all to the discovery that somebody incredible—like Jesse James or Super-man—was my real old man. We looted drugstores of all their comics: I walked out of them with my arms full of terror, war, and crime magazines Kitty had always forbid. And as I marched along the hot asphalt, half believing a midnight clock would strike, turning all my unbelievable goodies into plump vegetables and squeaking mice, Bart danced beside me, crowing, "There, see how *easy* it is? See how *nice* I am? Isn't this fun?" And although I hadn't realized it then, I understood it now—there had been tears in his eyes as he accompanied me back to the motel. Oh, I was blind to it, of course. I felt like some perky old son of a bitch who had just pulled off the great Brinks robbery.

At the motel, I impersonated an obnoxious little pasha while he orated the comics to me. He also read the newspapers out loud, especially the sports pages. We watched television propped against pillows, chain-sucking Cokes up through pep-permint straws, Bart's arm around my shoulders, hugging me close. Whenever a commercial came on, he said, "This ain't bad, ay Marcel? Please, you've got to remember me. Tell Kitty I'm all right. Tell her I'm a good Joe. She can't keep us apart forever. I just want to be your pal . . ."

We wrestled. He yanked the mattress off our bed, relegated the frame to a corner, arranged pillows around the mattress on the floor, assumed a position on all fours, and growled at me: "C'mon, you chickenshit little creep." He swiped at me with a lion's paw, and I jumped back, nervously giggling. "I'm gonna crush you, squeeze you to death, kill you, eat you, and shit you out in little blond-haired turds," he promised. But then I caught him unawares and, unleashing a shrill and thrilling shriek, I pounced upon him eagerly. For seven years I had been waiting to tackle a father. He hollered and grunted theatrically, rolled and tossed and tumbled me about, initiating the first of those play-wrestling sessions that I would remember with such fondness many years after. I laughed until I cried, while he threatened to give me a forehead knuckle torture, or a black-and-blue bicep nuggie attack, or a painful sternum drilling. Always, at the last possible second, I flung him away; he crashed clumsily against the flimsy walls, and collapsed in contorted heaps, dramatically groaning. With me astride him triumphantly, Bart gasped, "Don't hurt me, Marcel. I give up. I never knew you were such a tough little bastard." But just as my imagination crowned me the heavyweight champeen of the world, he would give a heave, jouncing me off onto the mattress. Before I could recover, he had made a claw of his right hand. With his left hand, he executed a motion at the underside of his wrist as if pulling a string on a lawn-mower engine. In this case, he was starting up his "hydromatic ball hooker," whose motor usually caught after three yanks. Then his clawed hand started jiggling terrifyingly, while he sputtered, imitating its gasoline-driven works, and I squealed hysterically through my giggles, trying to flee before those savage fingers ripped apart my crotch.

Of course, the man was on edge. He might even have been dangerous. At heart, he had no idea how to relate, other than to lavishly shower me with forbidden fruit: "A Milky Way every hour gives you power!" he cackled insanely as I obligingly stuffed my face. Each night we called a justifiably frantic Kitty; I assured her I was okay, and Bart explained that all he had ever wanted was minimal visiting privileges to his own flesh and blood. And Kitty was all sweetness and light on the telephone while cops traced our calls.

I don't think Bart slept at all during that first crazy time we shared. Whenever I opened my eyes, he was usually seated upright against some pillows in our large double bed, just staring at me while sipping coffee from a Styrofoam hot cup. I believe every night he watched me sleep. And toward the end his haggard face developed a terribly haunted mien. "I'm a worthless idiot," he desperately told me then, saying words I did not hear, really, until this morning more than twenty years later. "But you're okay, Marcel. I need to spend some time with you every now and then, because there's a few things I can pass along that are valuable. And one day you'll appreciate them. And you'll protect them better than I ever could because you're much tougher than me. I can tell that already."

Back in the present, my door opened and in walked the devil himself, flushed and panting, naked except for a black, European-style bikini and Spanish rope-soled slippers. And in one hand he carried a pail of water.

Lazily, I said, "Top of the mornin' to you, Pop."

At the edge of my bed he set down the pail, stooped over and gripped the iron frame under my mattress. As I blurted, "What the hell?" he heaved upward, dumping me over with a single powerful jerk, executing the job so thoroughly that he actually yanked the frame out from under the mattress and tipped it over on top of me. Then, even before the springs had quit twanging (even while wings of the erupting sheets still battered the air), he grabbed the bucket and doused me.

"You son of a bitch!"

Roaring with laughter, he said, "Up and at 'em, Sleeping Beauty! Only the rich and the very decadent sleep this late! We got work to do!"

"Up yours, motherfucker!"

Infuriated, I struggled to free myself from the drenched mess. But sheets were wrapped around my legs and an arm; my other hand was thrust through the old-fashioned springs of the bed frame. By the time I released myself, thoroughly apoplectic and determined to commit patricide, he was gone, already loping downstairs, and trailing behind an admonition:

"Breakfast is nearly over, Marcel. Move your *ass!*"

"I'll kill you!" I shouted defiantly. But my declaration ended in a sputter of laughter. And by the time I had shat, showered, shaved, and hit the kitchen for morning victuals, I felt wonderful.

As usual, Bart held court at the large table while demolishing great quantities of food: cantaloupe, eggs, sausages, toast, and nearly a dozen cups of coffee during our brief breakfasttime. Bart was incredibly adept at juggling a half dozen conversations at once. When I arrived he was discussing a stunt car —he would drive it that afternoon—with Monte Gershwin and a tight, wiry man in a greasy blue jumpsuit named Gil Brenner. He was also grilling Eddie Cobalt about the legalities of the Marcia Gadbois rattlesnake-bite case. And listening to general kvetching from the rectal realist, Bubba Wilson, and the Rolfer, Lily Enright.

While I drummed up Cheerios, juice, and Sanka, the stunt and special-effects people voiced their concerns about Saturday's parachute jump. "The winds in that fucking gorge are incredible," Monte Gershwin said. "It'll be like trying to piss in a hurricane getting down between those cliffs."

Bart said, "I'm not worried about the winds, I'm worried about the water."

Gil said, "We'll stretch a net across the river fifty yards from where you're supposed to land. We'll have poles, life preservers, the whole schmear."

"But what if the wind blows him below the net?"

"Heaven forbid. That'd be almost out of the shot!"

"God won't let the wind blow me out of the shot," Bart said serenely, picking a sausage up in his fingers and popping it into his mouth. He wiped his greasy hands on his bare chest. "If he does, I'll sue. Can I sue God, Eddie?"

"What makes you so sure God is a *he*?" Lily Enright asked sarcastically.

Eddie said, "I called up Union Pacific this morning and their rep, a kid named Tommy Blaine, said they're gonna cancel our coverage. He claims there's a clause says we hadda defang the snakes before they ever even crossed the Arizona line."

"Is that possible?"

"I don't think so; I'll read the agreement in L.A. next weekend. It's against SPCA rules, as I remember."

"Meanwhile—?"

"Meanwhile, we've run into a little problem from a local group called The Friends of Chamisa Valley. They claim Cliff's gonna trash the Wild River section of the Rio Grande gorge with his helicopter. They actually filed in court yesterday evening for a restraining order to keep him, and our cameras, out of the gorge."

"Who the hell are The Friends of the Chamisa Valley? Screw them, we go in there anyway, whether they like it or not."

Betty Malenkov barged in fuming.

"The bleeping Safeway is all out of cherry Jell-O!" she shrieked, slopping some coffee into a Styrofoam cup. "Can you believe it? I got a hundred and twenty lunches to prepare, and they're all out of cherry fucking Jell-O!"

Bart's secretary, Connie Alexander, stuck in her head, piping merrily: "Folsom at Universal just called. He's furious about the rattlesnake bite. He says he spoke with Tommy Blaine at Union Pacific, and they're claiming no responsibility. He also said Blaine told him the parachute jump was going to be filmed with a dummy, and under no circumstances was *any*body going to jump off that bridge."

Bart growled: "The audience knows it's a dummy if you use a dummy!"

"But he says Blaine says the contract says we promised to use a dummy."

"So what? So we promised. So we break a promise."

"If you get killed, they're not responsible."

I said, "Pop, what's so important about this idiotic movie that you gotta risk your life in such a dumb stunt?"

He reached over, snagging my chin between thumb and forefinger: "Marcel, you wouldn't understand, really."

Lily Enright said, "Do the Proper Authorities know you're going to roll that car this afternoon on the bridge?"

"I'm not gonna *roll* the car, Lily." Bart grinned impishly. "Bullshit, you're not gonna roll that car."

"I'm just gonna skid it sideways a little, that's all."

"What if you miscalculate and sail through a guardrail?" Lily croaked hoarsely, a regular Madame Doom.

"Then it's a good shot," Bart said. "It's important always to go out on a good shot."

"Tommy Blaine will shit a brick."

Bart asked Gil Brenner: "Did you guys replace the windshield?"

"Does a bear—"

" '—shit in the woods?' "

"Yeah, we replaced the windshield."

"So what I want to know," Lily rasped in her gravel voice, "is who took a crack at my poodle last night?"

"I saw Jerry down there with his fifteen-inch hard-on trying to fuck it around midnight," Mel said, entering the kitchen and heading for the coffeepot.

"You got the wrong party," Bubba Wilson said. "Jerry and Veronica were on the roof doing eggbeaters last night when the cops arrived."

Lily growled, "Lookit my bruise. One of those flatfoots grabbed my arm. How do I sue for police brutality, Eddie?"

"Flatfoots," somebody hooted. "When were you born, in the Jazz Age?"

"What're eggbeaters?" I asked.

Jerry Fazzina appeared in the doorway, decked out in garish Hollywood-Hawaiian cowboy togs. He also carried a fencing foil, and wore a protective screen mask. He said, "On guard, Bart. I want your ass in the side courtyard!"

My father leaped up. "Connie, bring me my swords!"

I turned to Lily Enright, asking, "Is it always like this?"

"Yup. This is how movies get made, kiddo. The magic illusion cast by the silver screen."

Gil Brenner grumbled, "He's crazy to roll the car on that bridge. He's crazier to jump off that bridge, if you ask me."

"So who's asking?"

Monte Gershwin said, "Mack Sennett would have loved it."

"Mack Sennett's been dead for half a century."

"Well, then, would you believe Yakima Cannutt?"

On his way through the kitchen, the cameraman, Mel, said, "But the man has a touch of class. Unlike the rest of you androids connected with this puerile exercise in futility."

I located the duelists on the courtyard lawn near the derelict swimming pool and the Ping-Pong table. Bart had added a screen mask to his bikini-sandal wardrobe. Seen close up and in action like that, his muscled body looked surprisingly solid and healthy. His legs had grown a trifle thin compared to the rest of his bulk, but he moved easily, and with an aggressive coordination that amazed me, given his propensity for self-abuse. But he had always possessed fantastic regenerative powers. Bart was one of those people who never slept until noon, no matter how plastered they had gotten the night before. His willpower could suppress any hangover. And besides, mornings, with his intense athletic and outdoors style, were my father's time. How he hated rising late. Especially given his obsession to repair any nighttime carousing damage as soon as it was humanly feasible to do so.

Give him credit. After appearing exhausted to the verge of comatose collapse just hours ago—here he was, dancing vigorously around the lawn, clanging foils with a strange little man wearing one-way shades, a silken pineapple-and-cockatoo sport shirt, an enormous Concho belt, flared slacks, and cowboy boots.

Behind them, lasciviously blatant in skimpy bikinis, Kathy and Veronica played Ping-Pong. A cassette recorder on the ground beside the table blared out David Bowie tunes. In the music room behind us, Frank Wilson was rigged up to his cardiac-bass paraphernalia, playing rock-blues riffs on his treble Fender to the magnified, echo-chambered beat of his own heart, an eerie three-pronged muffled thumping. Dragging its heavy tail, the peacock wandered obliviously about the court-yard lawn, pecking desultorily at insect tidbits.

Mel poked his head out the music-room door, calling "Bart? Telephone." Discarding his foil and mask, my father trotted inside. He returned a few minutes later, absolutely furious.

"I don't believe it!" he cried. "I'm running a circus for brain-damaged mongoloids! Charley Watson just told me that Teddy copped some acid last night and took all the rattlesnakes out to the mesa and let them go! LSD, for crissakes! I got a hundred thousand pickles written into the budget for cocaine, and that dumb schmuck's got to go and pull a peace-love-groovy on me! Psychedelics!" he spat derisively, adjusting his mask and attacking Jerry with a vengeance: "The curse of the working classes!"

Almost immediately, Connie Alexander appeared, saying "Telephone!"

Puffing from the exertion of whacking at Jerry, Bart said, "Tell whoever it is I'm busy. They can call back later."

"It's Bruce Dicus in L.A. He wanted to speak to Eddie, but I can't find Eddie. He says Tommy Blaine called Folsom, and Union Pacific is talking about canceling on the picture right now for breach of contract. Folsom says if you don't use a dummy tomorrow afternoon for the gorge leap, he'll pull you out of the picture if you survive. He also says a lawyer claiming to belong to Marcia Gadbois is talking a quarter of a million already for the rattlesnake bite. And he wants Teddy fired, as of this minute. Another thing he wants to know is how did you manage to blow it with The Friends of Chamisa Valley? They actually called him, in L.A., and made like we were planning to strip-mine the entire valley with our movie cameras. He also apparently heard a story that we threw a poodle in an empty swimming pool and were taking potshots at it all last night. I told him it wasn't a deliberate shooting gallery, there was only one shot fired, the dog wasn't hurt, the cops didn't arrest any-body, and you know what he said?"

"I can hardly wait."

"He said, 'If anybody gets arrested out there, I'm holding that candy-ass B.D. personally responsible.'"

My father never stopped attacking. "You tell Bruce I got dummies up the ass to drop off that bridge tomorrow. You tell him I'm dropping Charlie McCarthy, Howdy Doody, and Kukla, Fran, and Ollie, into that gorge tomorrow afternoon. I don't care what you tell him. Tell him we've built a six-foot-deep papier-mâché gorge and we're gonna drop a GI Joe and a Ken doll into it! Tell him I just bought a half dozen fuzzy Steiff rattlesnakes, and that we're gonna use dachshunds instead of Dobermans for the cannibal dog scene. Tell him I'm gonna retrieve the poodle from the swimming pool and mail it to him so that he can personally shove the little mutt you know where!"

"What'll I really tell him?" Connie asked, giggling.

"Tell him I'm *sorry!*" Bart slashed dramatically at his opponent's foil. "Tell him Boy Scout's Honor I'm not deliberately trying to set him up for a heart attack. Tell him we're three days ahead of schedule, at a saving of billions of dollars, and Brad says we're getting a winner. I don't care what you tell him. Tell him to mail me a carton of Thorazine."

"Will you call him back?"

"When I'm ready." And Bart drove Jerry back so relentlessly the strange little director tripped over the peacock—which squawked—and went sprawling.

Bart loomed over him triumphantly, one foot comically placed on the man's stomach, his foil point touched against Jerry's chest. "Beauty and youth triumph over age and ugliness once again!"

Both Ping-Pong players shouted "Yay!" and clapped. Disgruntled, Jerry said, "Suck on it, Bart. Now lemme up. I gotta go direct something that, in the loosest sense of the word, we're calling a movie."

Shannon Markson called out of a second-story window, "Eddie phoned from the Holiday Inn. He says a half hour ago

Teddy was arrested by the Pueblo cops for wandering around on Indian land, and they won't let us bail him out."

"Get somebody to feed the Dobermans, and find me a dozen more rattlesnakes. C'mon, Marcel, let's go have us a *workout!*"

And, grabbing my arm, he literally dragged me at a run through the mansion and out the kitchen door.

His morning regimen unfolded like the summer Olympics. He led me to the corral, and, before you could say "Casey Tibbs," we were galloping through the purple sage, my old man bareback on a glistening black nag, myself saddle-borne and clinging to the horn for dear life.

Bart really knew how to ride a horse, I'll have to admit. Seeing him astride that Arabian, I would have gaped in awe had I not been preoccupied with saving my own life. But still, I caught flashes of his style and exuberance, his monumental body loose and glistening as the horse galloped flat out, the only way I had ever seen my father ride a horse. How he hated to trot or canter!

When I realized I would live a lot longer by swallowing my pride, I reined in and just watched him go, running so hell-bent-for-election the dusty wake seemed to spring up far behind the horse's hooves, outdistanced by a goodly twenty yards.

What if they hit a gopher hole at that breakneck speed? I wondered. But I knew that to Bart it didn't matter. The accident would be like totaling his motorcycle. And, observing him as he veered, circling to head back toward me, I again felt close to tears, wishing that—like some high-country fisherman from the mystical Andes—I could cast a net around my father and pluck him from his own life, setting him down tenderly on a foreign shore where he might begin again, discovering a reason for his energy, and living to a ripe and productive old age among people he loved . . . who would return the loving compliment in spades.

I thought, *My God, but this man could be so beautiful!*

The horseback riding phase of the Bart Darling Memorial Decathlon Event lasted barely twenty minutes. Before I could even begin to digest the impact of our Arabian steeds in that lovely sage on a sunny day at seven thousand feet ringed by majestic mountains, we were in the Mercedes again, heading for town.

While he spoke to me—gesticulating fervently, his fierce little eyes everywhere but on the road—Bart also piloted us through so much dangerous congestion and frantic activity that it felt almost as if we were in an airplane dodging through a gauntlet of ack-ack flak.

Talk about anarchistic little cities!

Chamisaville's only rhyme or reason seemed to be energy. Progress—in any way, any style, at any cost! You could tell it had once been a lovely little adobe town, but quite obviously a once-solid community was being unconscionably trashed in a mad rush for bucks. Action for the sake of nothing but action was the order of the day: no plan at all guided the overall growth. An ugly strip development was taking over; construction boomed everywhere. Yet the town was blatantly impoverished. Cracked sidewalks and horrendously potholed streets indicated an unmonied tax base. Water bubbled up through cracks in roadway macadam. Because only two main arteries ferried all vehicular movement through the so-called tourist Mecca, traffic was impossible. A congestion, formed by ten times the automobiles Chamisaville could reasonably handle, kept us stewing in aggravating jams for long dusty periods.

Bart told me that in the rush to transform farmland into recreation and retirement developments, Chicanos were disappearing before an in-migration of middle-class whites and their different priorities and values. "Land that cost five hundred bucks an acre eight years ago is going for ten grand an acre today," he said. "Nobody local can buy if they want to hang around. This place, in another five years, is gonna be a you-wouldn't-believe-it honky-tonk mess."

"It doesn't have to be that way."

"Ah, what the hell—that's life."

"It still doesn't have to be that way."

"Tell it to *them.*" Bart included the outside world with a short sweep of his hand. Then he swerved into a parking space by the recently completed, already-deteriorating community recreation center.

"What's here?"

"They got a diving board," he called over one shoulder as I ran to catch up.

Noisy children crowded the overchlorinated water, but Bart could have cared less. He rented me a bathing suit and disappeared. By the time I entered the pool area, my father was already down at the far end, doing dives.

For an old man, he sure could cut the mustard. I stopped cold, flabbergasted. Absolutely fearless, Bart catapulted off the one-meter board time after time in rapid succession, executing dives—learned by rote in his youth—with an almost teenage finesse. And not simply swan dives and jackknifes. Bart had graduated from being a country-club pool rat to competing for Harvard, and naturally he had specialized in the most theatrical acrobatics, dives with severe degrees of difficulty and much flashy twisting and spinning: inward two-and-a-halfs, backward twisting double somersaults, reverse one-and-a-half flips with twists. Such aerial displays had always triggered onlookers' "oh"s and "ah"s, not so much over his grace and form, as over the breathtaking complexity and near-violence of his executions. Bart's powerful frame attacking airborne maneuvers always gave the feeling he might lose it completely, crashing against the board while rapidly spinning, or whacking his face, thighs, or stomach against the brick-wall water with frightening force—that's how Bart and his fans got their kicks.

But at forty-seven years of age? He was doing it, though, brazenly showing off. Every time he geared for a dive, at least half the swimmers stopped and followed him off the board. His huge body literally battered the air, and I found him terribly uncomfortable to watch. I held my breath. With every dive he seemed on the verge of losing control. Once my heart almost stopped when I believed he would smack the board. Instead, he jerked out of a tuck spin at the last moment, throwing himself sideways. I thought I heard his toenails tic against the board on his way to the water. And oh how he loved that, scaring people, making them flinch over his danger.

"What do you think, kid?" Winking at me, he heaved out of the pool beside the board, still refusing—at his age—to use the ladder. Damned if he would make a concession to energy conservation by exiting from the water like other less-macho beings. "Ain't I beautiful?" Four times he thumped his gut, proving it was still as hard as anthracite.

I said, "You aren't beautiful, you're scary. You're also crazy as hell."

"I know how to live, Marcel. I'll never slow down. I'm practically immortal—!"

Off again, Bart grunted as the board flung up his heavy body. He executed a reverse dive, a one-and-a-half, again missing the board by inches and entering the water cleanly.

When his head broke the surface, I said, "Let's see you do something simple, Pop. Something pared down and classic, like a back dive in layout position, or a swan dive. No histrionics, no danger, just something graceful."

"Graceful?" He slithered onto the deck and banged water out of one ear. "What's the percentage in graceful? How many tickets can you sell with graceful? I ain't in business to put people to sleep, I'm in business to give 'em cheap thrills; that keeps 'em happy—"

I tried to push that arrogant son of a bitch into the drink when he wasn't looking, but he must have been expecting my move. Bart had an instinct for that, an eye in the back of his head. Sidestepping my thrust, he chopped away my arms, gave me a bump, and stuck out a leg, tripping me. I belly flopped loudly on the tepid water.

Squatting by the edge, grinning his Kirk Douglas grin, he

bragged, "Marcel, you may be a lot younger than me, but don't ever forget, I wrote the book . . ."

Right there it happened again. I could see it plainly even though he caught it halfway to the surface and attempted a deflection. Something had lurched inside his body, and it must have been painful. He sucked in half a breath; all color drained from his scarred face, leaving that skin as transparent and fragile looking as the meat of a jellyfish. The perpetually startled blue eyes under his ponderous brows looked truly surprised, then instantly they glazed over with hurt. Until quickly, forging an enormous effort, Bart flung aside that inner pain, muttered "Holy cow," and sat down.

"Are you all right?"

"Yeah, sure." He gulped, forcing himself to breathe naturally. The pain had been sharp enough to force a tear out of each eye. Then color flooded his face again, restoring some tan to his shining cheeks. "Of course I'm okay. It's just sometimes . . . probably a fucking ulcer. Let's get out of here, it's too crowded."

Yet he rested there a while longer, afraid to move, I suppose. I swam to a ladder, climbed out, and sat down beside him, swishing my legs slowly in the water. He stared at a spot directly in front of us, captured in a blue mood and seeming small again, somehow flaccid and feeble.

"Pop, I don't know what you think you have to prove."

"To tell the truth, Marcel, I don't know either. I must be getting old," he said morosely.

A moment later he said, "All my life, you know what I've been? A five-star asshole, that's what. I've been a self-indulgent prick to absurd extremes."

"No, that's not true . . ."

"I don't really know if I had fun, or if any of it was worth it," he said. "Like, one thing that always puzzled me is how come nothing ever really jelled? I mean, here I am, pushing fifty, and I don't know how to add any of it up. Do you think it's *supposed* to add up? Do you think I'm supposed to have some kind of *feeling* about what I did all my life?"

He wasn't asking to hear an answer, and so I gave him none.

"I mean, what do you do if you reach seventy?" he said, honestly bewildered. "How do you figure out if it was worth it? How do you know what's the point?"

I remained silent.

"Sometimes, Marcel, I experience this overwhelming sadness for what might have been. Sometimes I have an almost crippling nostalgia for things I never knew. Sometimes I want to kill myself because I never had a family, I never gave you bottles, I never went walking together with you and Kitty in a park. I never had the courage for that kind of responsibility. I was such a coward . . ."

I shook my head, afraid if I talked I'd start blubbering. Kids chattered and shouted, leaping in and out of the water; cannonball sprays geysered toward the ceiling. A red-and-blue rubber ball bounced over the heads of a dozen children. The lifeguard blew her whistle and issued warnings not to run, not to dunk, not to jump in at the shallow end.

Bart suddenly grinned. "Holy mackerel!" he exclaimed ruefully. "In another minute I'll be flagellating myself with birch whips and crawling on my hands and knees to some goddam religious sanctuary somewhere. Let's get out of here, I'm supposed to be producing a frigging movie!"

In the Mercedes he was animated again and excited about the upcoming stunts. Turning in at the Sundance Trailer Court, he explained, "We gotta pick up Lorraine."

"I thought she couldn't stand watching you do gags."

"Oh, that's just her style. She complains a lot."

Parking behind her battered convertible, Bart bapped shave-and-a-haircut on the horn. A moment later, Lorraine appeared in her doorway. Her scraggly hair was in curlers; she wore a navy-blue T-shirt, dungarees, and sneakers, and had a guitar on a strap slung over one shoulder.

"Bart, didn't you ever learn to call for a lady by knocking on her door? Land sakes alive boy, where were you brought up, in a fucking barn?"

"Can the chatter and move it!" he said. "We're on location at the bridge."

"Big deal. What's on the menu today—suicide? Murder? Rattlesnake bites? Head-on collisions? Should I bring my knitting to mark the heads as they tumble?"

Bart said, "I'm begging you . . ."

"Your sincerity is overwhelming."

"Lorraine—!"

"Oh shoot . . . wait a minute." She popped back into her trailer and emerged seconds later minus the guitar, her curlers mostly hidden by a powder-blue bandana, a lit cigarette dangling toughly from her lips, a large purse slung over one arm, and wild round white-bordered Lolita sunglasses hiding her eyes.

Bart cupped his hands, making a sound like trumpets blaring a fanfare; Lorraine stuck out her tongue and gestured obscenely by slamming her fist into the crook of her arm. Before I could react, she had slipped into the back seat. "Drive on, Jeeves," she said scornfully. "My time is valuable."

We headed north, leaving behind the chaotic boomtown atmosphere. At an orange blinking caution light, Bart swung left, heading west toward the small airport and the bridge over the Rio Grande. On either side of us a serene, undisturbed mesa of uniformly high sagebrush plants intermittently broken by stubby juniper trees stretched away. The blue and cloudless sky seemed inordinately surreal.

Bart exclaimed, "Sometimes this landscape gives me the same feeling I had when I lost my virginity! Her name was Angela. I wish I could touch my lips to this land the way I touched my lips to the velveteen hollow of her throat!"

Lorraine said, "Stop the car, I'm gonna ralph!"

"Wait a minute," Bart protested. "People back east spend

millions of hard-earned dollars every year just for the privilege of glimpsing a landscape of this caliber!"

Caustically, Lorraine said, "Sheepshit, lizards, plague-carrying prairie dogs, and rattlesnakes. What a bargain!"

She was smiling behind those glasses. A moment later she reached forward and lovingly snapped Bart's right earlobe with her middle finger. He said "Lay off, woman!" and grabbed for her hand, but she withdrew it quickly, laughing.

"Uh-huh," she teased. "Looky-looky, but don't touch."

In a highway turnout east of the bridge a group of film people were gathered. At least a dozen cars had assembled there, including two state police cruisers, their emergency lights flickering. There were several portable toilets on hand, also a mobile changing room. Fifty yards north of the parking area, in a bare spot on the mesa close to the edge of the gorge, a helicopter idled, its blades lazily scything the still summer air. On the walkway midway across the bridge, a group of technicians labored to set up a net to catch my father when he staggered from the escape vehicle and leaped over the waist-high guardrailing. On the western access to the bridge another cop car was parked on the shoulder, its flashers twirling. Closer by, arranged along the south side of the highway, were several pickups, a large flatbed truck, and two camera vans. Also along the southern shoulder several men were piecing together sections of track on which to run a dolly shot the second Bart skidded to a stop and headed for the railing.

Bart eased his Mercedes onto the shoulder. As we got out, people flocked around Bart like buzzards after a choice tidbit of carrion. There followed more of the same old hysteria: after a spat with Jerry Fazzina, Rick Bates (the actor who played the pusher, Tony Phelps) had locked himself in one of the portable changing rooms. The state police warned Bart not to try and roll his vehicle, and he assured them he only intended to pull off a controlled skid. Eddie Cobalt had six messages from the Coast, including an "equivocal" death threat by Millie's boyfriend, who did not want his girl to bare her chest in any grade-B thriller, no matter what she had signed beforehand. Betty Malenkov wondered if Bart thought vanilla custard was a viable substitute for cherry Jell-O. The head of The Friends of Chamisa Valley, a tall, horsy woman by the name of Abbey Wilson, and her five followers on hand insisted that the helicopter could not enter the gorge. The walkie-talkies necessary for coordinating the timing of the automobile stunt with the various cameras shooting the scenes didn't work. Bart grabbed a gopher named Morty and sent him back to town with the driver, Julian, for batteries.

All the special-effects crowd was located around the bright-blue Ford Bart would use for the stunt: Randy, Bill Sholokoff, Gil Brenner, Monte Gershwin.

Bart scrutinized the tires, then dropped to the ground. On his back, he wriggled underneath the car, inspecting something, asking questions, tugging on various reinforcement bars. After that, entering the car by the passenger-side door, he buckled himself into the seat, adjusted his body, fiddled with the seat belts to see how fast he could unstrap himself, tugged on a crash helmet and grimaced, muttering "I hate these things." Then he quickly checked out the steel reinforcing bars and plates that would keep the auto from crumpling when—or (officially) *if—* he turned over.

Jerry Fazzina said, "When you come to a stop, how long will it take you to get unstrapped, junk the helmet, and make it out the door?"

"It has to be almost instantaneous. As soon as the car stops, you start the dolly."

Jerry said, "But what if—"

"Listen, if I get laid up, we make a sandwich with a close-up anyway. But we should try for one continuous take. I roll over, stagger out, the cop car squeals to a stop at the mouth of the span. I fire a shot or two at them, they fire at me, I go over the railing—just like that, no break: bam, bam, bam. After we've done the scene, we'll do some close-ups, although maybe that'll be taken care of by one of the other cameras on the first take—how do I know?"

"What happens if Rick won't come out of the changing room for the close-ups?"

"Who does that pansy think he is, Greta Garbo?"

Michelle said, "It's ten-thirty already. This shot is scheduled for eleven. Will we be ready?"

"Who knows? Ask Johnny H."

"Holbein isn't here yet."

"What's the matter with him?"

"It's his asthma again. He had an attack last night."

"Well, while we're waiting let's drop a dummy into the gorge. Devon? Check with Randy, will you, and make sure the parachute pack is around so I can don it for the gag."

Lorraine by my side, I joined a group that followed Bart and the stunt boys onto the span. An enormous Harley 1200 motorcycle came roaring up the highway from the east; it skidded to a stop in the rest-area gravel. Resplendent in a do-rag and dark shades, naked to the waist except for a bunch of Nazi necklace paraphernalia, Cass Attaturk jumped off and joined us. Shannon Markson was camped on the rickety stoop of the mobile changing room, pleading with Rick Bates to open up so that he could be powdered for the close-ups. A stream of muffled but thoroughly vile invective issued from inside. A state cop toting a crackling walkie-talkie also joined our band, advising Bart and Jerry Fazzina and Mel that they only had until eleven-thirty before the police would have to clear the highway again. And Abbey Wilson, growing increasingly testy as it became evident her group was being ignored, threatened: "We'll throw ourselves on the highway! We'll lie down in front of your automobile! We'll block the camera on that little train track!"

"Try it," Bart said good-naturedly, "and we'll toss you and your people into the gorge."

Two men, attached by safe ropes to girders under the roadbed and to the guardrailing, were completing work on the net that would catch Bart when he jumped over the railing. Ten feet long and only six feet wide, the net looked hideously small to be the only thing standing between my father and the river eight hundred feet below.

Lorraine retreated into the middle of the road. She couldn't stand by the railing—it made her dizzy. As for myself, I left the crowd gathered around the net and leaned against the railing, feeling queasy as I confronted the gorge.

The river was a tiny, milky-green ribbon down there. Graceful scallops of white water fanned off boulders in the stream. Sheer cliff walls descended five hundred feet from our level, then were broken by enormous volcanic jumbles leading to the water. In places, the river was flanked by flat, grassy strips, seldom more than twenty yards wide, I guessed. On one of those narrow patches of grass, Bart hoped to land tomorrow when he did the parachute gag.

Appalled, I approached Lorraine.

"What do you think, Marcel?" Arms folded, she sucked nervously on a cigarette and, in between exhales, loudly cracked a wad of gum.

"I think he's crazy. I don't understand how they can let him do it."

"He's expendable. He's only the stunt man."

"He's also the producer."

"Associate producers will come out of the woodwork like worms after a rainstorm."

"But doesn't anybody realize—?"

"They all realize, but nobody's talking. Nobody's even thinking about it. But on another level, I'm guessing that everybody thinks this might help salvage the movie. It'll all be on film. And believe me, you can really pack in the public hand over fist with a real death shot. I bet you some publicist already has a campaign mapped out to coincide with the funeral."

"But all this fuss about using a dummy?"

"It's for show. To make sure everybody's covered. We've all known—the studio, the actors, the crew, all of us—we've known from day one that Bart was going over that railing with a parachute on his back. I heard Folsom and Universal even gave him an extra five grand under the table, cash, to make sure he disobeyed all the contracts, all the publicity, all the insurance adjusters, and hit this treacherous canyon in the flesh."

"I don't believe it. I don't see how Bart—"

"It's something real."

"But—"

"It's why I love him, I suppose. It's why I hate him, also. And now it's why we aren't together anymore."

"I don't mean to be thick, but after yesterday, watching you two together, I'm not sure I understand the rift."

"The only thing I had to bargain with for his life was myself. I thought maybe I could prohibit him from jumping into this gorge by threatening to leave him if he did. I played my cards, I calculated the risk, and I guess I'm about to lose."

"What if he jumps and survives?"

"Doesn't matter. If I stayed with him he'd never take me seriously again."

"And the kid?"

"The kid goes, that's part of the bargain."

"Jesus . . ."

"Nobody wins in a situation like this."

"Suppose at the last minute he decides not to jump?"

"Then maybe we're together, and maybe we'll have the child. Maybe he'll hold it against me, and we'll stay split up. Personally, I think it's hopeless. I can't change that now. I shouldn't even be here today. I should be on a fucking bus for Nashville. I should start *some*time in my life to take care of business . . ."

"I don't see how there could be any alternative for Bart. I know he loves you. He's desperate for that child."

"Love," she said disgustedly. "Oh sure, he loves me. But you don't know Bart, Marcel." She was watching him. They had brought a life-size dummy to the center of the bridge, and were preparing to fling it over the railing. Mel had a portable videotape camera with which to film the descent. Crew members, hangers-on, state police—everybody had lined along the span's northern sidewalk, eagerly awaiting the drop.

Lorraine said, "C'mon. We might as well watch."

At the railing, we wedged ourselves between Veronica, Connie Alexander, and Lily Enright. Lily said, "I wouldn't jump into this lousy crevasse for all the money in Switzerland." On that note, Bart said, "Let 'er rip." Cass Attaturk, Bill Sholokoff, and Gil Brenner gave the sand-filled construction a heave, Bart yanked a ripcord as the dummy went over, and somebody yelled "Bombs away!" Then it became silent on the bridge. All we could hear was the wind sighing through girders underneath our feet and the hum of the videotape Porta-Pak.

The dummy had fallen halfway to the river before the gaudy yellow-and-white parachute unfurled. As it fluffed full of air, the body jerked, spun around crazily, then straightened. Immediately, some sort of wind shear caught it. As if it were zipping down an airless tunnel, the rig skidded toward a rock wall. It stopped just short of disaster with a rough jerk and rocked back and forth. Then the parachute collapsed on one side, indented as if struck by a huge fist. What happened next, I couldn't really follow. Just as it appeared the parachute would fall straight toward the river, it was carried into the cliff. The dummy slammed against rocks; the half-deflated parachute was ripped open, and the body bounced down a steep incline, ricocheting off boulders—spraying sand—for about fifty feet before the chute hit another kind of thermal, inflated, and swung out from the gorge walls attached to a considerably lighter burden. A moment later, what remained of the rig landed in the river, and was immediately gobbled by frothing white water, a violence difficult to imagine from our height. It seemed as if the bright yellow chute and its cargo were ingested by the milky-green water as casually as a goat might chomp up a dandelion.

Bart opened his mouth before anyone else. Laughing, he signaled for Cliff to helicopter a clean-up crew down there. For everybody else's benefit, he said, "No sweat—it's a piece of cake. Now come on, let's shoot this fucking car scene."

Lorraine looked ashen. "A piece of cake!" she said. "Did I hear correctly? The man is a bigger imbecile than even *I* believed!"

They cleared the bridge. John Holbein, who'd just arrived, and Bill Sholokoff, who was ramrodding the stunt, had megaphones and were shouting numerous instructions. Walkie-talkies crackled. Bart and Randy and Monte Gershwin made a few chalk marks on the asphalt; Bart lined up the chalk spots with pillars on the bridge, markers indicating where he must brake, spin, wind up, and bail out. Technicians clustered around the various camera units, making sure everything was ready. Then Bart strapped himself into the blue Ford, tugged on a crash helmet, and blew a kiss in our direction. Lorraine stared at him, quietly shaking her head. All cars were removed from the far side of the bridge and from the approach shoulders. A few local and tourist vehicles traveling the highway were halted by police roadblocks. Bart gunned the car east along the highway for about seventy-five yards, U-turned, and made a dry run for the bridge. Almost onto the span he hit the brakes, flipped his wheel, I suppose, and, with a furious screeching, skidded the car sideways for some twenty yards, smoke hissing off the rubber streak left by his tires. Almost as soon as the car had stopped, aimed back east again, he was out the passenger-side door minus his helmet. The police car to be used in the film screeched to a stop at the entrance to the span, and two actors dressed as cops jumped out with their guns drawn as one camera dollied up the track, and a van, with another camera mounted atop it, swerved to a halt just behind the cruiser. Bart pointed at the cops, shouted "Pow! Pow!" ran to the railing, and jumped over.

Lorraine shrieked. I cried out *"No!"* I think almost everyone on the location gasped. He had not said he would go over in the test run.

Shuddering, bitterly angry, Lorraine turned away, saying

"I can't watch any more of this bullshit. To hell with him. He probably even thinks he's funny."

Using a rope ladder hooked onto the guardrailing, my father reappeared, his face as animated as the Fourth of July, giving the V-for-Victory sign. Never had I seen him looking more exhilarated. He was flushed with the kind of triumph I would never understand, his life somehow enlarged by a moment of pure action, of scathing—nevermind if ridiculous— emotion. By having the guts to jump over that railing with only a flimsy piece of webbed material between himself and a gruesome death, he had risen above us all. I imagine his heart sang as he teetered on the edge of his own existence. Yet I would never know if the rush came from flushing his tubes with a terror of blowing the stunt and losing his life, or from teasing us with the athletic flim-flam involved. I've always believed that the so-called danger some people face, placing the rest of us mere mortals in their debt and in awe of their audacity, is actually—usually—much safer than entering the corner bucket-of-blood for a beer.

The technicians gathered, compared notes, made adjustments. Bill Sholokoff erased some chalk scribblings and added others. Somebody let air out of the dolly cart's dune-buggy tires. Others unraveled long tape measures and noted the distances between their apparatuses and the car.

Lorraine wandered off the highway into the sagebrush; I followed her. On a slight knoll about a hundred yards from the scene, we found several lichen-covered rocks and sat down, enough removed so that the movie chaos was only a muffled puttering on the still, bright air.

I asked her, "Why would he choose to do a stunt over the child? Last night he said the only thing he truly wanted in life was to be father of the kid you're carrying."

"Pride. Stubbornness. A fear that if he gives up this one thing that has made him special he'll just blow away in the next stiff breeze."

"But if only . . ."

"I'll tell you a story," Lorraine said quietly. The helicopter rose out of the gorge, settling to earth not far from us. Everybody cleared off the bridge, camera units and trucks backed up, technicians made last minute run-throughs.

"It's about how I got these little scars on my face," Lorraine said. "It was homecoming, my senior year in high school. I was the queen, and naturally I had a date with the king, a guy named Bruce Merklebach, a guard on the football team. I did my flaming-baton routine at halftime—I was a majorette, back then . . . very pert, very peppy . . . and we won the game. Then at the dance we reigned, Bruce and I, and were very beautiful —all that crap. When it ended we took off driving and drinking, and naturally the old moment of truth arrived along about two A.M., when, having wrestled what he could of my nonexistent tits out of my strapless, Bruce commenced growling about going all the way. Which I wanted no part of."

She paused, flicking ashes off her cigarette, reflectively observing as preparations for the careening-car shot wound down.

"Naturally, he mooned and crooned, whined and cajoled, pleaded and begged. Then he became threatening and insulting, but I held my ground. So finally he told me to drop dead and laid down rubber, dumping me in the middle of nowhere. Not a big deal, you understand. In fact, par for the course—my course, anyway: I had the toughest twat to penetrate in Cavendish County. So I dried my tears, stuffed my pathetic little chest back into the lovely white gown he had ruined, and started hoofing it, searching for a telephone."

Bill Sholokoff shouted "Go!" and Bart popped the clutch, lurching into a fast speed almost instantaneously. And although I know at least a hundred onlookers were gathered at various points along the highway, in recollecting the event I remember only that speeding blue Ford. Fact is, I felt as if I were the only witness to my father's dramatic flight toward that narrow bridge. I heard faint gunshots—they sounded like caps. Just as it reached the bridge, the blue Ford shuddered, its front end nosed down sharply, and with a screech of wheels that emitted smoke as the vehicle lurched sideways, Bart went into a short skid and then tipped over. The Ford did one and a half rolls, landing upside down and grinding along for perhaps twenty feet on the barely crumpled hood.

I don't recall shouting. Instead, I remember the look on Lorraine's face as she observed the somersault. Eyes narrowed, lips pressed together tightly, she neither flinched nor gasped, nor gave any other indication of her feelings at that moment. Hard-ass and bitter—I don't believe I had seen such a toughened and controlled visage.

Cameras moved up as the police car screeched to a halt. Bart crawled out the passenger side door lugging the briefcase full of loot and a gun. He staggered a few steps, apparently confused, and then was brought to his senses by the movie cops firing blanks. Jerked around, he aimed at them and fired a couple of shots. Then, in a crouch, he dashed to the railing, unleashed a final volley, and vaulted over. I heard Jerry Fazzina shout: "Cut! Beautiful! *Shit!*" Bill Sholokoff made an excited motion like a dramatic baseball umpire calling a third strike as he shrieked: "Dynamite!"

Very tightly, Lorraine said, "The first house I came to— just a little three-room frame shack on stilts like they build near the bottomlands—had a light burning. There weren't any dogs barking, so I gathered up my skirts and trotted toward the front porch. I reckon I was still maybe forty-five yards shy of my objective, though, when the old geezer who lived in the place loosed off just once with some .20-guage birdshot, and six or seven pellets hit me in the face; another dozen peppered my front. But the funny thing is, even taking into account the surprise factor, that blast didn't knock me down. I mean, I stopped all right, dumbfounded, you can be sure. But I didn't fall down. I guess I was too drunk. And also nearly out of range."

Bart had scrambled back onto the bridge in no time flat, exultant, of course. In fact, everyone was dancing. He'd pulled it off perfectly. Crew members fell into each other's arms, doing the congratulations up in spades. Then a great bustle began to entice Rick Bates onto the bridge, so that they could shoot some close-ups while the car was still upside down.

Lorraine said, "Instead, I screamed. I was so furious it didn't even dawn on me I'd been hit. I screamed, *'Who you shooting at, you asshole?—I need to borrow a phone!'* And this terrified old Beelzebub's voice leaped out of the porch darkness, shouting back at me: 'One step closer, whoever you are, and I'll stick this other barrel up your nose!' But I didn't care, I wasn't afraid, nothing. I said, 'Fire away, mister, because I got to use your fucking telephone, and you and your stinking little popgun cain't stop me!' And I walked right into it, expecting him to blow my head off in the next second, but it didn't matter. I was so goddam mad and feeling so fierce I didn't care. And I felt exhilarated, too. And that son of a bitch didn't have the guts to fire again. So I walked up to him, covered with blood, and stomped right past him without a word and into the shack, and you know what?"

"What?"

"That pathetic shitheel didn't even *have* a telephone!"

I said, "And . . . ?"

"And that's the way he is, too—Bart. It's one of the things we got in common."

6 I went through the rest of that afternoon in a daze. Simply spectating the logistics of coordinating the bridge scene had left me exhausted. With weary awe I observed my father's every move, as he and Jerry Fazzina, John Holbein, and several other functionaries manipulated that ungainly crowd of film people, hangers-on, ecology protestors, ersatz advisors, egomaniacs, cops, and sundry characters through the tortuous exercise of getting some usable film in the can. The entire production seemed like a wild reincarnation of the myth of Sisyphus. Fantastic amounts of energy were needed just to blunder several feet forward. And, despite the nearly crazed hullabaloo of the operation, the overall impression was of an event locked in near rigor mortis. A single progressive step required a downright overwhelming amount of frenetic activity swaddled in the mind-boggling boredom of endlessly waiting around.

At the heart of it, Bart shouted, cajoled, laughed, taunted, teased, raged. He knew all parts, all idiosyncracies, all personalities of his scatterbrained machine. He tinkered delicately with some people and bullied others unmercifully. Occasionally, he oozed politesse. At least once he threw a conniption and wound up foaming like a rabid dog. One minute he threatened to bugger Rick Bates personally if the actor wouldn't shelve his ego trip and perform. In the next breath, he was incredibly obsequious while trying to flatter Jerry Fazzina into a camera angle he thought might be better than the one Jerry wished to shoot. He badgered Julian in French, and conversed in a foreign technical lingo with the special-effects crowd. He renegotiated the loan of a Cessna when the plane's owner had last-minute apprehensions about allowing its use for the airport gun-battle scene. No detail escaped his scrutiny. He double-checked bullet-hole squibs taped under a false fuselage panel to make sure they would go off exactly as Jerry wanted. And he insisted on double and triple checks on actors' clothing to be sure it corresponded with outfits worn in other segments.

I was flabbergasted by the amount of human energy consumed in order to produce what would ultimately be perhaps a money-making, but also an inordinately trivial, work.

At one point I said to Lorraine, "I don't see how everybody can take this so seriously."

"These people are earning a living, Marcel. And some of them, including your father, are actually having fun."

It was true, I suppose. Despite the relentless trauma involved, my father, the cameramen, the grips, the actors—everybody did seem absorbed in the work. They loved their lighting and their special effects, their machines and their props. They got off on how it all looked—the illusion—and anxiously wondered if the audience would believe the bullet holes and the blood. They were fascinated by the timing involved in the film. And they dug the rhythmic power involved in prodding a small army of talented and emotional cripples toward a finished product.

But nobody cared much for the picture itself, the story line, the message; not one of them would have wasted a breath dealing with the question of whether the end result would be art. The underlying aesthetic presumption was that their movie would perhaps clean up at the drive-ins and be long forgotten tomorrow.

" 'Art—?' " Bart snorted, during a brief lull after I'd made a snide comment. "I just blow-dried my hair, ate two Big Macs and a Coke for dinner, picked up my teeny-bopping bitch covered with Tattoozies, and drove my glass-packed Camaro to the local drive-in collecting great head to the acid blasts of Humble Pie, and you're asking me to ball my stoned chick with 'art' up there on the silver screen—? Holy fuckin' toldedo!"

Around five o'clock, while they were still on location at the airport, Lorraine said, "Marcel, I've had it. Let's borrow a car and make tracks." So we located the Mercedes and left without bothering to interrupt a battle royale taking place between Bart, Jerry Fazzina, Rick Bates, and Cass Attaturk over the proper way for Bates to crouch and hold and fire his gun. The last words I heard as I revved up the car were Cass Attaturk's—he hollered: "Who the hell told you you were some kind of cowboy? You looked like a fuckin' faggot Roy Rogers in that last shot!" Rick Bates yelled back at him: "What the fuck do you know about guns, Mr. Know-It-All?" *"I've killed people with guns!"* Cass literally screamed. *"I'll kill you too, you fuckin' pansy, if you don't do this right!* I GOT A REPUTATION TO UPHOLD!"

"He's got a reputation to uphold," I said.

"They all have reputations to uphold," Lorraine muttered grimly. "The entire United States of America is gonna lynch Cass Attaturk if Rick Bates doesn't hold his gun in the proper manner for killing a man. Shit. It makes me want to bawl."

I heard somebody cry shrilly from the heart of the argument: "Well, if you're not gonna be authentic, *what's the point?"*

Abruptly, the deserted highway welcomed us aboard: we drifted through mellifluous silence, flanked by peaceful sage, under a cobalt sky. Lorraine slumped and began making weird faces, stretching her eyes open, grimacing her mouth as if to howl. She contorted her lips every whichway, scrunched up her nose, and assumed a dozen mobile grotesque expressions.

I asked, "What are you doing?"

"I'm stretching my skin. The wind, the sunshine make my face feel so tight."

"I thought you were in agony."

"I am. You don't know how sad I am."

"We could go to a bar, someplace low-key, and I'll buy you a drink."

"Nope, take me home. I gotta shower, I wanna shave. I feel clammy, hot, dusty, obscene. I don't know why I watch that crap, I really don't. It's like I'm a junkie; I've got this incredible sadomasochistic streak inside. I don't understand it at all. All I do is sit there, boiling inside, until I hate him. All day I wanted to bury an ax in his skull. I can't stand it, I can't stand *any* of it!"

She broke off, facing away from me, gazing out the window.

I said, "You're upset."

She sniffled. "Bright deduction. What'd you go to, the Sherlock Holmes Academy for Junior Crime Busters?"

"Hey . . ."

"Oh, let's drop it." She scrabbled in the glove compartment, looking for Kleenex, found an old greasy A & W napkin, and blew her nose.

"All those egos!" she wailed bitterly. "They actually think they're important human beings! They actually think there's a legitimate reason for that horsecrap they're perpetrating! They actually get uptight over what camera angle to use, or over whether they're being upstaged or not. Jeez! As if it matters! Do me a favor, stop the car, would you, I'm gonna be sick . . ."

I braked and pulled over. Lorraine opened her door, leaned out, and vomited. Awkwardly, I touched her back, saying "I'm sorry." In between heaves, she whimpered, "Don't be sorry. God hates an apologist. And anyway, I deserve everything I get, and then some. In my whole life I never got anything I didn't ask for."

"I'm still sorry. It's no fun . . ."

"Hey, Marcel!" She straightened up, ghastly pale, her face tear-streaked, her lips bloodless. "You're a nice guy, okay? I bet you're a gentle and compassionate human being. But you're way out of your league around here, you know that? Your white suit won't wash with these people."

"I thought Bart wanted me . . ."

"I did too. I thought maybe you could help stop him. Now I give up. I don't think anyone can head him. I don't care anymore, either: screw him. I got my own life to live. He's just another beautiful son of a bitch, and a month from now it won't matter one way or the other."

"Do you really believe that?"

"Yeah, that's why I start crying every hour on the hour." Lorraine lit up yet another cigarette.

I said, "You'll kill yourself with so much smoking."

"Do me a favor, go judge Nazis at Nuremberg, eh?"

"All right, I'm sorry."

"Quit fucking apologizing! I can't stand it. One thing about your daddy I admire the hell out of, is he never grovels. It'll be a long time before I meet anybody that arrogant again."

"His arrogance will get him killed tomorrow, won't it?"

"You saw the gorge. You saw the dummy fall."

"But it's special, isn't it? The fact that he's going to do that. Even in a clunker of a film like this one."

"Special? Don't you mean indulgent? And stupid? It's like being shot to death in a bar by a stranger in an argument over who gets first pick on the jukebox."

"You're pretty harsh."

"I feel harsh. I'm twenty-seven years old, and it took me a real long time to commit myself to a man. You may not know this, but it's a nasty jungle out there for a girl like me: the good pickins are hard to come by. Granted I may not look like Ava Gardner, but I'm fucking choosy. Know why? Because I know something about myself; I know I'm worth it. I know I'm not just another cunt in a screwing pool, I'm somebody special. I deserve the best, and I got a right to ask for the best. So I spent a long time playing it cool before your old man wandered along, and when he did—"

Her whole face lit up with a tough, humorous glow.

"And when he did—?"

"Well, for starters, the man had class . . . he was exciting . . . and dangerous. I dunno—he's funny. He's innocent, he's cynical, he's a baby, he nearly ripped me apart the first time we made love. He scared the shit out of me, and I have never scared easy. I thought he wanted to murder me. And then suddenly he was the most tender man I'd ever met. All this strange, warped love gushed out . . ."

She hesitated as I pulled into the Sundance Trailer Court, halting behind her jalopy; I switched off the engine.

"He has so much energy," she said fondly. "But you never know from one minute to the next what his weather will be." She grinned. "I think he's the only shitheel I ever met who never bored me."

Lorraine stubbed her cigarette out in the ashtray. Then she pursed her lips, her attention held by two kids arguing over a stickball game. Eventually, with bitter finality, she said: "Well, there's a lot of fish in the ocean."

Opening her door, she got out. "Come on in, Marcel. I got beer in the fridge. You can even use the shower after me, if you want."

The dilapidated trailer was furnished with a cot, a ratty armchair, a bunch of orange crates and cardboard boxes, and a purple wall-to-wall Styrofoam rug. Her prize possession was an enormous color TV console.

"Be it ever so humble—" she joked, disappearing in back, leaving me to my own devices. I found a six-pack of beer in her refrigerator and pried out a can. While Lorraine showered, I lazed in her lone armchair, sipping on the beer with my eyes closed, letting the tension engendered by the day's film activities drain. Repeatedly, I pictured Bart rolling that car on the bridge. I saw it from a great height, as if I were in a helicopter hovering over the scene. Each time I replayed the gag in my mind it was executed exactly as I had seen it happen that morning. Only it took place in absolute silence, and in a remote way erased all sense of violence and danger: a toy car skidding and flipping on an erector-set bridge, harmless and cute, funny and entertaining, a clever trickster's gambit. I almost drifted asleep, remembering that stunt; Lorraine's voice startled me when she reappeared.

"It's all yours if you want, Marcel. There's even a little hot water left."

Seated cross-legged in front of me, she wore a faded pink terry-cloth robe. Her hair was wet and slicked down; she held a beer in one hand. She looked funny and nearly demure, like somebody's 1950ish-style teenage sister. Even the beer struck a dissonant note: Lorraine seemed very young and from a culture a millennium and a million miles removed from the coke-tooting machinations of my old man's Hollywood menagerie.

I said, "How did you guys ever get together?"

"Who—me and Bart?"

"No, you and Errol Flynn."

She smiled. "Oh, I was singing in a place, in L.A. You know, just another dive. And he sauntered in one night dressed like some kind of vomit-riddled Hell's Angel: shit-kickers, dungarees, a blue-jean jacket sawed off at the shoulders. That bit. He was drunk as a skunk, just riding his motorcycle around the city, I learned later, and he chose my dive by accident."

"I can't imagine him being anything other than absurdly obnoxious, under those conditions."

"No, strangely, he wasn't that bad. I mean, for one thing he listened, you know? He actually *liked* my music. A lot of guys, if they dig a song, they fuss and holler and raise a big macho stink, but not Bart. Instead, after every number, he staggered up to where I was sitting, and crammed a five-dollar bill into a beer stein I had on the amplifier for tips. About the fifth time he tucked one of those bills into my glass, I said 'Hold on, mister, just what do you think you're doing?' "

"And in his smooth, debonair, impeccably aristocratic manner, my father replied 'You wanna fuck?' "

"Actually, he said, 'Lady, you just tend to the singing, and I'll handle the economics.' And he added, 'Soon as you're finished crooning, ma'am, I want us to go out and scout up a justice of the peace, because I love you and I want to get hitched.' "

"Just like that?"

"Yup. So I knew right away I was dealing with a real lulu."

"How come you weren't completely turned off, right from the start?"

"Well, maybe you don't understand something about your old man, Marcel. He's got a funny powerful way about him. Granted, he was plastered; he also looked unhappy as hell, and he seemed like a terribly affecting, touching little boy. I guess you could say he came on strong as a terribly vulnerable, poetically wounded person. Like, you know, he wouldn't be able to make it through another week if I didn't personally shore him up, saving his ass in a million considerate little ways every day, starting from that moment forward. Because somehow, despite all his obnoxious hype, wealth, and gross power-tripping, he was damn near incapable of surviving in the *real* world."

"Now you know better."

"No, now I know there isn't anybody, not even me—and I'm special, believe me, and Bart knows it. He knows he lucked into Eldorado in dungarees and sneakers when he tripped over me—but not even I can help him. The man won't let anybody creep close enough to save his life. Even though he spends half his awake hours begging folks to snatch him back from the brink of the chasm before he topples over."

I said, "But anyway, back then. That first night."

"Oh, I suppose he must of given me a hundred bucks in five-dollar bills. And he stayed until the end of my last set. By then, he was the only person left in the joint. I finished my so-long song; he had his head buried in his arms, passing out. I killed the amps, put away my guitar, sat down at his little table, and touched his shoulder, waking him up. I ordered amaretto from Pat the bartender and grilled Bart a bit: Who was he? Why all the money? In that vein."

"And it was love at first sight."

"Hah! The man was a basket case. In fact, he was so babbling drunk he could barely string three sentences together and call it a conversation. Ultimately, I hoisted him up, led him outside to his bike, and bid him a fond adieu. He straddled his big old sickle and kicked it over, and I reckon that would have been that."

"Except—?"

"Except, shit—he was so polluted, and so exhausted, and so demoralized he could no more have driven that huge motorcycle than he could have sprouted wings and flown home. I was walking away when he popped the clutch, lurched forward, crunched into a nearby car, and tipped over, the bike landing on top of him like a dead elephant."

I burst out laughing. Lorraine giggled herself, remembering.

"He cried out 'Help,' in this tiny little voice, like he didn't expect anybody to hear him, or, if they did—so what? But I went over and said, 'Mister, you are an unholy mess, you really are.' And you know what he replied to that?"

" 'Marry me. I love you.' "

"Two points, Marcel. Well, I told him I wouldn't marry a mess like him, but I knew how to drive a hog. And, in the interests of humanity, if he wanted, I'd be glad to pilot his machine home with him on the back of it. Granted, it took a while, but eventually he wriggled out from under the Harley, and that's what I did; I drove that monster off to his mansion with him on the seat behind me, clinging for dear life."

"Where did you learn to drive one of those things?"

"I had a brother was a motorcycle nut until he went bananas over the stock cars that eventually killed him."

"So you drove him home, he invited you in to look at his etchings, and—"

"Huh-uh, not this vestal virgin. I may look like a pushover, but believe you me, sugar, I'm the hardest fucking lay this side of the Vatican. Real early in my drab life I figured out that fast cocks are a dime a dozen, and a cheap snuggle is a bad investment. Nobody ever sucked me into the immortal 'quickie,' leastways not after the first couple of times."

She spit tobacco flakes off her tongue and wagged her head vehemently.

"But I would imagine that Bart—"

"Oh sure. Naturally he tried. Though he was incredibly awkward about it. I suppose because I wasn't the usual fare he was accustomed to lugging back to the manse. He invited me in, of course. And naturally, I was curious. I mean, I'd figured I was gonna wind up in some east L.A. hovel and here I was in Brentwood amongst the palm trees, the swimming pools, and the private guards. So naturally I followed him inside. I actually went for a three A.M. skinny-dip in the pool. And I was even thinking 'Wow,' like, you know? I mean, here this drunk schmuck lays a hundred bucks on me, two weeks wages in a single night, and next thing I know I'm floating around in Jacuzzi heaven and all I'm smelling is the jacaranda and the bougainvillea, or whatever it was they had growing in that posh neighborhood. And I'll admit, I'm talking about a girl who was pretty damn *hungry*. I mean, my life wasn't easy . . ."

"So you stayed the night."

"Yeah, I stayed. But on my terms, not his. And that really freaked him out."

"Your terms being—?"

"Well, he grabbed for me in the pool, and I told him to bug off. Then he tackled me on the patio, and I told him in no uncertain terms that I was nobody's casual piece of ass. And if he didn't like it he could lump it. In spades."

"Pop must have loved that."

"I don't know what he thought about it. Mostly I stunned him. Because he just backed off, fell down, and passed out. And come morning he was the politest damn tomcat I ever met in my life. He drove me home to my Watts hovel. And, while I'm getting out of the car he says, 'If you want, you can come and live with me.' I said I was too old to be impressed by fucking Jacuzzis in fucking kidney-shaped swimming pools. And he whined back at me, you know what he said?"

"I could guess . . ."

"He said, 'You don't understand, lady. I'm just a victim of circumstances. But I'm actually a real human being.' "

"That'd be Bart. Did he look up sorrowful-eyed, like a plaintive puppy, and scuff the earth shyly like a country hayseed pregnant with timid sincerity?"

"Más o menos. I countered by saying everybody was a real human being, what made him think he was so special—money? Then I did an arrogant, stupid thing—I handed over all the cash he'd stuffed in my beer stein the night before."

"Oh-oh . . ."

"He ripped it up into little pieces and scattered the confetti on the ground by his Mercedes."

"Wow."

"Yeah, I thought so, too. That was our first big fight, right then and there. I called him every name in the book. I went berserk. I laid into him about all the poor people on my block, and how much that bread would have meant to any of them. I called him a sick, capitalist, warmongering pig, and said I hoped he choked to death on all his money, or had a fatal accident on his fucking motorcycle."

"And . . ."

"And right in the middle of my tirade he nodded at me and grinned, tipped an imaginary hat, and quietly drove away."

"How, then, did you ever manage to get together again?"

"Well, first things first. I collected all the pieces of those five-dollar bills and laboriously taped them together. Then I went back to work."

"And he came in again?"

"Every night for three weeks. Only now he arrived stone-cold sober and dressed real decent. He sat way in the back, and maybe once a night, after a song he had liked, he would unobtrusively sneak up front and drop a quarter or a fifty-cent piece into my beer stein, bow real formally, and shuffle all hunched over and obsequious back to his table. And he was always gone by the time I finished my last set. He never hung around for a drink, or for a brief conversation."

"I don't believe he could hold himself in check for that long."

"Listen, Bart can do *anything* he has to do in order to get whatever it is he wants, if he wants it badly enough."

"I still can't guess how you guys finally merged."

"I took the initiative. I went to his house."

"Without an invitation?"

"Yup—cold turkey. I just traipsed on over there—I took a taxi to his mansion on a Saturday morning and rang the bell. Two women in slinky silken bathrobes were sitting at his glass coffee table, beside the chlorinated kidney, eating grapefruits when I materialized in my sneakers, dungarees, workshirt. They made me look about as glamorous as a goat turd. They also had tits like Mt. Olympus spilling out of those frosty lamé gowns, and faces cribbed from a Vogue magazine. I thought, 'Lorraine, what in tarnation are you doing here; you are so far out of your league it isn't even funny; these people are going to take you to school, and when it's over you won't even feel as high as whaleshit.' But you know what that cocksucker did? He introduced me to the bims like I was the Queen of Sheba, and then he told them that him and me had things to discuss. And they got the hint. They were professionals at Getting the Hint. Two seconds later they had evaporated into thin air, and we were alone. And I actually felt sorry for *them*. And he said, 'Lorraine, what took you so long?' "

"And you replied . . ."

"I said, 'Listen, Daddy Warbucks, I'm not gonna be anybody's Eliza Doolittle!' "

"You actually said that?"

"Yeah. And you know what he did? He picked up one of those half-eaten grapefruits, and bashed *himself* in the face with it! And that's when . . ."

She paused, eyes downcast, making patterns in the ashtray with her cigarette.

"And that's when—?"

"Fuck it, Marcel. It's all water over the dam."

I said, "How did you decide to have a kid?"

"Decide? Who you trying to kid? Nobody *decided.* It just happened. The usual accident. I wouldn't of decided to have a kid with Bart any more than I would have decided to go for a ride on the back of his motorcycle of my own free will!"

"But it seems important to both of you. So why give it up so easily?"

"Listen," she said slowly. "Listen very carefully, Marcel, because I want to make sure you don't leave here with the wrong impression about me. Or about what you might or might not think I have done, good or bad, to your father. You listening carefully?"

Dutifully, I nodded.

"All right. For starters, I believe children are too important to be taken lightly. I don't know how or why I developed that attitude, but it's something I've known almost instinctively ever since I was a pig-tailed brat growing up in a family of snot-nosed hooligans. Up until I met Bart, I think I'd had three or four abortions, because I always knew I was with the wrong guy, or with no guy at all. Or I didn't want to get married. And I sure didn't want to have a kid alone, either. I don't think bearing children is a solitary endeavor; I think it's something belongs to at least two people. And when I finally have a kid I want him or her to be brought up by a mother and a father; I want it to be part of a family—got that?"

She stared at me, holding it for a few seconds, boring fiercely into my eyes in a no-nonsense way, willing me to understand exactly the nature of her belief.

"And I'm not bearing my child as the widow, or as the outcast mistress, of Bart Darling," she said emphatically. "I'm nobody's martyr."

She added: "And I'm not going to bear a child for a man who's lost his respect for me, either. Which is what would happen if he makes that jump and survives, and I go rubbing up against him like some brown-nosing little kitten with my purr machine working overtime."

I said, "Is it possible you're going too far?"

"It's the only terms he would understand. It's the only way I could live with myself. Believe it or not, Marcel, sooner or later, if I work hard enough, I can do it right. I can have a child —and a relationship—on my terms, I really can. And I can do it because I believe in myself. That's no joke. And I'm not gonna take secondhand crap," she said angrily. "I'm not gonna settle for less than the best. I refuse to lower my standards for anyone."

"I imagine that makes for a pretty tough life."

"It's okay. I never expected less."

"In the meantime, you sing in that dumb bar and nobody listens."

"No sweat. I'm perfecting my art. So what if they don't listen? I sing every song as if that's the first time I ever sang it. Because I'm a professional. And just because everybody else is sloppy is no reason for me to be sloppy. Believe me, I'm never going to fall into the bag of lowering my sights, and my criteria. Let somebody else sidle up to second best, that's not my shtick— Hey, you know what?"

"What?"

"I'm beginning to sound like a fucking evangelist. Which means it's time for you to take a powder."

"So soon?"

"I'm tired of being with you, Marcel. I'm also sick of hearing my own voice. It's been nice, but let's not push it—fair enough? We both have other chores to do. My philosophy is to always quit while I'm ahead."

"All right, I'm off. Thank you."

"Don't thank me," she joked lazily, "just throw money . . ."

I walked out the door, into the curiously misty trailer park, where I paused for a second. The evening was still, literally imbued with inactivity for a moment. It seemed captured in a magic fist, held more precious than it had ever been clasped before. Lorraine's trick, I suppose: the gift of a very special lady.

Then I got into the car, and went in search of my father. I found him at the Big House, surrounded by the usual retinue, and fuming. Seldom had I seen him so enraged. Shortly after Lorraine and I left the airport, Rick Bates and Cass Attaturk had started a heated argument. The altercation ended when Bates called Attaturk a "flaming faggot," and Attaturk slugged him.

"And broke his fucking jaw!" Bart wailed at me when I tried to unobtrusively sneak through the kitchen, where he was in conference with John Holbein, Jerry Fazzina, Bill Sholokoff, and assorted others. They were knocking down some pretty rough stuff. At least two dozen bottles cluttered the table—half hard liquor, half tonics and sodas—with another dozen beer cans and bottles thrown in for good measure. Background music for the confab came from the piano room where Frank Wilson's heart was hooked up to his triple-amp system: the house trembled from the eerie thudding of his primitive cardiac tom-tom.

"It's about time *some*body broke it," Lily Enright said. "Not only can't that prima donna act his way out of an egg-salad sandwich, but he's a very arrogant human being."

"He's my main man!" Bart threw his arms around like berserk helicopter rotor blades. "I got three quarters of a picture in the can with him the principal fucking *thespian,* and I need the son of a bitch to wrap up the picture! There's not five scenes left in which I can shoot around him."

Jerry said, "Bart, we'll find somebody looks like him. We'll fake it until the jaw subsides a little—who's gonna notice? We can even leave holes and matte him in later. I mean, nobody would miss the son of a bitch."

Bart actually tore at his hair. "But he *speaks.* He has a nude love scene. Who can duplicate that shlong? He's supposed to seduce Marcia, remember? It's supposed to be sexy. How's he gonna look sexy-looking with his mouth like Quasimodo? How's *she* gonna look sexy, speaking of problems, all puffed up like the Pillsbury dough dolly from a rattlesnake bite?"

"Write a different ending," Eddie said. "He parachutes into the gorge and kills himself. The audience will clap."

Veronica said, "That's like writing a movie about Abraham Lincoln, where he never gets elected as president."

Bart scooped a handful of peanuts out of a nut bowl and flung them at her. "What does Rick Bates have to do with Abraham Lincoln? Oh Jesus," he moaned, "that's what I like about you people. A bunch of atavistic Einsteins!"

John Holbein raised one eyebrow. "Atavistic? What do you mean, 'atavistic'?"

"It's a *word,* John. Get it? It doesn't have to *mean* anything, it doesn't have to be *in context.* It's just a word, it's a noise, it's a sound, it's emotional, it conveys a state of *emotion,* y'know? Jeez!"

Jerry Fazzina said, "Makeup will have him looking like new. Nobody will know the difference."

"In close-ups?" Bart couldn't believe what he was hearing. "He's got jaws and cheeks the size of cantaloupes! He can't open his mouth because it's wired shut."

"Write in a fight," Bill Sholokoff suggested. "No problem. The audience will eat it up."

"I already got enough fights in this idiot picture to sink a battleship. And anyway, half the scenes left to shoot don't occur chronologically at the end of the picture. It wouldn't work."

"Still, he parachutes into the gorge, he hits some rocks, he barely comes out of it alive, he winds up with a face looks like pulverized catfish. That'd work."

"He can't even talk, dumbbell. He can't even open his mouth."

Brad Oughton wandered in, smoking a pipe, looking altogether too nonchalant.

He said, "Don't worry about a thing. I'm a genius with a

cutter. I can edit him out of the entire film, if you want. Nobody will notice the difference."

Bart said, "Ha ha. I'm rolling on the floor."

"I earn a living."

Lily said, "Wait a minute, Brad. You don't just earn a living; you're a genius!"

"Sure," my father said, really ugly, now. "That's how come he's working on this picture."

Brad said, "Fuck you, Bart," and walked out.

"Go ahead," Connie groused. "Alienate everybody. See if you can make it impossible to finish this turkey."

"They don't care how you dump on them, Connie, as long as they get their daily dope ration."

Lily said, "You don't have to be this unpleasant, Bart. It's not in the script."

"What am I suppose to do?" he complained. "I got a crew right out of a cuckoo's nest! I hire a gaggle of uninhibited go-go dancers who're supposed to throw their big tits around like Polacks in a watermelon patch, and suddenly they're talking lawsuits if so much as the imprint of a nipple against a T-shirt makes the final cut! I hire a retard to watch the snakes, he drops acid, sics them on one of my leading ladies, frees 'em all before their big scene, and winds up in the hoosegow! So I order more snakes and they arrived on this afternoon's bus. Only that lame-brain Julian, who's supposed to pick them up, forgets to for three hours, and they all suffocate to death! If I was making a Fellini movie I'd be in like Flint, but I'm not making a Fellini movie! Still, for two billion dollars a day, this is supposed to at least be a crew of professionals! Instead it's like the Ted Mack Hour versus the Special Olympics around here!"

Pouting, John Holbein said, "Speak for yourself, Bart. You're getting solid gold to run this show."

My father asked nastily, "What's that supposed to mean?"

Flustered, Holbein tried to wave him off. "C'mon, Bart, why all the hysterics? This is a picture. These things happen."

151

Bart threw in the towel. Wearily, he changed his tone of voice, murmuring barely audibly, "Well, I guess times have changed. It used to be people cared about the craft of making movies. Even B movies . . ."

Lily Enright said, "Aw, can the onions and garlic, Bart. What do you think you are, on a picture like this, an artist?"

She spat out that word, artist, incredulously. As if the mere notion were absurd.

"At least we could do it well," Bart said quietly, and, I thought, also dangerously. "At least it could be artistic garbage."

Unaccountably, my father seemed deeply wounded.

"Integrity at this late date?" Lily exclaimed in a huff.

Jerry Fazzina said, "Get off it, Bart. Garbage is garbage. Bill's right: it's no problem, forget Bates, we can fake it; nobody will notice the difference."

"*They* will," Bart said doggedly. "What do you take the audience for, total morons?"

A half dozen voices chorused, "Yup."

Bart faced each of them down, his fiery gaze flitting quickly from one to the other. They all dropped their eyes, embarrassed by the non sequitur created by these farfetched aesthetic considerations. Remembering his declaration on art earlier, I wondered what kind of a game he was playing.

"You can fake anything," Veronica said defiantly. "That's what movies are all about."

Bart said, "You people are full of shit." He wasn't joking, either. I had never heard him address anyone in that tone of voice. He really meant it, and he didn't care how much he offended them or how many of them he offended. So what if they realized the profound scorn he held for their talents?

After a long, steaming silence, he said, "Even garbage should have some redeeming molecule."

Nobody commented. They were all embarrassed. They had never seen him drunk in quite this way before.

Shannon Markson entered the kitchen, bubbling over with

the latest good news. "Craig Heller's in town; he flew into the capital this afternoon and drove up. He's staying at the La Fonda."

"Big deal—Craig Heller, Craig Schmeller. Am I supposed to know him?" Bart poured another drink.

"He's Millie's boyfriend. He says he's six-three, weighs two hundred and seven pounds, and has a black belt in karate."

Befuddled, Bart snapped, "Who's Millie?"

"The one who gets torn to shreds by the Dobermans."

John Holbein grunted, "Art, no less."

Bart said, "Eddie, call the cops."

"They're all busy," his lawyer said. "They are preoccupied with Teddy and Cass and investigating rumors that we were shooting up Lily's dog, and trying to figure out how to bust this entire crew for possession."

Bart said, "Come on, Eddie. No shit-can chamber of commerce in any shit-can little town like this is going to sic its pigs on a movie crew. Do you know how much bread we are sinking into this pathetic little pastoral ghetto?"

"Art," John Holbein grunted again.

Bubba Wilson and Charley burst into the kitchen. "Hey, everybody," Bubba cried, as distraught as anyone I'd seen during my brief Chamisaville stay. "Does anybody know artificial respiration? My brother just electrocuted himself!"

Bart threw up his hands: *"Why me, God?"*

A general hysteria followed, sort of the Battle of Shiloh as choreographed by the Marx Brothers. Inadvertently, Frank Wilson had spilled half a bottle of beer on the floor at his feet, and he wasn't wearing sneakers. The jolt had knocked him down, and out. When the kitchen herd arrived he looked blue, his eyes were only half open, and all you could see were the whites because they had rolled around into his head. My father dove onto him as if to kill him. Bart yanked the body out straight, slapped his face, tore open his shirt, listened to his chest. Straddling the unconscious man's waist, he pressed down hard with his palms against the sternum. And then suddenly

whacked him several times, so hard I thought for sure he meant
to murder the idiot for plunging them all into yet another inane
predicament. Leaning over, he then performed a savage grunting mouth-to-mouth. In between breaths, he gasped, "Did anybody . . . call a fucking . . . ambulance?" Veronica was sobbing.
Lily Enright muttered caustically: "It serves him right, the
idiot. A cardiac bass, for crissakes! He couldn't even graduate
from kindergarten!" John Holbein kept muttering, "What next?
What next on this cursed picture?" Jerry Fazzina said, "I don't
give a damn who croaks as long as they aren't one of my actors.
I'm going to Acapulco after this is over and I'm never returning
to the United States." Connie Alexander said, "Acapulco's a
mess; even the air costs a dollar a minute to breathe. *I'm*
heading for Mazatlán." Bill Sholokoff said, "Mazatlán? You're
nuts. There's a drug war going on there. They murder tourists
for breakfast." "That's in *Culiacán,* idiot," Mel said. "Mazatlán is still all right." Eddie Cobalt said, "Bullshit. Mazatlán is
wall-to-wall tourists. The place to go, if you don't mind being
a little primitive, is San Blas. Americans haven't destroyed it
yet." Bubba said, "Holy shit, you *did* it, Bart. *He's breathing
again!*"

Mesmerized by these follies, I could only look on stupidly
as two emergency medical technicians burst into the room and
took over. In half a minute Frank was gone, the ambulance
siren wailing away into the distance. A crowd of everyone from
my father to Julian and Kitty and Brad Oughton and Doris the
bookkeeper milled around, performing postmortems. It goes
without saying that Bart had redeemed himself from his kitchen
debacle: suddenly, a whole new deference to him characterized
their manner. An actual real-life drama had occurred, and my
father had proved his point. Obviously, some of them resented
him for it, but they couldn't attack him now. In the background, telephones continued ringing, and various emissaries
kept entering and departing with messages from (and for) the
outside world:

"Folsom at Universal called again for the eighty-millionth

time. He's shitting alabaster cupcakes. He says if you don't phone him in the next fifteen minutes, Bart, and explain what the devil is going on here, he's gonna send Bruce Dobos to Chamisaville on a morning plane to personally tear your heart out."

"Folsom at Universal!" Bart gestured helplessly. "I'm down in the bleeding swamp trying to pull eggs out of pregnant alligators with my bare hands, and that smug cocksucker sits up there in his Naugahyde fuckatarium smoking genuine Habanas and trying to tell me how to run the show. I wish he would come himself to this barnyard and get a little horseshit on his sealskin Hush Puppies, I really wish he would!"

I asked Betty Malenkov, "Who's Bruce Dobos?"

She said, "He's . . . the Hit Man." She said it with such a spaced-out awe, as if everyone in the universe knew everything there was to know about the Hit Man, that I found myself unable to ask her for more information.

Next, Shannon Markson trundled in with the good news that, "Rick Bates just skipped the hospital. All he had on was one of those green gowns. A nurse there says he went crazy. He told them he was gonna find Cass Attaturk and beat him to death with a rubber chicken."

"He can't get Cass; Cass left town," Charley informed her.

"Whaddayou mean he left town?" Bart clawed through the air like a leopard after a gazelle, almost landing on Charley's neck. "I'm paying him two hundred dollars a day to make sure all the blood and gore in this picture is authentic! He can't leave town; he's under contract! Form a posse—Bill, Randy, Cliff! You guys, grab a truck, go find that pint-sized sadist and order him back to me!"

"What about Bates?"

"Who cares about Bates? I'm gonna write him out of the picture. Where's Bubba—Bubba? Where the heck is he? He was here a minute ago."

"He went to the hospital in the ambulance with Frank."

"Call the hospital! Jesus Christ! I need him tonight. That

self-indulgent creep is supposed to be revising the script so we can work around Bates's jaw. Call him, threaten, get him back here. I want him to siddown with Brad and me and Jerry and figure out the alternatives."

"Mr. and Mrs. Gadbois have checked into the Kachina Lodge," Connie Alexander informed him. "They're talking a regular battery of lawsuits."

Bart hee-hawed like a donkey. "Call them back, tell them I'll countersue. Tell them she was balling the snakekeeper against all the rules and all the regulations. Tell them she cost me one snakekeeper, all my snakes, and two hundred grand in delayed filming. Tell them she's also a cokehead and I'll turn her over to the fuzz if they so much as make a legal *peep* in my direction."

Betty Malenkov raced in breathlessly: "Has anybody seen Johnny H.'s inhaler? He needs it quick! He's upstairs having an asthma attack and he'll suffocate if we don't find it. He thinks he lost it in the confusion around Frank!"

Bart asked, "Where's Julian?"

Kitty Spencer said, "Veronica sent him to the Seven-Eleven for some Tampax."

"Call the Seven-Eleven. Send him to a drustore—is there a drugstore open in this town after six P.M.? Get hold of a druggist, shanghai one out of his bed if you have to, find another inhaler, I can't afford to lose my assistant director!"

"Bubba Wilson called back from the hospital. He says screw you, he's not rewriting anything tonight, he's not moving from that hospital until Frank is out of danger."

"What's the matter with everybody?" Bart laughed insanely. "People in this business used to be dedicated professionals!"

"Did anybody tell you that Gadbois's lawyer also hit town with the mater and pater? They're apparently talking a quarter of a million dollars."

"Talk is cheap."

"Word has it the constabulary isn't gonna let you make

that jump tomorrow. They're not even gonna let us drop a dummy off the bridge. They said after you rolled that car this afternoon—"

"How much do they want?" Bart asked. "Eddie? Where's Eddie? Michelle, do me a favor, be a sweetheart, go find Eddie —huh? Oh, hi, there you are. Listen, Eddie, fill a suitcase full of money, would you? Go talk to the fuzz. Clear this matter up. I'm gonna be at that bridge tomorrow morning at eleven, and the helicopter will be there, too, not to mention three cameras on top of the gorge and two at the bottom, and I sincerely don't want any pigheaded gendarmes strutting around telling me I can't dive into their gorge, okay?"

"The Friends of Chamisa Valley claim they'll have an injunction by ten."

"I'm not worried about them. Christers! Yuuuccch!"

Allison said, "Who's Craig Heller?"

"What's-her-name's boyfriend, the chick who gets murdered by the Dobermans."

"He keeps calling. He wants to talk with you."

"Gee, I'm so popular. I could get a complex. Tell him: Gosh, I'd really love to chat sometime, but I'm so darn *busy.*"

"He says if you won't talk to him, he's going to kill you."

"Enemies," Bart joked. "Every time I fart, an enemy lands at my feet."

"He says first he's going to smash your kidneys. Then he's going to tear your ears off with his bare hands. Then he's going to bust both your legs and dislocate both shoulders. Then he's going to break your neck."

"Tell him I'll throw him to the Dobermans."

"By the way, one of the Dobermans is sick. Jack thinks maybe Teddy poisoned them before he copped acid."

"Is there a vet in this town?"

"Yeah, we already checked. But he's on vacation this week. Shooting bobcats."

"Make him an offer he can't refuse."

Then Bart said, "Brad, enough of these petty irritants. I wanna look at Tuesday's rushes. Let's set 'em up and roll 'em, okay? I'm tired of talking shop."

Brad said, "They never got here."

"Uh, run that one by me again?"

"They came into the capital on the three-thirty plane from the Coast, and Freddy swears he got them onto the three-fifty bus, but they weren't on the bus when Julian went to pick them up at five."

"I don't believe you're telling me this, Brad."

"We've threatened the airlines, we've threatened Freddy, and we've threatened Trailways," Connie Alexander said. "They put out a tracer. A kid down there thinks maybe they'll be on the eleven-o'clock bus tonight."

"But if Freddy personally saw them onto the bus . . ."

"Unfortunately, Freddy says he didn't actually put them on himself. He says he trusted the guy in the capital to do it, because the operation had gone without a hitch so far."

"Call Freddy. Tell him he'll never work in Hollywood again."

"That's what Tommy Blaine says about you. He says Union Pacific will never underwrite another picture that you even get within pissing distance of."

"Tommy Blaine will fall all over himself to insure my pictures when he sees the kind of money we make with this clunker."

"Suppose it never gets finished? Folsom is talking about folding the whole shebang tomorrow."

"He can't fold it tomorrow. He's got two million plus sunk into it already. Folsom would no more fold a picture after that kind of investment than he would send chocolates to his mom on Mother's Day!"

"Lily, I don't like to carp, but your charming little poodle just bit Gil Brenner on the finger."

"Which finger?" Lily asked calmly.

"His trigger finger!" Randy said irately.

"At least it wasn't his social finger," Bart said.

"The mutt *mangled* his finger!" Randy blurted irritatedly.

"So tell him to sue me. Call my lawyer. Drop napalm on my head!"

It went like that for a while. And then things quieted down. People drifted off and never returned. It was late. The phones jangled intermittently for another half hour, then went silent. There was work to do tomorrow, lots of it, and, to keep up the frenetic pace, people had to get at least a semblance of rest. Veronica and Jerry started making out in the dining room; Bart stood in the kitchen doorway for a moment, observing them wearily. But as Jerry bent her over the table and hiked up her dress from behind, my father drew the line. "Hey you guys, not here; do me a favor, would you, and keep it private . . . ?" Muttering huffy apologies, they tottled off. Until all at once it was two o'clock in the morning, and Bart and I were alone in the brightly lit kitchen. The air still reverberated from the day's activities. Drunkenly, Bart pushed himself up, snapped out all the lights, and sat down again. Catching bright starlight and the reflections of a nearly full moon, the aluminum table gleamed icily like the surface of a frozen pond. Opening yet one more beer, Bart sucked on it lethargically, out of habit instead of out of need or enjoyment, just going through the motions.

Only then did I realize he had made no move to visit Lorraine—nor had he mentioned her name in the past handful of hours.

I was touched by his bulk, the sag of defeat in it, the set of approaching age in his slumped shoulders. I also thought of Lorraine, in town at the noisy, crowded bar, singing her songs and playing that beautiful guitar while nobody listened. My father seemed a woefully vulnerable and impotent man. I found myself wishing with all my heart that something could make it all right between him and his hillbilly girl friend.

"I guess she's probably done for the night," he said, his voice hoarse, devoid of the arrogance that had carried him through the long day and hectic evening.

"What time does the bar close?"

"Oh, they usually throw in the towel by one o'clock. Chamisaville is no Apple."

"We had a really nice talk this afternoon."

"Mazeltov." But he sounded disinterested. "What did you talk about—cloning? 'Little House on the Prairie?' Nixon?"

"She told me how you guys met. And then mostly about herself, her feelings, how she'd like things to be."

"She is a tough little bagel, Marcel." Bart was slurring his words, lisping a little. Same as last night, his voice echoed sheer exhaustion. It was painful to watch and listen to.

"She's also full of it," he added. "She don't know nothing about nothing. She thinks she's the Queen of the fucking Nile, but everything she knows I had to teach her."

"Don't make that jump tomorrow, Pop. It isn't worth it."

"Nothing is ever worth it. That's not the point. The truth is, you got to stop wanting it all to be worth it. 'Cause nothing, at heart, is worth a hill of beans. Honest. Still, you have to pretend that it is, otherwise . . ."

"Otherwise what?"

"Otherwise what's the *real* point of hitting sixty-one home runs? It's absurd. *Finnegans Wake?*—talk about gibberish-riddled chain jerkers! There's nothing, really, out there that means birdshit. Another baby in the world? Don't make me laugh, you'll split my colostomy bag. It's born or it isn't born—so what? That's just what this planet needs, is another mouth to feed. I mean, what makes us think we're so important in the first place? You know why we got trounced in Vietnam? 'Cause we had the incredible audacity and arrogance to believe we were more important than the Vietnamese. So they ran us right out of the ball park!"

He stopped, I said nothing. I figured, let him run down, and then he could sleep. And tomorrow—

And tomorrow the man might kill himself.

160

Morosely, Bart said, "I wish I could have it back again."

"What?"

"You know . . ."

"No, I don't know."

"Oh, that feeling I used to have . . ." He paused, listening to something in the night.

"What feeling, Pop?"

"I wish I could buy it—isn't that funny? If it cost all the bread I had, I wouldn't care; I'd be willing to buy it."

Again he stopped, waiting, listening to the sound of his own words, laboriously planning his next statement.

"I'd do anything, just not to have to run on the *lack* of feeling, you know? The lack of interest. And the lack of excitement. I'm sick of manufacturing feeling with this hysteria all around me that passes for creativity. Or film making. Or whatever the hell it's called. I just wish I could recapture that feeling . . ."

Since he didn't elaborate, I finally asked again: "What feeling exactly . . . ?"

"Exactly?" He thought that over for an eternity before saying: "All right, you asked for it—I'll tell you. It's that feeling I used to have as a little boy, lying awake at Dolphin Bays shortly before dawn on Christmas morning. Am I getting through? I bet you had it too, once upon a time, if Kitty ever let you. When all the stars are still out, and you're excited almost to the breaking point, anticipating the gifts downstairs. When you still believe in Santa Claus, and your appetites are so easily understood and assuaged. Assuaged? Well, you know what I mean. Jesus!" he exclaimed in an almost terrified whisper. "Wouldn't it be incredible to experience once again what it felt like to believe in Santa Claus?"

I said, "You really have something with Lorraine."

"Yeah . . . uh-huh . . . granted . . ."

"Then why wreck it by parachuting into the gorge? It's like

Veronica said: it'll be easy to fake it. That's what the movies are all about."

He focused on me with one eye open, the other oddly squinted. "All my life I have faked just about everything except that. As such, it may not seem like much to you, but it sure means a lot to me." He giggled. "My last tattered vestige of lowly pride . . ."

"She's serious. If you jump into that gorge, you lose her, you lose the baby. She really means it."

"I *know* she means it, idiot. *I'm* the one who shacked up with her for over two years, aren't I?"

"Then I have to admit I don't understand . . ."

Glib despite his fatigue, he said, "I reckon it's one of those inexplicable tragedies, Marcel. Call it Romeo and Juliet, call it what's-his-name . . . Perseus? No, Pyramus . . . Pyramus? Pyramid! Pyramid and Thisbe. See, if I don't jump, I got no reason any more to call myself a man. If she doesn't abort the kid and split when I jump, she's got no reason any more to call herself a woman. It's a crazy setup. Catch-22. We blew it."

"I think you're gonna jump because you're afraid. You're scared to death of taking a real, loving chance. You're terrified of the commitment."

"Heigh-ho. Heigh-ho."

"Pop, if you survive that jump you won't have any reason to survive."

"Well, that's just too damn bad, now, isn't it?" But then he softened. And eventually apologized. "I'm sorry, kid. I'm being stupid. I shouldn't talk like that. For some reason this is where my life got me to, and I don't know how to change it. I pull off miracles just rolling out of bed every morning. I'm too old to give up the only thing that allows me to respect myself." He looked sheepish saying it.

"But nobody really cares if you jump or drop a dummy. It's only you, not anybody else. Except Lorraine. And she cares a lot."

"Marcel, you're beating your head against a dead dog."

"But—"

He exploded, pounding the table with one fist so hard a tin ashtray jumped off and clattered across the linoleum floor. "Hold on a minute, God dammit, Marcel! Did it by any chance ever just even *once* occur to you that there's a whole bunch of complex reasons for why it won't work with Lorraine and me, having absolutely nothing whatsoever to do with this charade of tired psychological bullshit we've been hashing over half-assedly ever since your plane touched down? Did it even *remotely* occur to you that whether I jump into the gorge and bash my brains out or escape without a scratch, or she gets an abortion or decides to have a ten-pound, thirteen-ounce all-American bambino, that the thing is bitched, would be bitched, and always *has* been bitched despite the hearbreaking fact that we *love* each other? And nothing you are babbling and gabbling and getting self-righteous about is even halfway to first base of what's going down between her and me? Huh? *Huh?* Did you ever think of *that?* Now lay off, pisshead, I've had it up to *here!*"

Flustered, badly shaken, I said, "All right. I'm going to bed now. I'm tired."

Disarmingly, all his anger instantly dissipated, he grinned: "Bravo."

"What about you?"

"Me? I think I'll kind of hang out here in the darkness for a while. Catch this table, will you? It looks like a hockey rink. If I'm quiet enough, maybe some little gnomes wearing ice skates will appear and entertain me with their pirouettes."

"You should sleep, Pop . . ."

"Hey, *seriously,*" he said. "What are you gonna do, show up at the bridge tomorrow with a pair of warm pants and a bowl of chicken soup? There ain't no Jewish blood in you, Marcel, not a drop!"

"But at least sleep—"

"Ah, sleep. It unravels the knitted hearts of gargoyles."

"If you really jump tomorrow, though, and you're not alert . . ." I couldn't stop. I think I actually believed that if I stopped talking, if I quit endlessly repeating myself in an attempt somehow to save his life, he was—the second I lapsed into silence—a goner.

"A quick toot ten minutes en avant is all I'll need, kid. Now, go rest your weary bones. I'm sick of your Greek chorus. I feel like I'm in a Philip Roth novel."

"Are you just going to sit here all night?"

"Not all night. Just for a while. I like it when things calm down around this time. Feels good. Feels comfortable. I can almost relax."

"All right. Then I'm going . . ."

He interrupted my exit, however. "I wanna say something to you, Marcel."

I stopped, waiting. I think he meant to say one thing, to say something intimate, but at the last second he changed his mind.

He said, "I'm gonna tell you a profound joke about the meaning of life."

"I'm listening."

"Let's hope so. Okay. Here's the joke. There's this venerated old rabbi, see, over in one little Russian town or another —this happened long ago. What's a good little Russian town full of Jews, before all the pogroms? Like Chagall used to paint, with goats and clocks and sly-eyed fishes and burning flowers floating over the houses. And lots of fiddlers on all the ethnic rooftops?"

"I don't know, Pop. Does it matter?"

"Okay, not really, but, well . . . we'll call it . . . we'll call it . . . *Tolstoiville!* Sure, Tolstoiville. It's across the valley from Dostoevskiville, and about fifteen kilometers north of Turgenevburg. Sure. Bueno. So anyway, there's this venerated old rabbi in Tolstoiville, he's sick as a tick-bit hound on a hot summer day. In fact, he's ninety-seven years old and this looks like it—Eternity Junction. He's wasted away down to nothing:

he weighs maybe forty-eight pounds in his beanie by now, and all the young rebs and students and acolytes and what-have-you are gathered around his bed for the obligatory farewells. They're also looking for some final pearls of wisdom from the great man's mouth that will help them face life, and that they can transmit to the peasants of Tolstoiville, who are gathered outside the rabbi's house, waiting for his soul to depart its earthly prison. You with me so far?"

"A hundred percent."

"Thanks. I know I'm maybe a little hard to follow . . ."

"All your life you've been a little hard to follow."

He pointed his finger, winked mischievously, and shot me. "In fact, Marcel, all the young rabbis and divinity students and Yom Kippur candidates, the whole black-hatted, ringalet-sideburn crew—they caucus and decide to come right out and ask this wise old rabbi to tell them the meaning of life before he passes on. So this one young guy approaches the gasping old patriarch and says, 'Rabbi, Rabbi, please. Before you die . . . tell us the meaning of life.' "

Bart swayed, leaned forward, and his head began slowly to descend toward his folded arms.

I prompted: "The meaning of life."

He caught himself with a slight jerk. "Oh yeah. Right. They asked him that, and the old boy gasps and rattles and wheezes and gurgles like one of those machines in *Willy Wonka and the Chocolate Factory*—you ever see that movie? It was horrible, horrible. He bubbles and toils and troubles kind of like that, searching for an answer, and then finally, in a hoarse, weak voice made almost unintelligible by the death rattle in his throat, he says: 'Life is a river.' Okay?"

"Okay."

"Good. So then the young rabbis and the students and one or two assistant directors and the key grips, they all go outside to where the people, to where the entire population of Tolstoiville is waiting, and they make an announcement. They blow one of those horns, what're they called, those religious horns—the tofu?"

"The shofar."

"The *shofar!* That's it. Shit, how could I forget that? The shofar. Sho far, sho good. They blow one of them, you know, to get everybody's attention, and then they tell the assembled multitudes: 'We have spoken to the wise old rabbi; we have asked him to tell us the meaning of life before he dies, and he has told us. And the answer is—' "

Bart giggled and said, "May I have the envelope, please?"

"Pop—"

" '—and the answer is: *Life is a river.*' Well—"

He giggled some more, anticipating the punch line.

"Well, everybody in Tolstoiville, they look at each other. I mean, even the roosters and fishes and clocks floating around above the ethnic rooftops are puzzled. 'Life is a *river?*' '*Life* is a river?' 'What does he mean, *Life* is a *river?*' That's very ambiguous. It could mean this, it could mean that, it could mean nothing, it could mean something. But to a man jack they all agree—the rabbi's gonna have to elucidate a little on the pronouncement, otherwise it's not gonna be much good to anybody. Still with me, kid?"

"Yes sir."

"So the upshot is, the young rabbis, the students, the documentary film makers, the whole—what's that word? I always loved that word . . . the whole *mishpokhe!* They all go back inside, and gather around the dying rabbi's pallet, and beseech him. They say, 'Rabbi, Rabbi, please, tell us what you mean about life being a river. The peasants don't understand. *We* don't understand. It all seems very vague. Did you forget and leave anything out? Have mercy on us, Rabbi, and explain this enigmatic answer before the Lord calls you to his kingdom of clouds.' And you know what the dying rabbi replied?"

"No . . ."

" 'Nu, so maybe life isn't a river.' "

Bart sputtered, bursting into laughter. And all I could do, after I had ceased laughing with him, was stand there, astonished, waiting for him to run down. When he finally did, gasping and coughing, racked by hideous-sounding spasms, I said, "Pop, that's beautiful, and you're nuts, you really are."

He said, "Oh Jesus, I love that joke. God dammit. Hey, you know something? I'm glad you came, kid. I'm sorry it isn't gonna work out."

I actually heard myself say, "Don't apologize, Pop ..."

"One other thing."

"Yes?"

"Don't worry about me. I'm okay, really I am. You may not know it—how could you know it? But even though I whimper and complain a lot I am one tough old galoot. I truly am."

"I know that."

"All right. Now scat. Skedaddle. Beat it."

When I hesitated still, he added: "Take a fucking powder."

"Okay ..."

Then he said, "If I die, you can have her."

"That's not funny."

"Oh hell," he said forlornly: "I love you." He barely got it out, but I heard the words distinctly.

"I love you too, Bart."

"Bueno. Now please. Quit playing this scene. Because in one more minute it'll become maudlin, and then I'll really blow a gasket."

"Good night, then."

"Sleep with the fucking angels." He chuckled. "That's what Lorraine always says: 'Sleep with the fucking angels.' "

I retreated, moving so slowly I thought I'd never make it out of the kitchen. Then, locked in a strange and dreamy lethargy, I feared I'd never make it through the dining room. When I reached the music room, I heard his voice issue softly from the kitchen: "Ciao." The battered calico cat leaped noiselessly off the piano and followed me upstairs. It waited patiently while I sat on the edge of my bed, staring out the window, not thinking at all, but feeling a lot of things related to Bart: his genes in me, the life he would risk tomorrow, and the fact that he was going to lose Lorraine. Later, when I slipped under the sheets, the cat hopped onto the bed, nestling into the curve behind my knees.

I awoke in a spookily quiet house. My watch said almost three-thirty. A car near the kitchen door coughed and ambled away, leaving behind an even eerier silence. Lying in bed wide awake, I awaited an event. The summer night had grown slightly crisp; stars shone brilliantly.

When nothing happened, I got up and entered the hallway. The house was absolutely silent, vibrating from the lack of noise. I held my breath. A luster defined the darkness, as if the air had recently been polished by a fairy rain. My own fatigue added a tingling clarity to the mood. At the end of the hall, the door to my father's bedroom was ajar. Feeling a strong urge to look in on him, to make sure he was all right, I aimed in that direction.

He hadn't come up yet from the kitchen. I waited in the doorway a moment, picturing him downstairs, slumped at the aluminum table, probably snoring. Perhaps I should find a blanket or a jacket and drape it over his shoulders so that he wouldn't catch cold. But that might wake him. And sleep, I knew, had to be precious.

Several times, on my way across his room, I nearly tripped on the litter and fell flat on my face. On his balcony, seated at the old upright, I plinked out a song with one finger: surprisingly, the piano was in tune.

But I preferred the strange calm enveloping the house, and quit tinkering with the ivories. I relaxed in the bright summery gloom. Puffs of air riffled my hair. The scent of some evocative flower—apple blossoms? honeysuckle?—drifted by me on cool, sensuous currents. Suddenly the world seemed like such an innocent place. A sad, yet romantic complexity governed our lives, making even our most insignificant actions immortal. Shades of F. Scott Fitzgerald. I felt overpowered by a sentimental melancholy. No matter how twisted the venues of experience, life was incredibly beautiful. Dogs barked intermittently all around the valley. The night was so clear and quiet I heard mongrels yapping at the starry heavens from miles away. To the east and south Midnight Mountains formed an imposing, glistening bulk. And, high in the sky, I chanced upon the tiny blinking red light of an airliner heading west.

A soporific drug held the universe in its spell. I felt in love. Not with anything or anyone in particular, but with life in general. A mystical power to the moment nearly flattened me. I felt woozy. I sat very still, captured in a luxurious stupor, smiling and not moving a muscle because I didn't want the mood to dissipate. My body glowed as if on the verge of a subtle, yet destined to be infinitely extended, orgasm. Lord, it was sweet!

Abruptly, I realized my father had entered his room. He was moving around, stumbling against various obstacles, muttering under his breath, searching for something. *Please don't turn on a light,* I begged. I couldn't bear the thought of my calm being shattered by an electric brightness. Bart rooted clumsily about in the gloom. He nearly capsized, knocking an object loudly onto the floor when he flung out a hand, steadying himself. Laboriously, he fired up an incense stick. And scrabbled in a cardboard box unearthing a half-hour-size film can. His 8mm projector already pointed at the sheet-draped wall. Other objects clattered. Bart cursed intermittently while threading the film, yet his words held no heat. He sounded almost bemused. Next, he blundered around some more, fuddling clumsily through the darkness with a strange almost-coordination that never let him crash-land, although he constantly teetered on the brink. He clicked a tape cassette into a recording machine, and out came the fey piano music of Erik Satie. After starting the film projector, he settled onto the edge of his bed. Hunched over, peering forward, his chin resting in his hands, he was immediately held captive by the film.

And so was I. Lorraine appeared. It was a simple home movie, amateurly photographed and spliced together. They had taken it of each other. Snow was falling; Lorraine stood in the middle of a field, wearing a fuzzy coat, packing snowballs. She made three, took off her mittens, and juggled the snowballs, making clowning faces as she did so. Bart appeared. Lorraine must have slowed down the camera so that now, run at regular speed, his actions were old-fashioned and jerky, Chaplinesque. In seconds he did a whacky striptease until he was naked, and then rolled around in the snow, popeyed and exaggeratedly lathering himself with the white stuff; I could almost hear him shrieking. In the darkness, on the edge of his bed, Bart chuckled. In fact, he actually released a snorting guffaw.

Next, Lorraine put the finishing touches on an obscene snowman. She stuck an enormous red carrot in its crotch, and pointed at the carrot, making *Perils of Pauline*–style shocked faces. Soon she broke up in giggles. Then she knocked off the snowman's head with a haymaker and tied into the white body, hilariously destroying it in minutes.

Suddenly it was summertime. On horseback, they ascended into the high country. They reached a beautiful mountain lake. Puffing nonchalantly on a cigar, Bart landed a trout, pantomiming buffoonlike the motions of an expert fly fisherman. There was a close-up of fish bubbling deliciously in a frying pan held by Bart over a campfire. Morning came. Lorraine, in the nude and speeded up, dashed down a grassy slope into the lake, comically belly flopped into the icy drink, flailed away for two seconds, leaped up, and floundered hysterically out of the water, screaming in agony from the cold. A close-up of her—lips blue, teeth chattering, wrapped in a puffy goosedown jacket—followed.

Dozens of similar scenes came and went. They were lovely, touching, silly, sentimental, very funny, occasionally sad. Bart strutted down a mountain path after a hailstorm, doing a mummer's strut. Thousands of green aspen leaves littered the trail: they had been battered down by the summer storm. Lorraine came along the same trail trying to balance a frying pan on her head. Then she was indoors, playing her guitar, pensively smoking a cigarette. Bart gunned down a city street on his motorcycle, pulled over to the curb, killed the cycle, assumed an Arnold Schwarzenegger pose, and made a hokey muscle. Lorraine, in a bathing suit, stood at the end of a diving board, trying to summon enough courage to jump into a posh Los Angeles pool. A poodle tiptoed out on the board behind her. She shooed it back. And advanced to the end again, looking very nervous. She gave the finger to the camera, stuck out her tongue, turned her back, and pretended to blow a fart, slapping one buttock obscenely. Facing the camera again, she pleaded for Bart not to take her picture. And traipsed back to safety on the rear of the board. And then shouted angrily at the camera. At the end of the board once again, she closed her eyes defiantly, pinched her nose, and leaped awkwardly into the water.

And then there were some slow-motion scenes of my father doing his beautiful dives.

At the end of the film, Lorraine popped up wearing a McGovern T-shirt flaunting a peace dove, and sky-blue short-shorts. An eleven-year-old would have looked more mature. She stood in rich green grass, surrounded by the pristine white trunks and buttery trembling leaves of autumn aspen trees. Grinning on cue, she gave a clenched fist power salute, and a V-for-Victory sign. Turning, then, she walked away from the camera about fifteen or twenty feet, faced it again, executed a funny-cute "And away we go—" gesture, and launched into a dance closely resembling the one I had observed in the trailer park at the end of our journey back from the airport a couple of days ago. My father grunted, entranced by Lorraine's poignent hoofing. It didn't last for long. Her tiny figure on that sheet looked like a Jiminy Cricket: cute, heart-wrenching, and hopeful, too ... And then the movie was over: film leader slapped against the stool as the take-up spool spun around.

For fully five minutes, Bart made no move. But at last he prodded himself up, shut off the projector, and regained his bed.

Perched on the edge of it, same as before, in the identical posture, he stared at the darkened sheet. The Satie music continued—modulated, dreamy, thoughtful. I think Bart went to sleep in that position. Because ever so slowly he began tilting sideways, lowering onto his enormous bed, until eventually he was curled up in a foetal position on the very edge of his wide mattress. The Satie music ended shortly thereafter. My father was passed out at last. He began snoring.

I got up. Proceeding carefully, I crossed his room, leaving him there with his no doubt convoluted dreams. And when I lay down myself, I was almost instantly asleep. I felt as if I were drowning in the wonderful taffeta currents of some enchanted sea tide.

No matter what happened now, I knew something about my father that could give my heart ease. My childhood, my origins, my relationship with Bart formed in my grateful dreams like granted wishes. I felt almost as if we had been saved.

7

Come the dawn, reality always rears its battered head.

Lorraine's tattered automobile was parked in front of her run-down trailer when Bart swerved the Mercedes into the Sundance Trailer Court and braked in front of her grimy dwelling. He shut off the engine and then sat there, making no move to get out. He looked terrible this morning: hungover, sure, but worse than that. Life had deserted him, his body was devoid of energy. Truly defeated, without hope, when he spoke he could barely raise his voice above a whisper. Gone was that wild-man, wise-guy energy that had characterized all his early mornings so far. He was like a man who had lost the will to survive. I was shocked at the fragility projected by his body. His scar-tissue face seemed delicate beyond belief. The man appeared to be melting; his eyes had a more-than-vacant look. His big hands could barely grasp the steering wheel. A torpor had transformed him overnight. It was as if all his years of carousing, having finally added up just last night, had struck a mortal blow.

I said, "Well . . . ?"

"You go in, Marcel. You ask her to come out to the bridge. I haven't got the guts."

"Pop, it's your deal. Jesus. She's your woman . . ."

"If I go in there she'll tell me to fuck off. I know. You have to do it for me."

"I don't want to. It's not my business. It's not my place . . ."

Wearily, Bart said, "I can't get out of this car, I really can't. I'm sorry. Please"— and he was actually almost whining —"I've never asked you to do that much for me, Marcel. But right now I need your help. I don't want to do this stunt alone. I don't want ..."

His voice trailed off. He stared glassy-eyed out the windshield.

I said, "Well why do you have to do it at all? I don't believe how idiotic you are. It's ridiculous! What's the point of being so stubborn?"

"I'm damned if I do and damned if I don't. There are no winners in life, Marcel."

"Oh, cut the cornball bullshit."

"Well ... will you or won't you?"

"I won't. I don't believe the way you're acting."

"Fair enough." He waited a second, then weakly beeped the horn... waited ... and honked it again. Nothing happened.

"Maybe she's still asleep," he said. "Maybe I shouldn't wake her up ..."

I said, "Pop, you look awful. You've got no business—"

"Don't tell me what my business is," he interrupted softly. "I know what I'm doing."

"You look like a ghost. I've never seen you looking so ... so *flabby.* "

"Happens to the best of us, kid. Nobody gets out of life alive."

"Thank *you,* Paul Newman."

"Don't be disrespectful ..."

He tarried a while longer, hoping for a miracle, a peculiar asinine smile on his face as he continued gazing sightlessly through the dirty windshield. Then finally he leaned forward heavily, twisted the ignition key, and started backing up.

"Oh, hell, wait a minute." I gave up. "I'll go ask her."

"Well, hurry it up. We don't have that much time."

When I knocked on the flimsy door, Lorraine called out, "It ain't locked!" I entered her humble digs. She was sitting cross-legged on the floor before that big color TV console. It was tuned into a morning soap, although the sound was turned all the way down. She wore a man's white shirt, blue jeans, no shoes. Her guitar was tucked under one arm. A garish cut-glass ashtray occupied the floor in front of her; it was heaped with cigarette butts. The whole trailer smelled like stale smoke. A Tammy Wynette songbook lay open beside the ashtray. And Lorraine looked awful. Her eyes seemed smaller than usual, her lips even thinner, for lack of any mascara or lipstick. And there was that same hopeless vacant set to her eyes that I had seen in Bart: like we were all doomed, so what was the use of trying, anyhow? There was nothing she could do or say to affect or manipulate her own fate, or to change the inevitably bitched nature of things in general. Judging from the many stubs in that ashtray, and from the bruise-colored skin around her eyes, I doubt she had slept at all the previous night after her stint at the La Tortuga.

She said, "Don't you tell me I look awful, Marcel, or I'll kick your butt, I really will."

"I just came—" I started to say.

"He's out there, isn't he? Too scared to come on inside and speak for himself, isn't that right?"

I nodded. "He's out there. He's frightened. Lorraine—"

"Don't you 'Lorraine' me, Marcel. I don't want any part of it. You tell him I don't care anymore, I really don't. You tell him go ahead and kill himself, and good riddance to bad rubbish. You tell him that, go ahead. You tell him his head is so far up his rear end his goddam tonsils are clogging his nostrils, you tell him that for me, okay? I wouldn't want him not to get the point, know what I mean? Because that man is *thick* . . ."

About halfway through this tirade, large tears welled from her eyes and dribbled down her cheeks. At the end of it her throat was so dry and constricted her voice cracked, it almost squeaked.

I said, "He's sitting out there in the car like a condemned person. He can barely talk. He's afraid to jump, he's afraid not to jump, he's afraid of losing you; he can't see any way out of it. I've never seen him this emotionally hog-tied."

"You haven't hung around him very much, then," she said

bitterly. "Half the mornings I woke up beside that pathetic hedonist, I wondered if I oughtta give him artificial respiration or call for an undertaker. I'm through trying to argue him out of committing suicide. If that's what he wants to do, let him do it, and the sooner he gets it over with, the better. But I'm not gonna hang around idolizing his colorful self-destructive nature, not on your life, sugar!"

"Then I guess you're not up for a trip to the gorge?"

"What kind of a masochist do you take me for? I mean, hey. After these past two years I'm still supposed to truck on down to the cemetery and watch him bury himself? What does he want me to do, give him a big ole kiss before he jumps so there'll be a lipstick smear on his cheek if he happens to hit eternity? What kind of romantic bullshit is that? You people must think I'm a real fluffhead!"

Lamely, I said, "Well, he asked me to come in and talk to you."

"Fine. Now you've talked to me." She turned her head away because the tears kept flowing, she couldn't check them. "Maybe you could at least go out to the car . . ."

"Marcel!" she wailed, losing all composure, facing me with pain and fury in her already bloodshot and swollen eyes. "Will you please get off it? Will you please get the fuck out of here and leave me alone? And you tell Bart, from me, that only a gaddom . . . a goddam *eunuch* would let somebody else do his dirty work for him at a time like this! Now scram! I hope I never see either of you again! Did you hear me? *Make like a bee and buzz off!*"

"All right . . . I'm going . . ."

Back at the car, Bart said, "No deal, huh?"

"That's an understatement."

"She ain't worth shit," he said, starting the car. "She's just another two-bit cunt."

"Pop, if you don't shut up . . . If you don't button that fat mouth of yours . . ."

"What's the matter with people?" he grumbled lifelessly.

"Everybody's falling apart. Nobody has any *stamina* anymore."

In silence, we drove out to the gorge. The scene there was a tribute to the adage that "the show must go on." Apparently, the cops had been paid off; the environmentalists' injunction had been stayed; no black-belt karate expert leaped to dislocate Bart's shoulders. Cameras had already been set up and were ready to roll. All the battery packs were checked out, accounted for, in good running order. The man named Cliff was busy flying his helicopter in and out of the chasm. John Holbein's asthma was safely in check, Jerry Fazzina's hair was neatly combed, and all his cameras had been satisfactorily placed. Randy, Bill Sholokoff, Gil Brenner, and Monte Gershwin were poised to drop another dummy, so that Bart could analyze its fall, the treacherous currents, previewing his own plummet through space. Mel, Charley, Bubba Wilson, Veronica, even Julian and Kitty Spencer were milling around, waiting to be called for anything. Bart hadn't shaved, but as soon as we parked and he left the car, Kathy noticed and, ordering him to sit down in a chair by one of the portable changing rooms, she erased his splotchy five-o'clock shadow in seconds.

In fact, I don't know when I had seen the crew functioning so professionally, and with such a lack of niggling, dim-witted bumbling.

I puzzled over the scene, wondering why it was running so much more smoothly than anything else I had witnessed these past two days. And decided the change in attitude and vibes resulted from the fact that in this case no gimmicks were involved; no safety valves, no tricks, no make-believe. It was the Real Thing. And the entire crew was reacting to that. For a moment they were taking it seriously. Having no room for error, they were making no mistakes. Bart's willingness to risk himself had raised them above their own petty bickering for a moment.

Connie Alexander said, "If you want to watch, Marcel, there's a vantage point over there, on those rocks, that isn't in the way of any camera. You can see him from the moment he takes off to the moment he lands."

"I don't know if I want to watch."

"Suit yourself . . ."

I tarried near my father, reluctant to leave him, fearing that once I had walked away it would be my final good-bye, and I would never have another chance to say anything important to him again.

I had an urgent desire to say something, something with meaning—courageous, simple, relevant—both for him and for myself. Something that would stand up, if this were to be it—his death. But no words came to mind. Immediately, the whole frantic search inside my head felt banal. And the fact that he might die, that shortly he would deliberately risk his life in order to give careless, thrill-seeking audiences a cheap high, seemed very absurd, very unreal, very ridiculous. Beyond this dumb effort, the world was ultranormal, excruciatingly sensible. Ravens drifted through the sunny, unencumbered day. Nothing I could draw on would make the experience significant.

In the end, approaching him lamely, I shook my father's hand. "Well, Pop . . . good luck." When he tumbled to the expression on my face he replied, "Hey, don't fret kid, this is a piece of cake. Listen—" He punched his digital watch. "In an hour we'll share a bottle of bubbly at the La Tortuga in celebration . . ."

"Okay. I'll see you . . ."

We exchanged no hugs, no abrazos. I stepped back, but lingered a moment longer. Kathy brushed his hair, combing it differently. Ignoring her, Bart kept on chatting with Monte Gershwin and Bill Sholokoff. Veronica applied makeup so that his scar tissue wouldn't glisten. Then they huddled somewhat mysteriously, temporarily blocking Bart from view. I glimpsed enough to realize that he was probably tooting a couple of lines. When they broke the huddle, he sneezed. Kathy brought him a different shirt and pants, and, after tugging on basketball kneepads, Bart slipped into them quickly. Michelle appeared with the gun he had to be carrying, and Bart made a stupid gesture of committing suicide by touching the barrel to his temple and grimacing.

That did it. I crossed the bridge, walking to the outcropping of rock Connie Alexander had suggested. Others already there included Brad Oughton and Lily Enright, Eddie Cobalt and Doris the bookkeeper, and Betty Malenkov.

"I get the shivers just looking down there," Betty said.

Bart's lawyer agreed. "You ain't kidding. If I jumped over that railing, I'd black out in fear, I really would."

Doris said, "I don't know how Bart does it, I really don't. Not at his age. The man is peerless."

"He's an ice man," Lily said reverently. "He doesn't know the meaning of fear."

Incredibly, Doris added, "What's it like having a man like that for your father, Marcel?"

I shrugged, feeling queer, like an imposter. The aura surrounding this jump made me extremely uncomfortable. On the one hand, he could die. On the other hand, an event that deserved no credence was being elevated to an important position it in no way deserved. Somehow, all of us were being hoodwinked. It wasn't right to invest this gag with so much significance. I mean, given the context in which it would appear, given the reasons for doing it . . . The whole thing was a shallow gimmick . . . made grotesque by the realization that a man might die.

Irritated—and frightened—I mumbled, "I don't know."

They flung out the dummy. It fell quickly, the parachute unfurled. Nobody moved or uttered a word as we all followed the descent. No wind plied the gorge, and the dummy fell uneventfully, drifting but slightly. It landed almost perfectly on a narrow strip of green beside the river eight hundred feet below. Bystanders on the bridge cheered as tiny ants down there raced to gather in the dummy and the yellow parachute.

"Just like Bart said," Eddie Cobalt laughed nervously. "A piece of cake."

"Lord, I'll be glad when this is over." Lily Enright bammed her chest. "I don't think my constitution can take much more sensational crap. I'm gonna have a heart attack."

While the special-effects people went over Bart's parachute, and then strapped it onto his back, a local doctor and a male nurse entered the helicopter, which Cliff piloted into the gorge. When it had settled on a grassy level patch behind a main camera, he cut the engine and the rotars whirred to a stop. For the first time I noticed a county ambulance parked on the highway shoulder about a hundred yards east of the bridge. Walkie-talkies crackled, people up top communicating with technicians down below and with the camera north of the bridge on the lip of the gorge that would follow Bart's fall from that vantage point. Finally, all systems were go. Police officers stepped onto the highway at both bridge approaches, prepared to halt any traffic. Special-effects and makeup and camera people retreated from around Bart, leaving him alone near the railing. Jerry Fazzina positioned himself at one end of the bridge with a white flag on a long stick, waiting to wave it.

Betty Malenkov said, "Oh Jesus Christ, I can't look."

Tightly, Eddie Cobalt said, "This is it."

Connie Alexander murmured, "Oh Bart . . ."

And Lily Enright said, "God help him."

Jerry Fazzina shouted, "Are you ready?"

Bart laughed: "Ready when you are, C.B."

Jerry swung the flag out over the railing, so that all the crew members involved below as well as on ground level would see it and start their cameras. Bart had instructions to count to ten before leaping, so there was a pause at the start of the gag, a suspended moment during which I peered at him intently, angry and confused, bitterly scornful of what he was about to do.

My father seemed pathetically out of place in the center of that span, caught in the lazy bright sunlight of that bluebird day during perhaps his last minutes on earth. I was shocked to feel, at the core of my emotional turbulence, an icy disassociation from the outcome. It didn't matter, really, if he lived or died. Bart had never created anything worth saving— I could invest him with nothing more, no feelings of love. His defiance, his childish insistence on the deadly gag, seemed mundane, without importance. There was no foundation here for tragedy: he couldn't die. I knew that for a fact long before Bart went over the railing; I knew that the gag was duck soup. There was no risk, because in real life a parachute stunt was not where the real risk-taking lay. Bart had already decided against that, with Lorraine. And that is where the tragedy, or the sadness, or whatever you wanted to call it, lay. He had had a chance to put himself on the line, but had copped out. Because of fear, maybe. Or perhaps he simply lacked the tools, or the honest interest . . .

Jerry Fazzina shouted, *"Go!"*

Bart took a step. I raised my eyes. The sky was electric blue; several clouds were too white. A buzzard circled miles above the scene. I lowered my eyes. Doris gasped: "Oh dear God protect him." As he had the day before, Bart fired his pistol three times, hopped over the railing, and was airborne.

"Son of a bitch!" Eddie Cobalt exclaimed.

Connie Alexander whirled away, landing in my arms: "Oh please," she moaned, "don't hurt him."

I put one arm around her, convinced that they all actually wanted him to die. Then Bart would become legend, lending an importance to their lives because they had been present at his self-execution. It would enhance their careers, giving them extra credibility. The way they now talked of the feats and the deaths of famous stunt people like Orner Locklear and Frank Clarke and Richard Grace, they would talk about my father. With immaculate serenity, I watched him fall. The yellow chute unfurled immediately, fluffing full with a snap that arrested his descent almost before he had cleared the bridge. And he drifted down, swaying slightly, without incident. There was no wind, no treacherous current to swing him against sheer walls or the murdering boulders composing steep talus slopes. Instead, he fell straight as a plumb line, landing perfectly in the grassy strip beside the river, so close to the water that the yellow chute settled into a back eddy. And it was over. He had nailed the gag as easy as pie.

A dozen voices let out joyful whoops that seemed to lack oomph. Jerry Fazzina dipsy-doodled his white flag again for the cameras to cease rolling. Thirty people hightailed it to the bridge railing and looked down. The cops waved through a few cars that had halted during the stunt. An air of jubilant anticlimax took over.

"Is that *it?*" Connie asked fearfully.

"That's it."

"And he's all right?"

"I'll bet he isn't even scratched." Eddie laughed nervously, the way a man who is supposed to win in a walk laughs when an underdog takes his measure and he's being a good sport about it. "Oh do I love the brass balls on that son of a bitch!" His enthusiasm was lackluster.

"A piece of cake," Brad Oughton said sardonically. "What was everybody so worried about? A tiddlywinks match would have been more exciting. I wonder if I can even doctor it to make it look dramatic."

Bewilderedly, Betty Malenkov asked, "What now?"

"Well, who's got the storyboards? What's the next scene on the schedule?"

"It's supposed to be down there, with Rick. But he still looks horrible. Have you seen him yet? Cass must have belted him with a rock the size of Gibraltar!"

"Thank God Cass is gone. That minigorilla would kick his own mother in the crotch and pawn her Laetrile."

I retreated from them, feeling out of kilter in an almost menacing way. Anger bloomed in me, accompanied by a bitterness hard to fathom. I wanted a release, I wanted to slug somebody. It was almost as if I also had wished that Bart would perish in the gag. Somehow, he had cheated me too by succeeding so routinely. Cheated me . . . and Lorraine. And I suppose that was it. Out on the mesa away from the gorge, away from the crew, I realized that Lorraine was the emotional key. Put simply, a death *had* occurred during that stunt. His affair with her, and, now, their child. In short, relevant and profound connections—relationships, human beings—had been cavalierly discarded and snuffed out. And in exchange for what?

A fifteen-second parachute trip into the Rio Grande Gorge for a movie about dope pushers and homicides featuring rattlesnakes and Doberman pinschers.

I sat on a piece of volcanic stone. A pressure behind my eyes indicated tears wanting to come but unable to fall. Terribly tight, almost nauseous, I slowly kneaded my stomach. Nobody else was aware of what had been smashed; or, if they knew, nobody cared. The hit I got at that moment was bizarre, and right to the point. Bart among the strawberries, and Kitty already abandoned in that shabby motel room, at the moment of my careless conception so many years ago. Fist clenched, sweat drenching me, I couldn't even howl. The entire episode was too silly for words.

In a minute, the helicopter would rise from the gorge with my father aboard. But I had no desire to see him—not now, anyway. I wanted no part in the congratulations. Hurriedly, I crossed the mesa and the bridge, making it to the Mercedes without shaking too many hands, and drove off, heading back for town. My anger dissolved during that short journey. By the time I arrived at the Sundance Trailer Court, I was relieved that he had survived, and that relief was compromised by sensations of fatigue, loss, and intense remorse. That lives could be so seriously altered in such a matter-of-fact way left me breathless.

Hope springs eternal, of course. As I parked beside Lorraine's decrepit Chrysler, I dared to cross my fingers. Perhaps, faced with a cruel choice, she would change her mind. After all, nothing was irrevocable. Bart was alive and well, and what else mattered? Hadn't that been the point of her threats against him? Her only desire being his survival?

She was seated on the floor almost exactly as I had left her. Same pose, same guitar under one arm, same ashtray heaped full of cigarette butts, same TV tuned soundlessly to a similarly moronic program. But when I entered, her eyes were wild and alarmed, sharp with fear.

"He's okay," I said immediately. "He pulled it off without a hitch. There was no wind. He made it look easy."

Her eyes changed as abruptly as if she had taken a near-knockout punch. One second they had been fearful and expectant, the next moment they had become dull, almost disinterested.

"That's swell, Marcel. I'm glad."

"Lorraine . . ."

"I told you, don't do that," she warned. "I don't want to hear it."

"Okay, then. What now?"

"I've got a three-o'clock appointment in the capital."

"Oh."

"It's an abortion clinic. They're very nice people."

"You're still going through with it, then."

"What other choice do I have?"

"You could not do it. You could have the kid. You could talk with Bart."

"Talk. Hah."

"I don't understand why both of you are so pigheaded. You're acting like two-year-olds."

"He'd walk all over me, Marcel. You know that. I bet I'm one of the very few people that man never walked all over. And the only reason he never did is because I never gave him an opening. He could never find the door to my weakness. I was too strong. He never could figure out how to own me. But if he was to get away with this . . ."

"All right. I give up."

"Would you like to do me a very big favor, Marcel?"

"I don't think I can. I don't think I have the talent for doing the kind of favors you people want."

"I'd just as soon not drive down there alone."

"It's your bed," I said bitterly. "You made it, you lie in it."

"Bueno. Excuse me. I shouldn't have brought it up."

She smoked yet another cigarette. I glared dumbly at the television show, a soundless and mindless giveaway. Obviously, I hadn't the strength to deny her request. I didn't even have the guts to elicit rough payment for my generosity by making her feel really small before I gave in. I merely said, "Actually, for the umpteenth time, I apologize. If you want me to, of course I'll drive you down."

"Can we take the Mercedes? I don't even know if my car would make it."

"Sure. We'll take the Mercedes."

"Could we leave right away? He might stop in here on his way to lunch or something, and I don't want to see him. Not now, not anymore, not ever."

"I guess you're the boss . . ."

"First I'll take a shower."

While she showered, I sat in her lone easy chair wondering how she felt—what was running through her mind. I couldn't guess. Impossible to get a handle on her love for my father, on how it might have been between them. Or why it is that we are all programmed to be so fragile. Americans live longer than almost everybody else in the world, I thought, yet we have no staying power. No will to fight for these things; no real will to fight for what's important.

And like that: stupid analyses. Trying to fit this pathetic adventure into one category or another, miserably searching for plausible explanations. But I had gotten nowhere by the time she emerged from the back room, transformed as I hadn't yet seen her, wearing a simple white cotton blouse and a summery calico skirt, and no shoes. Her wet hair was plastered unimaginatively against her head. She looked tired and lonely, also summery and feminine and refreshing. A tough little waif, old-fashioned and clean, doomed and almost ethereal, and no-nonsense: a survivor.

"You mind if I bring my ax?"

"Of course not."

It was a muted journey. We didn't talk much. Lorraine had the guitar tucked under her arm, but she played no songs. Unhappily, she probed the landscape, the wide sagebrush plain, the far hills. Pretty soon the high gorge walls were zig-zagged by the shadows of a thousand twittering swallows. Awkward at first, the mood became pensive, not very threatening. Occasionally she faced me and smiled: I smiled back. "Don't be gloomy," she said once, "it's all right. It's not so bad. One thing I don't believe in, I don't believe that any good experience is just one of a kind and will never happen again. No loss is irrevocable. There are other people to love. This was no once-in-a-lifetime affair. When I'm ready for it, I'll have kids, and I'll have 'em on my terms, so don't worry about that, Marcel. I mean, don't worry about me."

"What about Bart?"

"He has magic. He's special, you know that. He'll survive . . ."

As we cleared the gorge fifteen hundred feet lower than Chamisaville, a muffling heat wave enveloped us. With the windows rolled down, the hot wind battering our hair, we cruised along at fifty-five, squinting against the glare. I soon began to sweat uncomfortably and asked Lorraine if she wanted to close the windows and start the air-conditioner. She said, "No way, Marcel. I like the natural air; I don't care if it's hot. I'm used to sweating. When I'm all shut up inside a car and the air-conditioner's on, I feel creepy and claustrophobic. I feel like I'm trapped in an icebox. Or in a coffin . . ."

She slipped back into her pensive mood, sightlessly scanning the landscape. The mountains looked dusty and inhospitable in the dull glare. Lorraine plucked a few aimless notes on the guitar, but did not speak again for a while.

Then, as we passed the entrance to the prairie-dog village, she said abruptly and nervously:

"*Men!* Jesus they can be pathetic human beings. You know what I did once? I took a course on how to be a masseuse. And the day I received my certificate I applied for what I thought was gonna be a straight job in a massage parlor. But the first night there the first six guys assigned to me asked for a 'local.' I told them to go organize a peter party in the parking lot. But when I finished work that night, the manager called me a self-righteous, uptight nun and handed me my walking papers. After that you know what happened? I wound up massaging two-hundred-pound old ladies with purple hair in a health spa!"

She laughed, but her laughter was thin: she seemed scared, and was talking fast, all at once, to keep her mind off the upcoming operation.

"Actually, when you come right down to it, Marcel, I don't know how I got through it all so unafraid of men. And unbitter, too. I don't understand why I don't hate the whole lot of you, I really don't. Did I ever tell you about my friend, Connie Martínez?"

"I don't think so."

"Actually, I didn't know her that well. I met her last year when we came to Chamisaville on R and R from the Coast for a couple of months. She was a secretary at the unemployment commission. Young—I think twenty-three, twenty-four—single, no kids. Her boyfriend, Roland García, he drove a butane truck. They were engaged, wedding to be last October, I believe."

She thought about the date for a moment, even though it couldn't have been very important.

"Yeah, it was slated for October. But anyway, one day Connie went to a local doctor to be fitted with a coil. No problem: she goes in, he performs the job, she walks out whistling. Only, after a while she started suffering a terrific pain in there, so she went back to the sawbones and had him remove the coil—but the pain wouldn't subside. Connie went back to the doctor; he said don't worry, nothing was wrong, the pain would subside. But it didn't. She went to another doctor, a man, too, and he said it was no cause for concern, she'd just had a bad reaction, that's all. But finally the fourth doctor she went to informed her she had an infection in both Fallopian tubes likely to make her sterile, a common enough occurrence when women who've never had children are fitted with a coil—a fact nobody bothered to tell Connie beforehand."

Lorraine raised her hand, making an obscene gesture at the mountains out there, although I suppose it was meant for the doctors, for all the men who'd ever oppressed women anywhere.

"Well, you can imagine. Connie slunk home lugging a sack full of pills and told Roland all about it, including the possible sterility part. Instead of sympathy, Roland smacked her all over the kitchen. They had a big blowout. The upshot was he hollered he could never marry a woman who might not be able to bear his sons! And with that he grabbed his engagement ring and fled. Indignantly, no less! Next afternoon Connie OD'd on the usual sopers, and two days later I attended her funeral."

She clicked on the radio, frowned, and immediately turned it off.

"You know why Bart actually liked to pull off at that dog town, Marcel? He loved to park out there, on our way to the capital or back, and make love. That's one thing about him I really liked: he was playful like that. You know? Most men—shit—they take their sex so damn seriously. But Bart was wonderful. I guess he was the only man I ever balled who could laugh right out loud while we were fucking."

" 'Was,' " I said sadly. "What's with all the 'was'es?"

"I'm building myself up, that's all. Don't take it personal."

"I won't, I understand. But—"

"No buts," she said fiercely. "Don't start that again."

She clammed up, keeping her face averted from mine. Turning off the highway ten minutes later, I slowed down, entering the outskirts of the capital. Lorraine played a single chord, and then, without striking another note, she sang one verse from a song with a haunting, forlorn melody:

Darling if
You want to leave,
I promise that
I will not grieve;
I understand
That autumn leaves
Always come tumbling down.

She cut it short, making a disgusted face and growling, "Shit, the whole world stinks. I wish I was dead."

After that, except for the times Lorraine gave curt directions, neither of us spoke as we maneuvered slowly through the small city's narrow streets to the abortion clinic.

It was a pleasant, two-story frame house on a residential street, shaded by tall locust and Chinese elm trees. Dandelions bloomed cheerfully on a small lawn; flowering lilacs brightened either side of the front porch. As we walked up the steps, Lorraine said, "Look at this, will you? Norman Rockwell would have an orgasm!"

Inside, the waiting room was more like a living room. Cool, clean, homey—it smelled friendly. The doctor's assistant who talked with us was more like a human being than a doctor's assistant. Her name was Claire, a warm and professional woman. She had already spoken over the telephone several times with Lorraine. Now, she briefly reiterated the process, and asked if either of us had any questions. We shook our heads, relinquishing all suspicions: Claire had the gift of projecting immediately that she was a trusted friend.

After Claire had synopsized the procedure, we had a little waiting time. Outside, we sat on the porch, myself on the steps,

Lorraine, her back to the wall of the building, seated on the wide railing, her head tilted back. She closed her eyes and seemed lost in thought. Two yellow swallowtail butterflies worked over the purple lilac cones. A magpie chortled high up in one tree. The day, the place, were inordinately peaceful.

Lorraine said, "Ask me what I'm thinking, Marcel."

"What are you thinking, Lorraine?"

"I'm thinking I'm crazy. I'm scared stiff. I'm a fool. This isn't what I want to do at all. I want to have a kid more than anything else I've ever wanted to have in my life."

"Then don't go through with it. You don't have to."

"But I don't want to not do it, either. That'd be suicide."

"Then I can't suggest anything."

"You don't have to suggest anything. You just have to listen, that's all. Though actually I want you to do one thing for me, and this is important."

"I'll try."

"If possible, I want you to convince Bart that I really loved him, and that I'll always love him. I don't mean to ask for any of that shitass stuff of being 'Good Friends' after all this—that's dumb. I don't expect him to harbor anything but a deep and bitter grudge. Fact is, anything less would be unhealthy. And an insult to the emotional logistics of a loving relationship. I know there'll always be a fire in one part of me that'll hate his guts for being so self-destructive he botched my love and killed the kid. But he's also beautiful, and I'd leap for the jugular of anybody who said he wasn't. He may come on like a horse's ass ninety percent of the time, but it's eighty percent bluff, don't ever forget. He drinks too much, takes idiotic risks, and immerses himself in irrelevant endeavors because deep down he's so soft and inept, a little puff of wind would knock him over . . ."

The tears were falling again, squeezing out through her closed lids. She sniffled.

"Oh shit, Marcel. This stinks."

"There's still time to—"

"Stop it," she moaned. "You're so, relentlessly, *predictable!* How come you can't be an *original* human being like your father?"

Immediately, she opened her eyes, looking both terrified and apologetic. "Hey, wait a sec, Marcel. I didn't mean to say that. Golly! What's the matter with me? I'm cracking up!"

"It's all right ..."

"The hell it is. Stop being so amenable. Nothing's all right. I'm acting like some kind of moron from Peyton Place. I should get the Denny Dimwit Fucked-up Female Award for being stupid. I don't know how I get myself into these predicaments, I really don't. I always think ... I always think ..."

It wouldn't come. Lips pressed together, she closed her eyes again, and, her arms crossed, hugged herself as if for warmth, quashing a shiver.

A robin landed on the lawn. I flashed on a childhood scene. I was hiding behind a boxwood hedge in the Dolphin Bays west garden with a string in my hand. Beside me, Bart hulked expectantly on his hands and knees. The string traveled through the bushes and crossed the tarmac driveway onto the enormous front lawn, ending at the stick holding up a box trap just beyond some croquet wickets. Bart was teaching me how to catch a robin. Lilac smell enriched the air, birds warbled, summer sunshine heightened the scent of mowed lawn grass.

Claire opened the front door, asking, "Are you guys ready?"

"I only regret," Lorraine joked unhappily, "that I have but one embryo to give ..."

I stood beside her in a small room dimmed by venetian blinds, while Claire and a doctor named Nancy Salazar performed a vacuum curettage. It didn't take long. An air of calm expertise from the two young women, both about our age, set us at ease as much as was possible under the circumstances. During the abortion, Lorraine breathed in laughing gas from a plastic mask hooked up by a long hose to a wall outlet. Claire helped perform the curettage and also questioned Lorraine occasionally about pain, discomfort, nausea. She stroked Lorraine's arm a few times while I held her hand; she touched Lorraine's belly to calm her whenever she flinched.

I think the operation lasted five minutes. And then they were gone, leaving us in that fuzzy dim room recuperating for a half hour. Through the slightly opened window we could hear the breeze sighing quietly in trees. The magpie was still chattering.

After a while, something broke inside me, and, still holding Lorraine's hand, I had to sit down. I felt faint and instantly apologized for blowing my cool. Eyes closed, her forehead damp with sweat, Lorraine weakly chastized me:

"Wait a minute, for the billionth time, Marcel, stop apologizing, would you please?"

"I can't help it. I'm so sorry. I wish this had never happened. How do you feel?"

"I've got cramps. It's funny. It hurt. I mean not *that* badly. But it hurt, nevertheless. That kind of took me by surprise, the hurt. God knows why, but I hadn't expected pain. I mean, such physical pain. These people really had me lulled."

"What about now?"

"I'm okay. It's just those cramps. But they're not too bad." She hesitated before adding: "And you know something—?"

"What?"

"I really don't believe it's over. And so quickly."

Her face split open with a bewildered, yet also triumphant, grin as she concluded:

"It was a piece of cake, Marcel."

Later, in the Mercedes going home around dusk, Lorraine told the following story:

"Forget how I got there, sugar, but I once found myself stranded in a tiny cowboy town where maybe fifteen people still lived, with nothing but the clothes on my back and six dollars in my pocketbook. I didn't even know the name of the place I was in. Flat out in the God damndest desert you ever saw, with a few sharp, bone-dry, treeless mountains in the distance. On one side of town an abandoned train trestle had snakeweed choking it. A handful of yellow railroad buildings had caved in nearby. The timbers of some abandoned stock pens were mostly splintered. Also a bunch of monstrous dead cottonwoods had crashed and were laying around like twisted whales. Then came the highway aiming straight north a hundred miles and straight south a hundred miles. And on its other side, one bar, a half-assed general store, and a crumbling adobe motel that nobody except me ever stayed in, I'll wager. Behind it lay a few deserted shacks, adobe ruins, busted corrals, a couple of stock tanks, a single windmill. There were a slew of big cottonwoods still upright, too, and their white fuzz was floating down in the hot spring sunshine and windless air like a right pretty, dreamy snowfall. It was lovely. And so quiet you could almost hear that cotton falling and the road crickling in the early morning heat. The fluff had built up on the highway maybe an inch or two because no car had been through since the prior evening. And in the distance those flinty mountains quivered and silently sizzled, and I'd just about had it. Like: There I was, standing beside the road, pregnant with a child I wasn't about to have, not at that point, no way, and about ten thousand miles from all my dreams, let alone a friend. See, it hadn't been but maybe four months earlier I'd finally started out higher than a kite for Nashville, Tennessee—Lorraine Luray, the Arkansas Nightingale—Bart told you about our first summer together, didn't he? And then there I was flat broke and knocked up to boot, way to hell and gone in the other direction, barely five minutes later. And don't ask me for how long, but it must have been half that entire morning I waited beside the road for an opportunity to stick my thumb out and hitch a ride. North, south, whichever way whoever it was that came along was going was just dandy with me. And while I stood there I thought about this famous country singer in her half-a-million-dollar mansion with fifteen bathrooms. And about that famous country singer with his guitar-shaped swimming pool and his fifteen-hundred-dollar rhinestone suits that weighed forty pounds, and his three-thousand-dollar mailbox. Also his twenty-thousand-dollar Bonneville Pontiac coated with silver dollars and unborn—*unborn*—for crissakes!—calf leather, toting real silver pistols for door handles . . . I just stood there running dreams like that through my baking noodle, all hot and itchy and hungover and feeling sick and then real dizzy. Until finally I heard a car tooling down the road. That is, first I heard the radio, way off in the distance, and a country song; I forget who was singing—a woman—let's say Kitty Wells; I heard that first, then the car, finally. And I stuck up my thumb when it still must of been a half mile away. And you know something? It never slowed down. That buggy just came blasting through with the radio blaring, and the girl beside the redneck driving bellowed out a hearty *'Get a horse!'* Then they disappeared into a big boil of all the cottonwood fluff that had been laying on the highway. It was like when you turn one of those Christmas paperweights with the snow inside upside down and then rightside up again. The air was feathery and white, and I couldn't help it, I burst out crying. Settling back down, the cotton got pasted to my cheeks, but I didn't even have the strength or the desire to reach up and rub it off."

Lorraine turned sideways to face me better. And, fixing her fiercely determined eyes on me, she finished her story by saying:

"That was the lowest, meanest, most hopeless I've ever felt. Maybe if you'd handed me a pistol right then I would of stuck it into my mouth and blown my brains clear across the country to the Mississippi. But I survived, all right. You always survive if you're willing."

When we reached Chamisaville, she insisted I drive her straight home to the trailer. I offered to stay for a while, but she said, "No thanks, Marcel. I wanna be alone right now. I gotta rest up for tonight."

"You're not going to perform tonight? That's crazy!"

"I need the money. And anyway, tonight I get paid. I can't pass that up."

"I'll give you the money. How much do you need?"

She laughed. "Marcel, you're a good guy, you really are.

But please don't worry. I'm a big girl, I can take care of myself. Now go home. And remember, the one way you can help me, if you're willing, is to inform that big lummox I did the dirty deed, and if he doesn't like it he can lump it."

"That's it?"

"Don't make more of life's incredible banalities than they actually are, Marcel. That's the word for today."

"Can I get you anything? Do you have food?" I opened her refrigerator: it contained a carton of milk, half a loaf of bread, some radishes, a jar of Cheez Whiz, three beers, and mayonnaise. "Listen, you can't eat this garbage. I'll go buy you something healthy."

Wearily, she said, "If you don't disappear from my life right now and stay out of it for a while, Marcel, I'm gonna call the cops. I mean it when I say I want to be alone. So take your Boy Scout act elsewhere, okay? I'm sorry. I know you want to help. Believe me, I'm grateful. I'm especially grateful you drove me down there today; I'm not sure I could have done it alone. But right now—"

"Stop. I can take the hint."

She smiled: "It took you long enough, though ..."

At the Big House, a curious calm prevailed. Supper was over. The house seemed almost deserted. I found Bart in the editing room with Brad Oughton and Jerry Fazzina. They may have been working earlier, but when I entered I caught them lounging around drinking beer, smoking a little dope.

On guard, but friendly, Bart said, "Hey, kid, what happened to you this morning? I called all over. How come you weren't on hand when we lifted out of the gorge?"

"I don't know. As soon as I knew you were okay, I split. I get tired from all the waiting around ..."

"Well, what's happening in the outside world?" he asked, more tranquil than I had seen him in a while and with that same friendly and bemused smile on his features.

"Actually, Pop, I drove down to the capital with Lorraine."

"And—?" His features were petrified in that almost-coyly smiling attitude.

"Well, you know. She got an abortion. It went all right. No complications."

Very quietly, almost inaudibly, he said, "That cunt."

Both Jerry Fazzina and Brad Oughton looked uncomfortable. Jerry said, " 'Scuse me a minute, Bart, I gotta find something." Brad said, "I have to take a leak." And—presto!—they disappeared.

Bart clicked on the Moviola. "Here's some footage on the chase out to the airport. It's not bad. What do you think?"

"I'm not really interested, right now. I'm tired. It's been a heavy day."

Leaving the Moviola running, he walked away from it. "I pulled it off without a scratch," he said. "I didn't even sprain my ankle. I landed perfectly. I always knew it would be like taking candy from a baby. I lead a charmed life."

"I'm glad, Pop. I'm really glad it went okay."

"Everything went okay today," he said quietly, crushing his beer can. "Without a hitch. Isn't it amazing how life can be so smooth and simple sometimes?"

I didn't know what to say, or how to respond to the edge in his voice. As I looked at him all I could think of was that Auden poem, "Musée des Beaux Arts," and its reference to the Brueghel painting about the fall of Icarus.

He said, "Well, what the hell. It's nice to know everything has been taken care of in an orderly fashion. I suppose I should give her a call."

"I don't know that she wants to talk with anybody right now."

He laughed. "Who are you, kid, her bodyguard? Her new amanuensis? Her fucking *agent?*"

"I'm nobody. I think she's tired, that's all. That's a rough experience. She wanted to rest up for a while."

"Well naturally. Of course. Me too, I think I'll rest up a while myself. Been a long day. Gotta keep sharp, you know. I have a one-day break and then I got to figure out how to help Jerry throw Millie to the Dobermans without having her black-belt boyfriend tear my arms out of their sockets. Busy fingers are happy fingers ..." he mumbled, and then he evaporated, leaving me alone with the whirring Moviola.

I slept uneasily, I had dreams. Lorraine sang her country-and-western tunes in a crowded, smoky bar; nobody listened. After each song, I put a dollar in her mug for tips; she avoided looking at me each time I did this. Then I circulated around in the bar, asking people to pipe down; they told me to fuck off. I blew a fuse, a fight developed, all hell broke loose. We escaped, Lorraine and I, and drove into the desert in the Mercedes. In due course, we ran out of gas, and started walking along the highway, Lorraine strumming her guitar and singing a lonesome song. No cars passed by, no gas stations loomed ahead. A rattlesnake beside the road buzzed a warning, and I jumped back. Lorraine said, "Don't be frightened, it's only a snake." Carelessly, she got too close, however, and the snake bit her on the ankle. Such a funny look transformed her features. "Dammit," she said. "That idiotic snake wasn't supposed to do that." I carried her into the desert, searching for a tree, for some shade. She started to puff up from the bite. I found a mesquite bush and set her down; soon it became obvious that she was dying. "Don't die," I pleaded. "Come on, have a heart, Lorraine." She smiled weakly. Her eyes grew heavy-lidded and sexy. "It's okay," she murmured. "Don't worry about me, Marcel. I can handle this. It's a piece of cake ..."

In the morning I was awakened by an urgent knocking on my door. "Go away," I moaned. "I'm still asleep. I don't want any. I'm broke. No peddlers allowed."

A woman's voice informed me: "There's been an accident."

I sat up, instantly riddled with apprehensions. An Arabian horse had tripped and rolled while Bart was galloping it at fifty miles an hour. He had totaled himself against a diving board.

Or he had been stabbed to death by Millie's angry boy-friend. . . .

"What kind of accident? Please come in."

The door opened; Connie Alexander said, "Your dad's in trouble."

"So what else is new?" I was frightened, but I tried to be funny.

"They've got him down at the country jail. He was ar-rested this morning about dawn."

"Is he all right?"

"Oh sure, you know Bart. Except for his pride, I guess. And of course, he really tied one on . . ."

"What happened? I thought he went to bed at eleven o'clock. I saw him go upstairs . . ."

"Just before dawn he drove over to that mobile-home park where Lorraine lives, doused her trailer in gasoline, and set it on fire. When she ran out of doors, he had a gun and started blasting. She claims he was shooting it at her, but he wouldn't do that. Not Bart. I mean, that's not his style. He was only pretending because he wanted to scare her."

After a five-second pause for the facts to sink in, I blurted: "I don't believe him! He's *crazy!*"

"No, he's not crazy," she said thoughtfully. "He just has all this energy . . ."

But I was enraged. "Oh no you don't, no excuses. That man is out of his mind! He pisses me off royally. He's like a baby! Things don't add up in his brain anymore. He's a menace to society. You can't condone his antics."

Connie said, "Don't be hard on Bart, Marcel. He can't help it. He has to do what he has to do."

"Bullshit."

She came back at me with her own flash of anger: "Believe it or not, *he holds things together!*"

I said, "Look, let's not fight. The first thing to do is get him out of jail."

"We only heard about it fifteen minutes ago. Eddie will

bail him out. He told me, Eddie did, to tell you about it. Maybe you want to go with him."

"Of course I want to go. Give me a second to get dressed. You're sure he's all right?"

"Word is he's alive, a little the worse for wear, but still one hell of an ornery cuss."

"And Lorraine?"

"She's okay."

"Where is she staying?"

"That's up for grabs. Nobody knows, apparently. She lodged a complaint and then disappeared."

Accompanied by Eddie Cobalt, Jerry Fazzina, Connie, John Holbein, and Veronica, I aimed Bart's Mercedes toward the county jail. We were held up in traffic: an army of backhoes, like enormous killer praying mantises, lumbered everywhere, attacking the town, knocking down old buildings, digging trenches, accidentally fracturing water mains in an orgy of road widening. Hot-tar mixes were going down; the stench was brutal. Steam mingled with dust and clogged everything, reducing visibility. Dozens of workers in fluorescent-orange hard hats wandered around, tentatively poking at the black molasses with leveling instruments. Another bunch lounged around, watching it all happen. It took us a half hour to travel the mile between Bart's crazy home and the courthouse complex.

Inside the jail, we encountered a fed-up sheriff. Bob Martínez had spent the last few hours coping with Bart's act, and although he obviously would have done almost anything to get rid of his recalcitrant charge, he was also fighting mad.

"Bail?" he said incredulously. "Nobody's *set* bail yet. And if I had anything to say about it, when and if it was set, it'd be so high he'd never get out of here. We've got that man for arson, two counts of attempted murder, assault with a deadly weapon . . . and not just on the girl but on at least six police officers who tried to arrest him. We've also got him for God knows how many counts of damage to personal property, starting with the girl's trailer and winding up with dents he put into the fender of my police car with his head. Not only that, but after we locked him up he went berserk and busted everything he could get his hands on. He also broke our mugging camera when we tried to take his picture. And he made such a fuss we couldn't even print him. You're lucky we felt sorry for the bum and decided not to kill him."

Eddie said, "I apologize, I really do. We all apologize. You people have been more than generous with us. I'm sorry this had to happen. Needless to say, just send us an itemized bill for all the damage, and there will be immediate restitution."

"Just like that?" Bob Martínez grinned. "Man, life sure is easy when you've got the bucks, isn't it?"

Eddie said, "Sometimes this sort of thing goes along with the movie business. People away from home, the tension of film making, you know—the pressure can get them. Most film budgets have a little something extra to deal with these emergencies."

" 'A little something extra'—is that what you call it?"

Eddie cleared his throat, suddenly all steel and ice, and said politely but very firmly: "What about my client?"

"You can have your client, mister. And good riddance. As long as you, and him, will sign these papers guaranteeing his appearance before Judge Chávez next Thursday at three o'clock P.M." Sliding some papers across the counter, he called back down a narrow corridor: "Ricardo, unchain the movie producer, will you?"

Bart was grinning his foolish, sheepish, little-boy grin when he emerged from the inner sanctum. He looked about as I had expected he would. A whopping shiner, messy hair, crusted blood on one ear, and dried glop in the grooves between his front teeth. The fragile, transparent scar tissue over his swollen cheeks was split in several places. His lips had swelled and cracked; his face and his hands were filthy. His turquoise-blue cowboy shirt with mother-of-pearl buttons was torn, blotched, wrinkled; his dungarees were covered with mud. Dirty athletic socks sheathed his big feet; both shoes had been lost in the melee. He was still tanked. Or anyway, woozy and staggering.

And obnoxious.

"They stole my fucking shoes," he griped.

"Shut up about the shoes," Eddie advised. "You're lucky to be alive."

"I shall return," Bart called triumphantly back at the glowering sheriff as we hustled him toward the exit. "I'm gonna come back here and dismember this jailhouse brick by brick! I'm gonna level it with my own bare hands, and I'm gonna stomp it into little pieces, and then I'm gonna *eat it*! I don't care if it takes me a year to eat it, I'm gonna eat the whole damn thing!"

Eddie ordered him to shut up. I begged him to shut up. Then I called back to the sheriff, "I'm sorry, he's still drunk, he doesn't mean it, I apologize for him."

The sheriff replied, "Don't worry about it. Gringos always make a lot of noise. It's their money."

"Jesus," Eddie griped, shoving Bart into the back seat. "What's the matter with you, man? You trying to get us all killed?"

"Just having a little fun," my father replied, mischievously trying to cuff Eddie, but missing by a mile. "There's no law against having fun."

Connie said, "I can't wait until Folsom hears about this one. Things aren't bad enough, *you* had to freak out."

"I'm not freaked out, Shannon. I just got a little tipsy and played a joke on Lorraine."

"Some joke. And people call me Connie, in case you hadn't noticed."

"Connie, Shannon, turn 'em all upside down and they look the same to me."

To Eddie, Jerry said, "Tell him to shut up, would you?"

Connie said, "It's all right, Jerry. I've never seen Bart this unhappy or this loaded."

"I'm not unhappy," Bart said painfully. "I'm having *fun!*"

Connie tossed her head. " 'Fun' he calls it."

"When I see Folsom, you know what I'm gonna do?" Bart giggled. "First I'm gonna smash his kidneys. Then I'm gonna tear his ears off with my bare hands. Then I'm gonna bust both his legs and dislocate both his shoulders. Then I'm gonna break his neck."

Nobody except Connie deigned to answer that. Bitterly lighting a cigarette and shaking out the match, she growled, "You and whose army?"

"Hey, hey, *hey!*" my father protested. "Smile, everybody. We're in a Fellini movie!"

"Alright already with the theatrics," Connie said.

"That's me," Bart hooted. "I shoulda been an actor. Suckled on the wings of a creed outworn."

Eddie said, "I'm a lawyer, and even I know that quote isn't half right."

"Hey Marcel." Bart leaned forward, tapping my shoulder. "Hey, kid, why the frost, eh? What's with the cold shoulder? Why so glum? Cheer up. We only go around once in life, so we gotta grab for all the gusto we can get."

Grimly, I said, "That's about it, too."

"That's about what?"

"A lousy beer ad."

"Oh dear, listen to the Boy Scout, will you people? My gosh, pardon me—pardonnez-moi—for breathing."

We drove in an awkward, semihostile silence for a moment, but Bart was revved up and couldn't keep his trap shut for long.

He tapped me again. "You shoulda seen your friend," he giggled. "You shoulda seen her face when she popped out the doorway of that flaming trailer and I started shooting at her! Did she shit a madonna? Do pelicans eat fish?"

"I don't think it's very funny, Pop."

"Funny? *Funny?*" he screeched. "Shit boy, you wouldn't believe how hilarious! I thought I'd die from laughing! Toward the end I couldn't even pull the trigger! Lord, that was beautiful! She rolled over in the dust, trying to dodge bullets she thought I was aiming right at her, like she was being tumbled in ocean breakers! God *damn* that was fun! She was shrieking and kicking her legs and shouting 'No no no no no no no no!' " —he made his voice squeaky, mocking her—"and I started laughing so hard I had to fall down 'cause my legs became weak! Shit, I wish I'd had a movie camera; that one was a classic!"

Connie said, "You pig."

Bart said, "Fuck you. You're fired."

"Thank God. It's about time."

"You're *all* fired," Bart snarled sloppily. "The whole lot of you. You don't know how to make movies worth squat, anyway."

Eddie said, "Bart, why don't you clam up before you actually alienate somebody."

"That's the problem," he sulked. "You're all so damn thick-headed I can't even offend you. Oh Lord," he wailed theatrically, "my kingdom for one sensitive film maker!"

John Holbein sneezed, gasped, cleared his throat, and looked a trifle blue around the gills; "I hate this country," he moaned. "I hate the juniper. I hate the sagebrush. I hate the goddam alfalfa. I wish we'd wrap up this turkey early and get ourselves back to some concrete."

Bart said, "I don't care if we finish the picture. I don't care about anything any more. Folsom can go suck raw eggs. Amen. I've had it. All you people, everybody, you're all morons. Morons," he howled. "Morons, morons, morons!"

Jerry Fazzina snapped, "And you're the king of the morons."

"King of the morons?" Bart looked hurt. "Only the *king*

of the morons? Oh no, not me, you sell me short, friend. I happen to be the ... Michelangelo of the morons!"

"Michelangelo of the morons," Connie said sarcastically. "You bet."

"Aw hey, c'mon you people. Lay off a little. I had a bad night, I feel crummy; how come sympathy around here is as rare as a Jesuit in a Cadillac? Jesuit in a Cadillac? Did I say that? Egads, we'd better hire this boy, he sounds like a writer!"

I said, "Are you going to apologize to her?"

"To who? I mean, To Whom? It is 'To Whom,' isn't it? I wouldn't wanna botch my grammar in front of you, kid."

"You know to who. To Lorraine."

"Lorraine? That name strikes a bell. Do I know a Lorraine ... ?"

"Hey Dad—!"

"Apologize be damned," Bart said. "I'm gonna smash her kidneys. Then I'm gonna tear her ears off with my bare hands. Then I'm gonna bust both her legs and dislocate both her shoulders. Then I'm gonna break her neck."

Connie said, "What's the shooting schedule today? It's not the Dobermans, is it? I'm not sure I could take the Dobermans today."

"Dobermans are tomorrow," Jerry said. "Today we go back to the airport ..."

"I'm gonna shoot those Dobermans," Bart said. "Marcel, stop the car by that sporting-goods store. I'm gonna buy a twelve-guage shotgun. That's the best way to shoot Dobermans."

"Moron," Connie said cheerfully. "I don't believe I'm your secretary. Better I should be your wet nurse."

"The *Michelangelo* of the morons. I've never been anything but the best."

When I pulled into the parking lot behind the Big House, everyone piled out of the Mercedes, relieved to be home. Everyone except Bart, that is. He sat in the center of the back seat making no move to descend.

I had started to walk away from the car. I turned back. "We're home, Pop. This is the last stop. Everybody out."

"I like it here, Marcel. I like it in the back of this Mercedes. It feels almost safe. The subdued pomp, the subdued circumstance—that's for me. And anyhow, I ain't going into that house. I can't face those people. What'll I say?"

"You don't have to say anything. Come on, come with me. I'll help you upstairs. Nobody cares. You'll take a shower, get some sleep."

"I can't sleep. What about the movie?"

"The movie will survive for a day without you."

"You don't understand, Marcel. Without me the movie will collapse."

Tiredly, I said, "Does it matter if it collapses?"

"It matters to me."

"All right. So what are you going to do?"

"I'm gonna sit here a moment longer, enjoying my place in the sun as the Michelangelo of the morons. Then I'm gonna get out, and go inside, and face them, and take a shower, and go on location . . ."

"I'll see you inside, then."

But as I started again to head for the house, he whimpered, "Marcel, don't leave me."

"What's the matter?"

"I feel awful. I got a headache. Something's wrong. I feel terrible. I don't know what happened to me this morning. It's awful. She'll never speak to me again. When I went over there, I only wanted to talk. I only wanted . . . Why'd she get that abortion?" he whined. "If she hadn't done that, we could have worked it out."

I said, "What's done is done."

"If it were done, when 'tis done, then 'twere well it were done quickly. If this assassination—"

Right there he stopped—in mid-sentence, in mid-breath. He didn't really look startled, just a bit puzzled. One hand, I suppose his right one, grappled for his left shoulder. Then his eyes opened wide, as I guess what must have been an incredible pain hit him. He went rigid, his eyes bursting out of his scarred face. He blurted "Oh—!" But even that was cut off, sliced in half as surely as if Bart had been beheaded. The autopsy later on said it was a massive coronary: everything in and around his heart cut loose at once. So my guess is he was dead even before lurching forward and sideways at the same time, until he was wedged between the rear seat and the front backrest, inches off the floor.

I was in a car accident once. As a passenger in a little TR-3 that collided head-on with a Ford Fairlane traveling fifty miles an hour. Fortunately, we were almost at a standstill. My friend driving had slowed for a left-hand turn the morning after a rough night at a Middlebury College house party. And that's when the old cliché that everything takes place in slow motion during a critical event was really driven home to me. Our accident took forever: later, I remembered every aspect of the collision as if my brain had filmed it at half speed. Our front end slowly crumpled as it slammed the Ford's radiator back through its block. Then our vehicle swung lazily away from the Ford as the windshield began to shatter. Parked cars crossed from my left to my right as my head ripped off the rear-view mirror. And, as we completed our swing aimed in the opposite direction, I headed slowly out the driver's-side door. Molasses-slow seconds later I finally floated almost weightlessly into the street. We had been struck head on, spun around, and banged thirty feet in the opposite direction inside of two seconds: the Triumph was totaled. Yet all I received from the adventure were a few bruises, a minor scratch, and a brief headache.

All this by way of saying I have no idea how long it took me to move toward Bart. The heart attack had occurred so abruptly there had been no time to register the act before it had ended. Probably he was already long gone by the time I found myself at the car, reaching for him. I grabbed for his arms and could find no handle: I think I wound up gripping his shirt at the right shoulder with one hand and latching onto his hair with the other. He gave a weird, lifeless grunt as I heaved with all my might, dislodging him from that car. I fell over backward, and Bart slid heavily onto my legs. Kicking free, I hollered "Help me!" and scrambled around and over him, flopping him onto his back. His wide-open eyes brought me up short. No feeling clouded them. They were empty: very clear, very still, very silent. I touched his hair; I placed fingertips against one cheek. His beautiful scar-tissue skin gleamed dully, a fragile, transparent membrane. Beard stubble scratched my palm.

I whispered, "Oh no." I called out again, "Please, help me! It's Bart! Call an ambulance!"

I listened to his chest and heard no heartbeat. It had been stifled in there, frozen solid, just as if an engine had seized. I heard no flutter, nothing. I felt for a pulse, but could find none. Then I pressed down on his chest as I had seen him work on Frank Wilson, released my pressure, repeated my actions . . . and then pounded his sternum frantically, aware all the time that I really didn't know what I was doing. Desperately, I hissed at him: *"Come on, Bart . . . Jesus, you son of a bitch . . . you can't do this . . . what's the matter with you anyway? . . . Breathe, God dammit . . . Come on, Pop, wake up, would you . . . this can't happen . . . PLEASE, YOU SON OF A BITCH, DON'T DO THIS!"* Frantically, I gave him artificial respiration, blowing as hard as I could into his mouth, down his throat, then heaving against his chest and stomach to force out the air that issued from him with a strange blatting sound: it struck my face stinking like invisible pus. Gasping for breath myself, hearing strange sounds like squeaks that turned out to be my own frightened exclamations, I tried the mouth-to-mouth for a few minutes, slapping his face, also, and then hitting him, hitting his shoulders, begging him not to die, threatening him, blaming him: *"Bart, for crissakes, you haven't even finished this movie!"* And swearing at him: *"COME ON YOU MOTHERFUCKER, YOU SHITHEAD, YOU ASS-HOLE, THIS IS STUPID!"* And I flailed at him, grabbed his hair and shook his head violently, tore open his shirt, the but-

tons popping, grabbed his shoulders and shook his entire body
—a feat I never could have accomplished under normal circumstances—but he only joggled, his head snapping around horrendously on a neck without tension . . .

I stopped, horrified by what I was doing, and certain,
anyway, that whatever I tried would be useless. Then I gave up.
The man had been killing himself for years. I had had my
chances to save him when he collapsed in the orchard on our
trip north from the airport, when he almost went down in the
courtyard that first night, when he blanched and caught his
breath in the swimming pool . . . but I had been afraid to
acknowledge his mortality then, and this time—as I had known
the split instant his Shakespeare quotation was cut short—
offered no second chance.

"Oh Bart . . ."

Gingerly, I embraced him, afraid to place any more weight
against his big body. I saw Lorraine doing her whacky, lovable
dance on that screen two nights ago, cricket-sized and heart-
breaking. And then . . . I don't know. I settled more heavily
against my father, solidly embracing him, holding on to him—
I guess the expression is—for dear life. I squeezed his unrespon-
sive flesh; I held on tightly to that suddenly diminished body,
so helpless now that it lacked all energy.

"What did you have to go and do this for . . . ?"

I had no idea what to do or how to feel, nor could I explain
my own emotions. I had an almost humorous longing to say,
"Wait a minute, please, there's something I forgot to tell
you . . ." On another channel I felt a weird relief: "Well, thank
God that's over." Too, I wondered in panic: "What am I supposed to do now? What happens next? What about the funeral?
Who must I call? Does he have a will? What about the movie?"

I held him that way, gently arranged against his chest for
a long time. I could feel his body cooling, changing, growing
heavy and unresilient. Magpies made noises in the cottonwoods; horses snorted and stamped their hooves. People mur-

mured; their shadows criss-crossed me but seemed no more significant than the sun-cast patterns of tree leaves. Life seeped out of Bart. It trickled out in slim sensual rivulets of heat or electricity the way smoke rises from a cigarette sitting on the edge of an ashtray in a quiet room. I almost could have sworn that tiny particles of energy composing my father's life-force tickled me as they flowed around my body or undulated up through me. I know that for a while I had a sensation of actively absorbing something from him, something real and warm, something mysterious and powerful and not quite of this world, causing a sensation like none I'd ever felt before.

A mysterious calmness came to hold my worst fears at bay. I loved that man so much. How grateful I was for the gift of holding him, of being with him now. Lying with my head against his chest, breathing quietly, I know that I absorbed his departing essence—call it his soul, call it what you will . . . I knew that it was a gift of his wonderful energy—made pure again by his death, and this transfer. And it was made possible not only by the love I had for him, but by the profound affection he had always held for me and never demonstrated, unable or unwilling—given the emotional miles that had always separated us, not to mention the real miles—to reveal it to me.

I embraced him as tenderly as if he had been my lover. I heard him plinking away at the balcony piano a few nights ago, thoughtful and exhausted, and no doubt frightened also. Simple, rare notes fell through my drowsiness like raindrops selectively chosen from the sky. And I heard his rough voice singing another verse from that song he had written for Lorraine:

At twilight or daybreak
Your face comes a-mingling
Among all my dreams that remain.
And I wonder however
A poor boy like me can
Get a girl like you out of his brain.

Fragments of the last few days glided through my mind. I heard him exclaim *"Time—?"* on the telephone long ago when he had called me in New York. I recalled, I could actually feel, the rib-crushing bear hugs with which he had greeted me at the airport. I saw him filming Lorraine and me while we picked apples, and I watched him piling fruit into her sweatshirt. Making a gun of his hand, he shot the peacock. *"What do you mean 'comets'?"* he wailed in the La Tortuga bar. We admired the wasted, beautiful trout under the southwestern stars and the moon; nearby, horses whinnied. One phrase repeated itself in my head: "Joe Blow from San Diego . . . Joe Blow from San Diego . . ." And then I saw him sitting by the edge of that pool like a little kid, asking perplexedly: "How do you figure out if it was worth it? How do you know what's the point?"

Eventually, it was over. All his life drained, and he left me. Whatever I could absorb, I had absorbed. He'd become a body—useless, clammy, a stiff.

At the start I had been alone; then I had sensed a commotion around me, I had felt their shadows on me. Their presence had died away as all my senses concentrated on Bart: my awareness had shrunk to include only my father and me. When I raised my head, then, and opened my eyes, letting the world flood into the intensely inner-focused being I had become, I was shocked by the bright daylight and the enormous size of things. And by the fact that I was outside, on the ground, beside the Mercedes, surrounded by people. Because, toward the end of that spell with my father, I had had no sensation of touching anything except him, or of being anywhere except with him. The experience had been like floating in water or in space, absolutely weightless, unencumbered and alone.

An ambulance pulled up on the outskirts of the circle. Two emergency medical technicians jumped out and took over: they had an IV in the body even before they had hoisted it through the rear loading doors. "Do you want to come with us?" one of the technicians asked me.

"It doesn't matter, does it? He's dead."

"Suit yourself . . ."

Something about his tone made me feel guilty. "I'll come," I struggled to say. He gave me a hand into the ambulance.

Just before the doors closed I heard Veronica blurt tearfully, "Incredaburgable!"

Somebody else cried, "When it rains it fucking pours!"

8 Aftermaths, of course, are always fraught with confusion. Being in shock, I honestly don't remember very clearly the details of what happened right after Bart died. They worked on him for a little while in the emergency room, then a doctor I had never seen before came in and pronounced him. Dazedly, I asked for the name of a funeral home, made a telephone call, and had them come for the body. Connie Alexander, Eddie Cobalt, Jerry Fazzina, and Bill Sholokoff went with me and helped select a cheap coffin. His corpse would be driven down to the capital for cremation, and, with my permission, Eddie took care of all those details. Then that part of it was over, and we all retreated to the Big House, made drinks, and milled around. I called the East Coast and told Kitty; she offered to fly out immediately, but I didn't want her intrusion. Our conversation was awkward and stunted. Bart was no great love of her life: she'd had little or no connection to him for years, especially since I'd gotten old enough to deal with him directly. Still, she offered some practical advice when, at a loss, I asked her "What do you think I should do next?"

"Call Arnold. Find out if he left a will. Arnold would know about the estate."

Uncle Arnold, Bart's elder brother, was a powerful Wall Street lawyer, a family man, a Calvinistic Episcopalian as steady as the proverbial rock. When I phoned and spilled the beans about Bart's death, he seemed unsurprised and not particularly moved about Bart, and yet genuinely concerned for me. "How are you taking it, Marcel?" he asked solicitously, and wondered aloud if I needed money. He confirmed there was a will. Its gist? Well, first off, Bart wished to be cremated, and wanted none of his "gloating" siblings or relatives or even friends at a service. I, his son, should dispose of the ashes however I saw fit. No tombstone either. "Please," he had written, "just let me disappear from the face of this earth." Other than that, his money, his stocks, and whatever could be realized from the sale of his things, belonged to me. "Hard to say how much that'll be," Arnold offered, puffing thoughtfully on his pipe. "But I would guess that it all might add up to a quarter of a million. Not much, I'll admit, but Bart had a bad habit of squandering just about anything he ever touched."

"What about a funeral? What do you think I should do with his ashes?" I suddenly realized that I knew very little about Bart, about his friends—if indeed he had friends—about their needs or desires to eulogize him.

"I don't know," Arnold said thoughtfully. "Bart and I sort of lost touch over the last thirty years. I haven't spoken to him a dozen times since the war. Naturally, the family will want some kind of service. A memorial, anyway. And out at the family plot at Dolphin Bays, of course. Yet as for a funeral . . ."

He ruminated carefully for a moment, while I simply sat there, waiting for him to come up with answers.

"You could respect his wishes, naturally. Or why not ask his movie friends there? My guess is something ought to be done in Los Angeles . . ."

We chatted a while longer. Arnold was all practicality. "I'll have a man from our firm, probably Towner Babcock, fly out the first of next week and help you start cleaning up the details," he said. "In the meantime you might start scouting around for an art expert to evaluate his collection: I believe he had some pretty valuable things stashed in that house . . ." Then we said good-bye, hanging up as if nothing out of the ordinary had happened.

Eddie Cobalt was on another phone, calling Los Angeles, informing everyone from Folsom to friends like Mac Ivory and Mort Cheesman that Bart had died. Myself, I tried to dial Lorraine. "I'm sorry," the operator nasaled, "but that number has been temporarily disconnected." No doubt thanks to Bart's arson job. So I drove over to the Sundance Trailer Park in one of his pickup trucks, but her battered vehicle wasn't parked in front of the charred trailer. The manager said that naturally she had moved, he thought into a motel—"Or maybe she's staying with friends."

I began a small saga then, a short-lived epic journey in search of Lorraine. I started at the La Tortuga, but the manager there, a tall, taciturn Texan by the name of Chris Robinson, said he had no inside track on her whereabouts. "She came in last night, did two sets, collected her paycheck, and then stood me up for her third set," he informed me matter-of-factly, without rancor. "I'll tell you something," he added. "She's a pretty little piece, that's for sure, and I hate to see her leave, because she could really pack them in here. But she'll never make it in the big time."

When I asked why, he said, "She won't kiss ass. She'd die before she'd suck cock. She won't even banter with the patrons. She's too goddam serious up there. All she's got going for her is her professional voice, and the fact that she *looks* like the cutest little honky-tonk chippy this side of the Alamo. But she has a shitty personality. She refuses to swallow a little of that pride of hers. She's got a brain, I'll admit, but she's always putting out vibes like she's holier than all the rest of us. Or like she's doing some kind of penance up there. She sings *down* to people, know what I mean?"

After that, I started driving aimlessly, pulling over wherever I spotted a hotel or motel sign, asking at their desk if she was registered. For a while, it was crazy. I wound up driving in circles. About the third time I stopped at a motel and had the clerk say to me, "Aren't you the fellow who was here asking for that same lady a half hour ago?" I told myself to wake up and put a little method into my madness. So I hunted up a pencil and an old envelope in the glove compartment, went to the north end of town, and began more systematically to track her, writing down the name of each establishment I visited. Several times I thought I spotted her car, and veered recklessly off the highway, or the main street, or a side road, only to discover that the heap in question was similar, but different.

It was a hot, tourist-infested afternoon: layers of dust hung over the crowded town. The smell of steaming fresh asphalt permeated everything. The sun was bright, the sky cloudless; glare reflected off shop windows and automobile windshields. I soon had a terrible headache. Pedestrians constantly darted across streets in front of me; I braked too hard, jerking myself about unmercifully. I spent intolerable minutes sandwiched between shimmering Winnebago campers that towered over me. I grew nauseous from their exhaust fumes. The town was cluttered with lowriders paneled in purple or glistening white angel hair with St. Christopher medals dangling from the rear-view mirrors. On the back of every tourist van an endless array of trail motorcycles and ten-speed bikes were appended. I had never seen so many decrepit hippy vans, largely Volkswagen buses, in my life. And the pedestrian traffic: midwestern tourist families in matching jumpsuits; local Chicano cornerboys and -girls looking sultry and discontented; a thousand various freaks looking sloppy, or phony, or cutesy-pie spiritual; old bowlegged farmers in sweat-stained cowboy hats and clean shirts, clean dungarees, and worn cowboy boots; a bunch of Hollywood vaqueros looking so clean they sparkled; and a lot of East Coast aesthetic, shabbily tweedy people—I suppose denizens of the renowned art community. It was a little like trying to thread my way through a bargain-basement Times Square.

I must have tried twenty motels without any luck. After the first dozen I felt like an exhausted swimmer simply trying to stay afloat. I had no hope of finding her, but continued the search anyway, just to be able to say I had done it. That is why eventually—inevitably—I saw her car parked in front of a garish Kentucky Fried Chicken barn and pulled over beside it. Her guitar, a battered suitcase, some cardboard boxes of clothes, and a few scuffed record albums filled the back seat of that funky convertible. Lorraine was inside, alone at a red-and-white checkered table, listlessly gnawing on a chicken leg.

"Well," I said wearily, "I found you."

Without glancing up at me she said, "I didn't know you were looking." Her eyes were real red, real swollen. She appeared jaundice yellow, mighty sick.

I said, "Did you hear about Bart?"

"I heard. It was on the radio. On the hometown news."

"Oh." And then: "What did they say?"

"They said he died of a heart attack. They said he was in town making a movie. They said he was a 'noted entrepreneur.' That's about it. They didn't elaborate."

I said, "I was there when it happened."

"I don't think I want to hear about it, Marcel. Right now I'm not sure I'm tough enough. This hasn't been what you would call a real good day. I'm feeling slightly fragile."

"I can't even cry about it," I said. "It doesn't seem real, yet. It's as if everything happened in a fucking movie. I keep waiting for some dam to break, but it won't. Everything has been so matter-of-fact and orderly. It doesn't seem momentous or tragic or anything . . ."

"I cried," she said quietly. "I drove out on the mesa and sat there for two hours and cried my heart out. For a while I thought I would die. I couldn't breathe. I almost blacked out."

"It's not your fault."

"That's not why I was crying, or why I thought I would die."

"It happened real fast," I explained. "It happened right after we bailed him out of jail. He was in the back seat of the Mercedes. Everybody else had gotten out. He was being funny, quoting Shakespeare, when it clobbered him. I don't think he even felt it, it was that fast. I tugged him out, and tried a heart massage and mouth-to-mouth, but it was hopeless."

"That must have been rough on you," she said forlornly.

"I don't know. It's like that cliché—'like a dream.' I can't put it together or really feel anything about it. I don't even know how to act. I feel like *giggling* all the time."

Lorraine said, "You know how I feel?"

I shook my head.

"I feel really whittled down to size."

When she lit a cigarette, her hands trembled; her fingers were badly stained by nicotine. She smelled like nicotine. She smelled stale and ashen and fatigued. I don't know when I had seen anybody that strung out. It was scary. Particularly for someone who barely weighed a hundred pounds to begin with. And her clothes, her T-shirt, her dungarees, her sneakers were dirty, too. In all she could have been just another doped-out hippy.

"Well—" Carefully, she split the paper matchstick with her bitten-down fingernail. "What are you going to do?"

"I don't know. I guess I'm supposed to hang around here for a while. I have to wait for somebody to fly out and help me take care of all the stuff in the house. Maybe I'll go to Los Angeles for some kind of service, I don't know. I'll have to close up his house out there. I really don't want to return to the Big House. Instead of a carnival, it'll be like a morgue. Eddie told me they have to finish the location part of the film. That's another week or ten days. He said tomorrow they wouldn't work, in deference to Bart, and maybe that would be a good day for a service here."

"I don't want to bury that man. He wasn't the kind of man you're supposed to bury."

"I sent the body down to the capital to be cremated."

"You should scatter the ashes."

"Where?"

"I don't know. In the La Tortuga Bar. In that fucking gorge. You could rent a plane and scatter them over the mesa. I really don't know, though—I can't even think about it."

I asked, "What are you going to do, Lorraine?"

"That's today's sixty-four-thousand-dollar question. I

don't have any money—I even lost last night's check in the fire. I also stiffed Chris for a set, 'cause I felt shitty, so I can't even go back there and demand another one. I guess it's up for grabs. Today I planned to drive around until I was so tired I couldn't drive any longer, and then I was going to pull off the road wherever I was and catch some shut-eye. And tomorrow I'll try and turn my brain on and figure out what to do."

"You can't simply drive around like that, with no rhyme or reason."

"I'm not going to accept a charity room at the Big House, Marcel, if that's what you've got in mind. That's not my favorite place right now."

"I have money; I'll get you a room. I can give you bread to do whatever you have to do, that's no problem. Apparently, I'm going to inherit everything he owned. Which should make me about half a millionaire."

"Congratulations."

"I can spring for a motel. I can give you enough to fly to L.A. or Arkansas, or wherever you want to go."

" I think I'm too tired not to take you up on that. I could seriously use enough bread for gas to the Coast. I have connections and friends there. It's easy to hustle jobs."

"You can't take off right now, not in the shape you're in."

"What do you want me to do, hang around Chamisaville revisiting all our old haunts?"

"But you can't leave now. You need a rest. Come on, let's go find a motel." She was crying again, quietly but steadily. Her thin lips were wrinkled bitterly. "Shit, Lorraine, you need to rest. You need sleep. Jesus."

When she got up, she lost her balance and banged against the table; I reached to steady her, and wound up accepting her waif's body as she slumped into my arms. And I held her like that, in the aluminum-bright, red-and-white-checkered atmosphere of the Kentucky Fried Chicken barn, while her body shuddered, and she gasped against my chest, and her big hands twisted the cloth of my soiled shirt. Some teenagers at a table across the room stared openly at us. A girl behind the order counter glanced at us surreptitiously, out the corner of one eye. I held Lorraine and heard the fluorescent lights buzzing and a grease bin back there sizzling . . . and the traffic outside that air-conditioned place. Car horns were distantly beeping. I held her for maybe five minutes, then she pushed away from me, mumbled "Thanks, Marcel, you're a good egg," grabbed a handful of napkins from a tin dispenser on the table, and said, "Let's get out of here. This place gives me the creeps."

She followed me south of town to an old-fashioned adobe hotel called The Chamisaville Inn. Located back off the highway a little, it was surrounded by sagebrush land. Vigas poked out of all the walls, lovely mud ramparts rambled over three stories. There were patios and courtyards, a few piñon trees, and weeping willows. Also tennis courts, a small swimming pool, and a pleasant outdoor terrace where you could have drinks at white tin tables protected by sun umbrellas. Her room was light and airy, with a large picture window and a fireplace. Even though it was summer, piñon logs were stacked beside the fireplace, for the nights could be chilly at seven thousand feet.

When she was settled in, I gave her most of the cash in my pockets, close to a hundred dollars. Lorraine said "Thank you," and sat listlessly on the edge of her bed, her head hung, totally defeated.

I said, "You should go to bed."

"I don't think I can sleep. I'm all worn out, but I almost know I can't sleep."

"You have to sleep."

"Why?" she asked. There was slight humor in her voice, a faint smile on her lips: "Will it unravel the knitted hearts of gargoyles?"

"You just need sleep. I know I'm useless, especially in any kind of crisis situation, if I don't get enough sleep."

She changed the subject. "Would you get me a drink from the bar, Marcel? That might help. In fact, you might ask them if they'd sell you a bottle."

"What of?"

"It doesn't matter. Anything. Southern Comfort. Blackberry brandy. Vodka. I don't care what it tastes like."

"You don't think you'll just make yourself sicker?"

"I'll make myself sick in a different way. It'll be a relief . . ."

I went into the bar and asked a recent transplant from Baltimore if he'd sell me a bottle. He was perfectly willing as long as I would pay the bar price, about double the liquor-store retail cost. I returned to Lorraine's room with a pint of apricot brandy and a cannister of ice. While I was gone she had showered and was now sitting in bed holding her guitar. I made us both drinks, and sat on the edge of the bed, sipping along with her. Occasionally, she stroked a chord. After a minute I could feel her relaxing a little; and I could feel it in myself, too, the draining of tension. Just before I really felt loose, I telephoned the Big House, and spoke with Eddie Cobalt to inform him of my whereabouts. He wanted to know if I had any plans for a service; the entire crew was pressing him; people were confused, depressed, in shock. I told him we would have a service, but that I would work out all the details with him in the morning because right now I didn't want to think about it any longer. Then I poured us both some more brandy.

Lorraine said, "Brother, a lot of water has gone over the dam since that phone call to you in New York."

I nodded, feeling peaceful and also, suddenly—I suppose at long last—very sad, cheated, dismayed. I could feel tears approaching as I never had before. It was almost like having an orgasm. They came from every area of my body, traveling up through my flesh and organs toward my head, with strings attached to every nerve in my body causing an almost exquisite pain. My face started twisting long before they arrived. My mouth wrenched open in that peculiar agony that presages crying, my eyes went almost shut, and the tears gathered steam like an enormous and powerful force within my body, searing me everywhere, doubling me over in pain, and then in grateful dismay when they finally broke. I heard a weird, wild sound explode out of me, half grunt, half screech, half agonized and frightening wail. I rocked on the edge of Lorraine's bed, shaking my head and making that noise with my lips shaped into a bawling snarl, and with the tears soaking my face, and then my shirt, while my whole body shuddered with gratitude for the release, finally, into a state of mourning. Vaguely, I heard Lorraine's husky voice soothing me: "It's all right Marcel. It's good to cry. It's okay." Her fingertips touched my shoulder, my arm, and I heard her sobs, too; she was crying with me.

We carried on for almost an hour. And when finally I had wept myself dry, I was so drained I felt stupified: I could barely move. I had never been that emotionally exhausted. I was so sleepy that only with a great effort could I keep awake long enough to pour us another drink.

"You stay here tonight," Lorraine said. "You can sleep with me."

"I won't touch you," I muttered stupidly.

"I know that, idiot. Lord, you're thick sometimes."

It took an incredible effort to swing around the bed and crawl in beside her. Immediately, we swung into each other's arms. Lorraine muttered, "Sleep with the fucking angels, Marcel." And we held each other all through that long and spellbinding night. Bart was everywhere. His pained, diaphanous face drifted through the dark, sweet-smelling air of our room like a nostalgic memory of romantic suicide. He grabbed me in a crushing bear hug, laughing boldly, but I could barely feel the pressure of his powerless arms. He galloped on an Arabian horse far across the mesa—or was that him? It might have been, yet I couldn't make the figure out exactly. And dreamt of a pale horse, a pale rider. I awoke shivering, clinging to Lorraine, who was still attached to me, her eyes flying open the instant mine did. She asked, "Are you okay?" and I nodded, and then we were drawn into our dreams again. Bart was holding a silvery trout in the mysterious moonlight. When he let go of it, it remained suspended in the air before him. He laughed and gestured, as if that floating fish were a product of his personal legerdemain. I reached for the fish but couldn't touch it. Bart hooted and slapped his thigh: this time he had really put one over on me. The Siamese cat leaped up, trying to swat the fish with a paw, but it couldn't. Bart said, "It's an easy trick, Marcel. It's a piece of cake. Even a moron could make a trout float like that." The moon came down out of the sky and balanced on his fingertip like a basketball. He spun it atop his finger with his other hand. And, making all kinds of comic, frantic faces as if it were going to fall off, he zig-zagged around, pantomiming panic and fear. But the moon never toppled from his finger. And he floated gracefully in the air, effortlessly turning somersaults and doing twists, his body naked, his tanned muscles glistening. He tumbled in a rainbow-shaped arc through the air, yet instead of landing in the water, he disappeared into an enormous grave.

I awoke with a shout. Lorraine squeezed me, and for the nth time whispered, "It's okay, Marcel. I'm here. Everything is all right."

"Listen." She cocked her head. I said, "It's raining."

"I love that sound."

I got up, opening a window, and stood there for a while, listening to the rain fall, striking leaves, dripping off gutters. I unlocked the door and stood in the doorway, feeling cool. Soft gusts buffeted my aching body. The straight-falling moisture was barely more than a drizzle. But it was persistent and seemed to be falling as if it would never end. The air achieved a brilliant cleanliness that was evocative and nostalgic, enormously sad and refreshing at the same time. I got back into the bed with Lorraine, and we lay there for a long while wide awake, listening to the rain, smelling it. Eventually we slept again, and I had further dreams of Bart. He flitted through a forest, barely visible between trees, like a mysterious native American from our country's early days. I wasn't even sure if it was him. I never caught enough of a glimpse to ascertain his identity.

I awoke a final time, while it was still dark out. I opened my eyes so cautiously that Lorraine did not awaken with me. The rain had ended: stars were out. A fine mist lay against the ground out there, a marvelous rich scent on the air permeated our room. Of damp sagebrush and damp juniper, wet adobe dust, and freshly cut lawn grass. Somebody far away laughed; a few dogs were barking. I could see a dozen bright stars out the door from my vantage point on the bed. Lorraine was feathery and warm in my arms, snuggled against me like a kitten. I touched my lips to her dirty hair, tasting it, smelling it. Her warm skin pulsed against my own skin, and I felt enormously protective. I wanted to cup her in my hand the way you might cup a tiny mouse. The air seemed made of velvet. All at once I realized her eyes were open, staring at me. She asked, "Are you all right?" and I told her, "I'm fine."

"That's good, Marcel."

She lifted her guitar from beside the bed, and settled it in her lap. Peepers raised a summer ruckus somewhere, in a distant bog. Closer by, crickets chirruped. Occasional raindrops dripped off the roof. A damp sagebrush smell on the air was like the Michelangelo of Sentimental Odors.

And I really was fine. I felt calm and whole and unafraid. I knew that everything would work out: I could handle it. I would not be confused. There would be a service here in Chamisaville, for the film crew—and after it I would release them from their guilt, and back into the picture. They could use the Big House for as long as was necessary. I would hang around until Towner Babcock arrived, and we would methodically close down the house, sell off Bart's things, place the house on the market. Then I would carry Bart's ashes back east and, against his wishes, inter them in the family plot at Dolphin Bays. For however he had rejected them during his lifetime, his roots had come out of that territory and those legends. At heart he had always been the marauding son of a robber baron, full of all the nastiness and adventure that implied, and imbued with an errant life-force that was both admirable and despicable, exciting for sure, and riddled with crippling contradictions he had never learned to overcome.

The regret, of course, was that he had never been fulfilled. His wonderful energy had been trapped in, and dissipated by, the anarchy of our times. Exaggerated in Bart, as in few people, had been the vitality, if not the answer. Today, and during the course of his lifetime, that vitality had all the makings of an enormous tragedy. And yet in the future . . .

And yet in the future, in that mythical future which will one day touch and transform us all, how wonderful it would be to reach a hand back through the pulsating filaments of memory and catch my father's fevered legacy, molding it in a way that no one has yet discovered, delivering his energy into historical times as different from today as today is different from two thousand years ago . . .

I said, "Would you do me a favor?"

"I can try."

"Would you sing a verse of that song he wrote for you?"

"I guess so . . ."

She played a chord, thought for a moment, and then sang:

> *Now the barroom's deserted,*
> *And I can't remember*
> *The first time you tousled my hair.*
> *But a ghost in the music*
> *Is drifting like smoke through*
> *A feeling that lays my heart bare.*

A protective serenity shielded me as I lay there, mystified by the calm, rain-soaked universe outside that open door, and by the sensation of having that tough little hillbilly beside me, my father's last love, perhaps his only true love.

"You sure you're all right?" Lorraine whispered.

"I'm positive."

"Me too. I'm okay, now. Thanks for sticking with me, Marcel. You helped me make it through the night."

9 I stayed out west, commuting between Los Angeles and Chamisaville for almost a month, going through Bart's things, closing down his houses, tying up all the loose ends. By the time I returned to New York, sycamore leaves freckled the sidewalks and scruffy lawns of Washington Square Park. A string of crisp blue autumn days welcomed me back to the fold. I had lost a semester at the university; my children seemed to have grown a foot during my absence. Especially in their presence I felt that I had changed: they regarded me obliquely out of big blue eyes which said as much. I had an impatience in my blood: I felt curiously dissatisfied with the rhythm of my life. I had lost something that I had never truly owned, not even remotely, and the injustice involved cached a persistent ache in my stomach that refused to go away. The loss deepened with every passing day: an impatience merged with my sorrow, making me uncomfortable indeed.

I visited my mother. During my short time away from Manhattan, Kitty's hair had turned gray. She assured me it had been gray for a while, I had only just noticed. Startled, I asked her, "How old are you now?" She told me: "I'm almost fifty." We went out to dinner at a little Italian restaurant on Sixth Avenue with old linen tablecloths and the menu written on a blackboard. The bond between my mother and I had changed significantly. She seemed almost matronly, and almost resigned. Still, her soft steely eyes struck me as being inordinately lovely. The light in them was like amethyst-tinged smoke captured in amber. I had once thought of them as very sexy. Now her eyes conveyed a different sense of personality. Over mussels and garlicked greens I found myself daydreaming, remembering the only time I had ever seen Kitty naked. It was at a Lefties' picnic up around Mt. Kisco in July one year, when, for some reason that remains obscure today, all the Communists—about fifteen of them—decided to have a skinny-dipping spree in a bass pond. I was really surprised by my mother's lush, curvaceous body. It was languid and smooth and snowy white. All my life I had thought of her as one of the most attractive and sensual women I had ever seen. Her sweet, sleepy eyes . . . a slightly pug nose . . . and all-American lips. She had always looked healthy, yet in a subdued, rainy-day way. Now, suddenly, it hit me that she wasn't young anymore. The generation that had birthed me was dissolving, becoming a nostalgic vapor that heightened the luster of my own youthful territory.

Toward the latter part of October, I developed an acute need to talk with Lorraine. New listings in L.A. gave me a phone number, and I dialed her immediately. She answered, and during the course of our conversation told me:

"I'm still alone, Marcel, but I'm okay. I'm working at a place called Jack's. They guarantee me forty a night, and that's not bad. I'm doing all right. I'm going back to Arkansas for Christmas."

I said, "I've just gotten a first release of some of his bread. I'm gonna send you fifty thousand dollars."

"I don't need it."

"It's just a chunk of Bart's money. I don't need it either."

"Thanks, but no thanks. It feels too funny. It'd be like payoff money to me."

I said, "You're being too stubborn. You're gonna keep yourself from ever really forging a breakthrough, Lorraine. You can't forever refuse to let good things happen to you."

That got her huffing. "Wait a minute, Marcel. You're talking through your hat as usual. When a real good thing comes along, I know how to grab it. I've taken some chances that'd make your hair turn white in a minute. And I've had a hell of a lot of fun in the process, believe me. I couldn't begin to tell you the kind of poetry Bart and I shared, and it was worth it. So don't start coming on as a Christer just because you can't unload fifty grand that's burning a hole in your conscience."

Incredibly, I heard myself saying, "Lorraine, you're an idiot! I hate your puritanical guts!"

She laughed, "That's the spirit, kid. Now you're getting the hang of it."

Twenty-four hours later, looking mighty pale, and feeling a trifle under the weather, I staggered out of a plane that had just landed at the Los Angeles International Airport. Downing a hefty slug of Jack Daniel's at one of the lounges, I rounded up a bouquet of colorful flowers and took a taxi to a nightclub called Jack's; six similarly monikered establishments were listed in the greater-L.A. phone books. On my fourth try, I pulled up in front of a simple-looking place on a nondescript boulevard and found Lorraine inside the half-deserted bar, quietly singing her heart out for a half dozen patrons paying little or no attention. I lacked the necessary gumption for marching up and dumping the wilted flowers in her lap; nor could I blasély tuck a C-note into her nearly empty beer stein. But when the set ended, she headed straight for my table, gave me a hug and a kiss, and asked, "What the hell are *you* doing here?"

"I don't want anything from you," I said quickly. "I just don't feel like losing touch."

"I'm not your kind of woman," she said gently. "And you're not my kind of a man."

"I know. That's not why I'm here."

"Just so long as it's understood."

"Believe me, it's understood. Stop being so defensive."

She grinned, then, and clinked her glass of amaretto against mine. "Cheers, Marcel. Here's looking at you, kid."

"Next set, do 'Amazing Grace.' A capella."

"Why?"

"Because this little overnight junket is gonna cost me close to a thousand dollars before I'm finished."

She laughed. "You're pouring money down a rathole if you think you can impress me by pouring money down a rathole."

"It isn't down a rathole. So why don't you shut up, have a little humility, and just do the song without making a federal case out of it?"

She raised her eyebrows and cocked her head, eyeing me with a bemused expression. "Why Marcel Thompson, I do declare. I believe you're becoming an obnoxious son of a bitch."

I started whining. I said, "Hey, Lorraine . . ."

She giggled. "Don't you 'Hey' me, sugar." Then she got up swiftly, returning to her guitar, switched on her own spotlight, unplugged the jukebox, closed her eyes, and launched "Amazing Grace," a capella. I'd never heard anything as dramatic and beautiful. Over that bar fell a hush such as I have rarely heard in any kind of a joint, anywhere. The bartender refused to shake up a drink or punch the cash register; nobody else moved, not even a chair squeaked. We were literally hypnotized, afraid to move. By the time it ended I was almost crying. Nobody even dared shift their weight until about thirty seconds after her last note had died away. Then Lorraine herself struck a guitar chord, heading into a sweet Dolly Parton song called, "I Will Always Love You." About midway through the set, I rose and quietly left, taxied back to the airport, and returned to New York. Next night she phoned, wanting to know, "Marcel, what in hell were you doing in Los Angeles?"

"I wanted to make sure you were all right."

"I could of told you that over the telephone."

"Maybe. But I wanted to see for myself."

"Jeez," she said affectionately, "what a jerk."

"You gotta understand something Lorraine," I said seriously.

"And what's that?"

"There's never any substitute for the real thing."

"You can say that again."

"There's never any substitute for the real thing."

She shrieked, and after we had hung up I was startled to find myself laughing and crying at the same time. The activation of his genes in me was like a newfound toy in my blood, a gift more precious than I ever could have imagined possible.

I was so excited and nervous I had to leave the apartment and take a walk around my territory. Although close to midnight, Eighth Street was still crowded with pedestrians. I motored along the Manhattan sidewalks at a snappy clip, almost like a sprinter wanting to break into a gallop at every stride, hustling arrogantly through that city as if at any moment I might grab it by the balls and twist hard, until I had all of Gotham down on its knees, hollering "Uncle!"

Talk about feeling high and brash and powerful!

Then I started feeling so jittery I had to sit down and rest for a minute on a Washington Square bench. The park was nearly empty. A few gays were walking their dogs. A loving but sorrow-stricken couple held hands and talked earnestly, their heads bowed together, nearly touching. I breathed heavily, trying to calm down; my heart was beating fast, almost murmuring. I wasn't quite sure if the emotion was anguish or exhilaration. I felt giddy, almost weightless, remarkably close to flight. All around me, and inside of me, I could feel Bart's presence. It was eerie. It seemed probable that he might materialize as a ghost in front of me, and I closed my eyes, frightened, trying to ward off the experience. Lorraine seeped around also, prickling faintly like fog particles against my burning cheeks. I could almost hear her talking to me, laying it down yet one more time for the record:

"Marcel, Bart came closer than anybody I've ever known. My time with him made me feel for certain that what I want is out there. Please understand: I never wished to trap him, or to make him change in a way that could hurt him. I just didn't feel like shouldering his need to kill himself into the bargain. I have never believed that the lust to self-destruct constitutes a viable freedom. I won't accept that. It's not the only way to be special in this world. There's no reason to be ashamed of a long and happy life. My future children and I are determined to reach a ripe old age . . ."

Me too, I thought almost euphorically. And I could do it, by God. *I was going to live forever!*

Bart was there, haunting the mists before me. Seated at a piano, touching notes that made no noise, he moved his lips but made no sound. He wasn't in agony, though. He seemed oddly contented. As if, now that his role in life—as hustler, buffoon, ass man, organizer, daredevil, and world traveler—was over, he had nothing more on the line, and could enjoy his life, finally, as a simple endeavor that demanded nothing more of him than an eager good will, and to be handsome, and to occasionally perform some silly miracle as he had with that trout, and the basketball moon.

Now that I had an assurance he would never leave me, it was time to say good-bye. With a wink at me, and a silly grin, he suddenly closed his eyes, assumed a twisted posture holding an imaginary mike, and, his face contorted in a wild, comic grimace, he abruptly ripped down one arm and made a fist, going into his Johnny Ray imitation:

> *If your sweetheart*
> *Sends a letter*
> *Of good-bye. . . .*

With that, he took off—poof!—airborne at last, arms spread as in his childhood fantasies. He cleared the Dolphin Bays lawn, the willow trees, the grass tennis courts, and the private beach. And, using the thermals expertly, gliding with more grace than a hawk, he proceeded out to sea, where, high above the gauzy Saturday-morning spinnakers of racing sailboats, he became lovingly lost among the gulls.